The Circle of Fate

The Drifter

by
Larry W. Batts

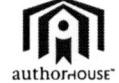

Bloomington, IN
authorHOUSE™
Milton Keynes, UK

AuthorHouse™
1663 Liberty Drive, Suite 200
Bloomington, IN 47403
www.authorhouse.com
Phone: 1-800-839-8640

AuthorHouse™ *UK Ltd.*
500 Avebury Boulevard
Central Milton Keynes, MK9 2BE
www.authorhouse.co.uk
Phone: 08001974150

© *2006 Larry W. Batts. All rights reserved.*

No part of this book may be reproduced, stored in a retrieval system, or transmitted by any means without the written permission of the author.

First published by AuthorHouse 10/16/2006

ISBN: 1-4259-6346-3 (sc)
ISBN: 1-4259-6347-1 (dj)

Library of Congress Control Number: 2006908820

Printed in the United States of America
Bloomington, Indiana

This book is printed on acid-free paper.

Chapter One
A Broken Promise

(October 17, 1995)

    He stood proudly with his shoulders back, a successful businessman, staring out his office window on the third floor of the Edwards Building in Richmond, Virginia. The night sky was illuminated with lightning as it tore through the darkness, accompanied by an orchestra of thunder. The rain was coming down with great fury, causing the drops to pound against the window like drumsticks against a cymbal.

    This witness to nature's spectacular event was a tall, slender, good-looking man. At six foot one with straight black hair and hard, chiseled features, he engulfed the room, a monument among the greatest of men. His dark blue eyes and full, immaculately trimmed beard completed the look of a powerful man — feared, liked, and respected by those who knew him. His accomplishments as a successful architect and investor had made him a wealthy man. Starting from nothing but a dream and ambition, he had spent the last ten years building his business into a multimillion-dollar company.

    As he reminisced about the beginning and his struggles against what seemed fantastic odds, he now stood here living his dream. He had gained great community respect, which is normally granted by such wealth. However his most valuable possession, forgotten along the way, was now threatening his very purpose of obtaining his goal. Through the years of hard work, diligence, and self-sacrifice, he was able to get his unstable company to a profitable state, but he unintentionally neglected the ones he loved. The last ten years rushed by in a blur with a string of late nights, working weekends, and broken promises. He was now faced with the most important decision of his life: retire or possibly lose his most prized possessions forever.

He turned his head and stared at the picture of his wife and daughter sitting on the corner of his desk. They were the fuel that had fed his burning fire of ambition that consumed the last ten years of his life. His wife, Janelle, was a very strong-willed woman, and yet very gentle, with a heart as pure as gold. She stood five foot five, petite with long black hair, green eyes, and a smile that would melt any man's heart. That smile was what captivated him one lonely night at Charley's Bar thirteen years ago. A few dances, a little wine, and she sank the hook; there was no escaping her. It was not long after they were married that his daughter Amy was born. She was a love child brought into this world by them. Her presence had strengthened their family bonds, bonds now weakened by time and threatened by success.

This tormenting feeling of regret overwhelmed him as he stood there staring at the picture. His wife was beautiful, and he remembered the fun they once shared. The last two months were spent in countless arguments about the business, broken promises, and how much time he spent at the office. His daughter was now nine and he realized how little he knew her. Last night, Janelle spent hours arguing about his persistence in avoiding Amy by hiding at the office, and how much more its importance seemed to be. How Amy was growing up without a chance to know her father. How he had made promises to her that he did not keep, and how this was affecting her.

A crack of thunder and blinding light brought his attention back to the window. As he stood there, staring into the evening sky, the same thoughts kept swimming through his mind. Trying to determine who was the best suited to manage his business; one he could trust, one who could fit into this environment and would make smart business decisions. He felt like he was traveling down different streets, but somehow the journey would always end up in the same place, much like traveling through the Twilight Zone. It seemed no matter how hard he thought, with all his choices, he would always come back to only one: his brother John.

John was his identical twin, not as ambitious as he had been in his life, but still a very strong and convincing man. He would make a good partner; he knew the business very well and could keep the company profitable. However, because of his brother's past, he was still haunted by his decision. Dubious as he was, giving up the business and putting John in charge was still the right thing to do. *Keep it in the family,* was his thought, as he truly loved his brother and had suffered with him in those trying times of the past.

John had taken a hard dose of reality and had been drowning in self-pity for what seemed an eternity. He was stung so hard by love that he closed off his life and receded into darkness, unable to see the light coming from those who loved him. He was once very ambitious, and with his strong personality, he had landed a very promising and lucrative career. Newly engaged to a beautiful woman with a promising future of her own, he was a man in his prime, and yet fate is so often cruel when you least expect it. Eager to surprise his young bride-to-be, he left work early one beautiful summer day, only to find her in bed with another man, a man he thought was his best friend. It seemed from there his life crumbled, leaving him stranded in the dark abyss of despair.

The image of them together, naked and writhing, filled him with a boundless and uncontrollable rage. He savagely beat his friend, almost killing him. One of life's cruel tragedies can take the joys of living and turn it upside down into an undeserved hell. John became a loner and withdrew from others, driven by hate, seeded by love, and twisted by fate. Like many before him, he buried himself in drugs, gambling, and alcohol, which only deepened his despair. Unable to keep a job or relationship for longer than a few months, it seemed there would never be a recovery. Making the decision to let his brother work in his company seemed to bring John from out of the gutters, off his path of self-destruction, and back to a safer lifestyle.

John was a natural, and he picked up the business immediately. With a head for finance and negotiation, he quickly increased profits and assisted in landing several lucrative contracts. In the last six months, he had made several improvements to the business with new and more cost-effective processes, adding his value to the company. Even though his brother showed great improvement over the last year, he still worried about him. The fear of John reverting back to the drugs and alcohol still plagued his decision.

The clock struck 7:00 PM and brought him back from his reverie. He had called his brother earlier to have a drink after work, and now he's late, again. In a rush, he grabbed his full-length raincoat and headed for the door, locking it behind him. He stopped for a moment as he gave pause and glanced back at his office door bearing his name. It seemed to be blurred and unreadable; he shook his head as if to gain focus, but it seemed to make no difference. His eyes moved from the name to the title: *President* that was etched on the glass door. For some reason, the print appeared to be very clear and in focus. *Maybe this is a sign,* he thought. *Maybe it is time for me to retire.* With a wry smile, he turned away from the door and headed down the hallway, not knowing how fate was soon to play its deadly game. From his cell phone, he called his brother John, confirming their engagement across the street at Charley's. With the weather being horrific, it gave him the opportunity to discuss his plans and relax before fighting the traffic home.

    He scuttled to the elevator and got there just in time to catch the door as it was closing. There were four others in the elevator with him, two elderly gentlemen, and one very lovely blonde wearing a very short red dress showing off her nicely shaped legs. The last one was a young man, a courier for Johnston's Courier Service. After a quick hello and a good evening he went back to admiring the young lady's legs. He always enjoyed admiring a beautiful woman, and was a sucker for nice, shapely legs. When the elevator door opened on the first floor, he was the first to exit. He picked up his pace as he glided through the corridor and out the front doors. In his haste to get to the bar, he had forgotten his umbrella. He shook his head disgustedly, tucked the collar of the raincoat closer to his neck, and dashed across the street in the blinding rain.

    The wind slammed the door shut as he whisked into Charley's Bar. In front of the main doors was the small dance floor where Janelle had once mesmerized him with that smile of hers. In front of the dance floor was the bandstand, and to the right was a small bar, used only when it was busy. Around the dance floor was a fenced corral with bar stools for extra seating. The main bar was on the east wall to his left and Tony, the bartender, was flirting as always, with two young lady patrons. Looking around, he noticed the bar was almost empty. A young couple was sitting at a booth on the back wall, the same one he sat in the night he met Janelle.

    One could never tell what they would find at Charley's. Sometimes the place was packed with standing room only, other times it's like it was now. He proceeded to his favorite table, close to the dance floor and in front of the main bar. From here, he could see everything that was going on and be able to watch for his brother, who also seemed to be late.

    The waitress, a small, thin brunette named Sandra, saw him come in and immediately headed toward his table. She was a very lovely young lady with her own streak of bad luck. She had a large scar, very visible on her right cheek, left over from her last boyfriend. He was a biker. One night here at Charley's, in a brutal, jealous rage, he broke a beer bottle across her face. His jealousy landed him behind bars for what everyone hoped would be a long time.

"How are you tonight Sandra," he asked. Sandra smiled that crooked smile, caused by the scar, that they all had come to admire.

"I'm fine tonight. How is your brother John doing?" she asked.

"My brother is fine. He'll be here shortly, if you're interested?" She smiled as he ordered himself a Bud Light and a Tom Collins for John, his brother's favorite drink.

The howling wind cut through the bar, splitting the silence as the front door swung open, exposing the silhouette of his brother. John noticed him sitting at their usual table and immediately yelled out, "Hey, Bo. You're looking mighty fine tonight." Although he hated it, John referred to him by his childhood nickname, Bo. He tolerated it only from his brother John and no one else. One night, long ago, his friends tried to teasingly call him Bo and decided not to try again, as they almost came to blows. Infuriated, he towered over his friends, fists clenched, while he shared some profound language with them, and they needed no further convincing.

Sandra brought their drinks over and set them down on the table, all the while looking and smiling at John. She seemed to always like John more, even though the two of them were identical twins. "Hi, John," she said.

John glanced into her eyes as he smiled, "Hello Sandra, how's your daughter Beverly?" "She's fine. Have you been doing okay?" Sandra asked.

John nodded his head but said nothing more. He always considered Sandra as a good match for his brother, John. He was unable to ascertain why John did not share Sandra's feelings. The conversation between them ended as quickly as it had begun. Sandra left the two brothers as she returned to take her spot at the bar. The brothers sat in silence as they sipped away at their drinks. John had noticed the strain in his brother's face and was compelled to speak up and ask the question," What's up, Bo?" John had become nervous from all the silence, for this was not his brother's normal behavior.

His fears were quickly put to rest as he listened to his brother's story of retiring and leaving the business with him. He was overcome with a plethora of emotions, from excitement to pride to admiration for his brother. He could not mask his surprise at the news, but he wished his brother well on his decision. John accepted the position with gratitude and pride. Being trusted enough to take over the business gave him back his self-esteem. They both sat there, discussing the turnover of the business, when and how it was to happen, when Bo's cell phone rang.

It was his wife Janelle; John could hear the anger in her voice through the cell phone as the words echoed across the table. "You promised Amy you would pick her up," Janelle screamed, as Bo carefully pulled the phone away from his ear. "Remember, tonight is the play rehearsal, and you promised you would take her. You forgot again, didn't you? You son of a bitch! She is sitting in her room crying her eyes out, again! You always do this to us and I'm the one that has to pick up the pieces, you asshole!" John heard the cursing very clearly and felt sympathetic grief for his brother, as he watched the changing expression on his face. He leaned across the table as he gently whispered, "Hey, Bo … I'm sorry," only to have his feelings brushed off by his brother, as he continued to be berated by Janelle.

"I'm sorry. I came over with John to have a drink. I needed to talk to him about something very important, important for us," he replied apologetically. The conversation continued, as he was dragged deeper into submission. Janelle hung up at the height of her fury. Her parting words: "I'll take care of it like I always do. I'll take her myself and when you get home, we need to talk." He immediately called Janelle back with the look of fear in his eyes, which was clouded by his anger. When she did not answer, his fear became more dominant, pushing the anger aside.

"What's wrong?" John asked.

"She has the Jeep and it doesn't handle well on wet roads. It hydroplanes too easy. John, I need to go. Can we discuss the business later?" he said as he stood up.

"Don't worry about the tab; I'll take care of it. Call me later," John replied as he hugged his brother goodbye.

Bo quickly disappeared out the door, wondering how he was going to explain the events of this evening. As John was paying his tab with Sandra, a voice from a table beside them said, "Is everything all right? Your brother left in quite a hurry!"

John turned his head and recognized an old drinking buddy. One he had shared his sad memories with, on many occasions here at Charley's. Later, after he went to work for his brother, he discovered that George was a chief competitor.

He respectfully nodded as he replied, "Hello, George. I'm afraid he missed his daughter Amy's play rehearsal again, and his wife is very upset that he broke another promise to Amy."

George gave his respect to John as he responded, "A broken promise is the hardest to redeem. It's the cause of many broken lives. Hopefully, he will be able to set it right before it's too late."

John thought for a moment before he nodded his head in agreement. "You're right, George. I do believe he is going to fix that tonight. In fact, that is what we were just discussing. I'm taking over some of his responsibilities so he can get back to the more important aspects of his life."

George respectfully nodded as he returned to drinking his beer. A moment later, he spoke. "Your brother is a good man. You need to help him, John, so he doesn't make the same mistakes I have made."

John, remembering George's stories, simply replied, "I'll do that, George." He smiled as he stood up to leave. "Take it easy, Mr. Stickler. Maybe someday soon we could have a drink together and reminisce about the good ole days."

George nodded. "I would like that, John. I miss your company."

John turned away and left Charley's as Sandra waved goodbye, but he did not notice her gesture or acknowledge it.

(The road south of Bo's House)

Janelle's face was crimson with anger, for this was not the first time he made a promise to Amy and failed to deliver. Her fury continued to distract her driving, causing her to forget the dangerous conditions around her. The speed limit was ignored, along with oncoming traffic, as her fury increased by every mile. She was now late for the rehearsal and feared Amy would miss it altogether.

The weather had unleashed its wrath on the poor, helpless mortals below. Like a pawn in a supernatural chess match, the rain and the wind bounced the Jeep around the road. Her knuckles had become white from clenching the steering wheel as she struggled to remain in control and try to hide her anger from Amy. Despite their valiant attempts, the windshield wipers were no match for the torrents of rain that barraged the vehicle. Janelle trudged on in the darkness, barely able to see the road, let alone what lay ahead.

Amy sensed the tension in her mother's voice as words continued to spew out of her mouth. Upset by her father and knowing what this was doing to her mother, she spoke up and said, "Don't worry, Mom; it's okay. I know Daddy is busy and I'm not upset anymore."

Janelle glanced toward Amy with empathy, knowing she was only trying to hide how she truly felt. Playing as if she was the mom, wanting to make her feel better. "Well, I'm tired of forgiving your father for breaking his promises, and when we get home, well; well, I'm going to have it out with him. Its time for him to let go of that damn company and start thinking of us instead," Janelle blurted out while she was trying to keep her anger at bay. "Things are going to change around our house or by God…" Sensing what she was saying and how her anger had turned belligerent, she quickly stopped the conversation and apologized. "I'm sorry Amy, but I promise you it will get better."

Amy remained silent not wanting to provoke her mother's anger any further. She sat in the passenger seat as she watched her mother drive. Janelle was still deep in conversation when the Jeep topped the hill at fifty miles per hours. "Watch out, Mom!" came a fateful scream from Amy.

Quickly breaking away from her conversation, Janelle glanced down the hill. At the bottom, she saw a car stalled in the middle of the road. Keeping calm and not panicking, she gently applied the brakes, but with the wet roads, the Jeep began to hydroplane, throwing it into a slide. Her heart began racing; her eyes squinted, trying to find a means of escape. Guardrails to the right, vehicle in front, another one coming up toward her from the bottom of the hill. There was no way she could abscond through this one; in a panic, she slammed the brakes to the floor. The tires locked, putting the Jeep into an unexpected spin, out of control, sliding down the slope to unrighteous doom.

Amy's screams brought a God-awful fear into Janelle as she leaned across the seat to grab and pull Amy close, as if she could use her own body as a shield to protect her daughter. Janelle held her tight as she watched the approaching destiny with horror in her eyes.

(The School)

It took Bo an hour and a half before he reached the school after his retreat from the bar, due to the rain and traffic. The rehearsals were over, and only a few of the parents and children remained. He recognized Amy's teacher, Sara, when he entered the auditorium. Sara was a tall, slender woman in her mid-thirties with large, beautiful brown eyes, long, wavy dark hair, and a full figure. She was very attractive and possessed a soft speaking voice. She was standing among some of the parents, and without any regards to their privacy, he interrupted them.

Looking horrified, he harshly asked about his daughter, Amy. Sara gave him an inquisitive look with a slightly tilted head, until she realized who he was. "Hello," she said with a very confused look on her face. "I'm sorry, but if you're looking for Amy, she isn't here. She didn't show up for rehearsals tonight." Terrified by the news, he dashed for the front door of the auditorium without even saying goodbye. His only thought was Janelle had been smart enough to stay at home and not attempt to drive in this weather. He again called the house, hoping for Janelle to answer, only to hear it ring until the answering machine picked up. Fear-stricken, he began to drive recklessly with no concern about the hazardous conditions. His car was moving like a blur against the shadows from the streetlights, on the winding and slippery roads. He had only one thought on his mind: getting home. Their last conversation kept coming back into his thoughts. It was the same conversation that had ended many arguments over the last few years — *"I'll take care of it like I always do."*

As he drove toward home, his worries began turning into anger as questions popped into his mind with no supporting answers. *Why did they not show up? Did she decide to stay home? Why won't she answer the phone?* He felt he had done no wrong this night. His decision to retire and give them back their lives together was the right step for their future. Janelle had no reason for losing her temper and yelling at him. She had some explaining to do, he thought, and letting her off easy was not on the agenda.

(Bo's House)

His anger began to subside as he neared the driveway of his small estate. He realized Janelle was not aware of his intentions of retiring, and tonight resembled nights of the past, where he had failed to keep a promise. When he finally arrived at his home in southern Richmond and entered the circular driveway, he had calmed down, as he worried about his wife's rage. In his rush to check on them, he decided to park by the front door instead of in the garage, where he normally parked. As he ran into the house, still worried, he inadvertently slammed the front door behind him. Once inside, he called their names. "Janelle! … Amy!" but there was no response, so he called them once again. The entrance to his home had a long corridor with wooden floors; the study, where he spent most of his time, was to the left of the front door, a few feet down the corridor. He walked to the small closet, which was also close to the front door, and removed his raincoat. He kept hoping as he was hanging up his raincoat that he would see his little girl running down the hallway to greet him. He closed the closet door as his eyes never left the hallway, still hoping, but to no avail. The large house was silent, except for the normal creaking noise of the wood floors as he walked.

When he approached the living room, at the end of the hallway, he glanced inside to see if Amy and Janelle might be asleep on the large leather like sofa in front of the big-screen television. This is where he usually found them on those late nights after work. The room was ghostly silent and there was no living presence. He sighed as he walked toward the stairs on the opposite side of the living room. Stopping at the top of the stairs, he looked down the small hallway toward Amy's room. He decided to check her room first, only to find it too was empty, as was his bedroom. He wandered aimlessly throughout the rest of the house, calling their names. As each room came up empty, his hope of finding them asleep somewhere weakened.

His search ended back in the living room, where the silence of his dwelling was choking him and leaving a lump in his throat. The only noises he heard were the sounds of his own heartbeat as it pounded against his chest, and the shortness of his own breath. With a sudden burst of energy and long, quick strides, his movement was blurred as he rushed toward the garage, hoping to find the Jeep. As he opened the door leading to the garage, his legs lost all their strength as he fell back against the wall. The Jeep was gone and he now felt completely helpless. His fears overwhelmed him, for he now knew something was deadly wrong. The only strength left in his body was used to call his brother John as he pushed the talk button on his cell phone.

John answered the phone only to hear the panicked voice of his brother. "Is Janelle and Amy there? She's not here! They never made it to school! I have no idea where they are."

With a calm and collected voice, John tried to reassure his brother, "Calm down. I'm sure she's all right. I'll make a few phone calls and see what I can find out. I'm sure she is fine, so relax and have a drink. I'll call you back as soon as I find out something." Feeling somewhat more placid and with collected thoughts, he walked back to the living room and sat down on the sofa, as he patiently awaited his brother's call. Every sound, every vehicle passing by would take him to the front door with inspiring hope, only to be disappointed. The more he sat and worried, the more he realized he needed to do something to occupy his time. Pacing and circling the living room seemed to ease the pain, when a sudden thought entered his mind to call Janelle's mother. As he reached for the phone, his cell began to ring. With childlike excitement, he quickly answered it. It was his brother John. "Hey, Bo … you need to meet me at Mercy Hospital."

Half-frozen with fear, myriad thoughts raced through his mind. Without any regards to his brother's feelings, he yelled, "What's going on?"

With a melancholy tone, John murmured, "I'll explain everything once you get here; see ya in a little bit." Frightened and ignorant of what had just happened, he threw his phone across the room, striking it against the fireplace mirror, shattering the mirror. *Oh great, seven years bad luck to look forward to,* he thought as he left the house, traveling at a high rate of speed with no reverence to his actions as he rushed toward the hospital. The rain had stopped sometime earlier, and the roads were beginning to dry. By the time he reached the hospital, his nerves were shattered. He parked in the emergency parking and ran into the hospital in search of his brother.

In the emergency room, he found his brother John standing beside Jack, the police commissioner and friend. Jack had his head bowed, as if he was trying to avoid eye contact. Trying to remain calm and self-collected, he spoke. "Please tell me everything's okay." John grabbed his brother's arms and eased him back toward a small chair, inside of the emergency room. With a soft touch, John pushed his brother into the chair. John was crying softly by the time he spoke to his brother again. "Janelle and Amy were in a car accident."

Not wanting to hear the rest of the story, he interrupted his brother in a low, shaky voice and asked, "Are they okay?"

John knelt down in front of him without saying any more, and he knew then the worst was yet to come. He held back his fears as he allowed John to finish telling him everything. John realized his brother was patiently waiting, but still hesitated slightly before he was able to continue. "Janelle died." Bo's heart sank into the pit of his stomach, as his eyes filled with tears. He sat quietly without saying another word, knowing there was still more to come.

John went on to say, "Amy is alive, but her condition is critical. She's been in the operating room for the last couple of hours. I'm not sure of her condition right now, but I'm sure we will know something soon. I'm so sorry, Bo." By the time John had finished telling his brother the news, he could no longer hold back his emotions. The two brothers clung to each other as both broke the silence of the emergency room with their cries.

An hour later, they sat beside each other as they patiently waited for some news about Amy. Police Commissioner Jack was pacing about the emergency room, waiting for the same news. Bo's heart was breaking with uncontrollable tears that would flow from his eyes from time to time. How he now wished he could take this night back and do it all over again. He put his hands over his eyes, covering them, as he tried to ease his sorrow. The small ER had been desolate and silent until it was broken by a deep voice that said, "Excuse me, sir."

Bo removed his hands from his face as he glanced up into the eyes of a heavyset man wearing a white gown. There was a stethoscope hanging from his neck, and the look in this man's eyes was not one of hope. His greatest fear now overwhelmed him, for he knew what the doctor's next words would be, even before they were ever spoken.

(The Funeral)

John, with Sam's help, made all the funeral arrangements. Sam was Bo's accountant and very close friend. It seemed Bo had given up on all hope of life, after losing that which he treasured the most. They tried to help him by keeping him away from any unnecessary memories, for Bo had not spoken a word since that fateful night at the hospital. On several occasions, John and others had tried to comfort him, but to no avail. John was concerned for his brother, and could see him sinking into the same abyss he had experienced many years ago.

The day of the funeral came, and it seemed everybody was there to comfort Bo and give respect for his loss. Without conscious thought, Bo aimlessly shook hands and was comforted by what seemed like thousands, and yet not a word was spoken. A nod here and one there was his only response. He acted as if he was avoiding the reality he was now faced with for the rest of his life. Not a single tear fell from his eyes, as the funeral progressed and they lay Janelle and Amy's bodies into the ground.

Chapter Two
The Drifter

(One year later)

He had the look of a man who had aged very quickly over a brief moment in time. The light streaks of gray in his beard and hair and small wrinkles in his cheeks showed his aged look. He stood like a stone statue, strong and distinguished, with the scorned look of a man drowning in grief. With the emptiness in his heart and the blank stare of his eyes, he stood looking out of his study window, as if he had a compulsory expectation of Janelle and Amy driving up in the Jeep. Staring out at the circular driveway occupied most of his time. It had been a year since that tragic night, and their deaths still haunted his dreams. The same thoughts chipped away at his mind until all other thoughts were vanquished. You could hear the muttering sounds as they echoed softly through the hallway, "It's my fault … I should have been there …   Just another broken promise."

His outgoing personality and optimism died that night, one year ago, now beaten further down by his memories, with its savage, relentless guilt. He had been teetering on a thin line separating reality from the realm of insanity. All those who loved and respected him gave no comfort to his darkened, lonely heart. They all tried to help, but their well-intentioned attempts only appeared to drive him deeper into seclusion.

One cool morning in November, his brother John came to visit. The gathering of the twins went well, until John accidentally brought up his wife and daughter. "You have to quit blaming yourself, Bo. The accident was not your fault. I understand you want to keep their memories alive, but you need to go on with your life … Janelle and Amy would want you to," John said, with as much sympathy and compassion as he could muster.

His approach was nothing but innocent, but he realized that understanding and sympathy in the past never seemed to work. His attempt to get his brother to realize how his life was affecting all those who loved him failed.

Bo lost control and blindly lashed out at his brother. His voice was filled with anger, and he did not realize the destructive nature of his tone, when he yelled, "I want you to leave! You have no fucking clue what I'm going through! Now get out!" All John could do was look at his brother in sorrow. He was taken completely by surprise by the anger in his brother's voice. The more he tried to regain his composure, the deeper the void became. Finally, and with reluctance, John left the house with those words still ringing in his ears. He stopped at his car as he glanced back toward the house hoping his brother would come to his rescue as he always did, but he was not there. With a look of despair in his tear-filled eyes, he slowly opened the door. John had never felt rejection from his brother, not until this day. He drove away from his brother's home with the semblance of a lost child, not sure where the journey would end. The twins were always close, inseparable, as if made from the same mold. What they both never realized was how those spoken words of anger would influence the rest of their lives.

With Bo's attitude and being swallowed up in his own self-pity, he caused his friends to desert him one by one, until they were all gone. He became a hermit in the midst of thousands, all alone with no friends, no family, and what seemed to be no escape. He longed to be free of his guilt, but his conscience would not release the bands of culpability. These feelings of aspiration drove him to run away from his business and home, which seemed to be his only recourse. There was no specific place to run; he just wanted to hide and escape his bonds of torture.

He called Sam, his accountant and old friend, and gave him explicit instructions on how to invest and manage his money. After a brief explanation of his intentions, he hung up the phone and began sorting in his mind the items he wanted to take. After careful deliberation, he decided to only pack a few clothes, leaving everything else behind, especially anything with attached memories. The only exception was Amy's Winnie the Pooh bear — the one he had given her when she was six.

After a few hours of packing and loading his Lincoln Town Car, he was ready to leave. The only item left to retrieve was in Amy's room — the only room he had not been in since her death. He climbed the stairway and slowly walked down the hallway to Amy's room. His heart felt heavy, pounding against his chest, causing him unbearable pain. He hesitated as he stood outside her room. With his head hanging low, he took in a deep breath, let out a big sigh, and slowly stepped into her room.

Winnie the Pooh was lying on Amy's bed, where it had lain untouched for a year. He sat down on her bed, picking up the stuffed animal, and held it in his lap, looking at it as he held his emotions at bay.

A short time later, being consumed by a flood of guilt, he stood up and left her room, closing the door behind him. He left the house and proceeded to his car, carrying Winnie the Pooh under his arm. Carefully, he placed the bear in the passenger's seat while he stood by his car for a brief moment, as if not completely sure of his decision. Once inside the car, he picked up the stuffed bear and held it close to his chest, giving it a big hug, as Amy used to do.

He closed his eyes as he remembered the day he had given Amy the bear, and how she hugged it so dearly. This became her most valuable possession and she loved it dearly. For the longest time, she carried it everywhere she went, never letting it out of her sight. Even till the day she died, she would not go to bed without it. He began clenching at the stuffed toy in a savage rage as the memories of that day returned.

(June 15, 1992)

It was a late Monday evening and Amy was sitting in his lap with her head on his shoulder. She had lifted her head, and in her soft, gentle voice asked, "Can we go on a picnic Sunday ... please?" He looked into her eyes and smiled, for he could never resist her. "Sure we can ... I promise." She smiled back at him, laid her head back on his shoulder, and fell asleep. Wednesday came and it seemed to be a normal day at the office, until a prospective client called to discuss ideas on a new building that he wanted designed. His plane would arrive Saturday night and he wanted to meet Sunday to talk.

The rest of the week was spent preparing for their meeting. When Sunday arrived, he ended up spending all day with the client, not leaving until late that night. On his way home, he stopped at a convenience store to buy a pack of cigarettes. Seeing the bear on a small display next to the counter, he felt compelled to buy it.

He hoped the gift would pay homage, and his beautiful little girl would forgive him. When she saw the bear, her face lit up with the largest smile that he had ever seen; he knew then that she forgave him. She took the bear from his hands, all the while jumping up and down with excitement. She squeezed the bear up against her chest, hugging it lovingly, and then she gave him the same great big hug.

He released the raging emotion, while he held back the tears that had formed in his eyes. He gave the bear a gentle kiss on the top of its head, before gently placing it back onto the passenger's seat. He started his car and drove away from his beautiful home, without even a glance back.

(Spring 1998)

He had drifted from town to town for nearly three years, not staying very long in any one place. His life had turned to a drunken state of disarray. Like a hobo with no boundaries or limitations, he drifted from place to place without any meaningful purpose. When asked his name, he would simply reply, "Call me the Drifter." Many nights he would stay in the bar until it closed, dragging his limp body outside after being forced to leave, spending many nights in some lonely motel. Every day had become the same as the last, like a bad perpetual nightmare. Instead of being able to succeed in forgetting his guilt, he carried the burden even heavier in his heart, like a knife permanently embedded, never letting him heal.

One night, in a sleazy motel, he lay in bed, drunk as usual. In a deep REM sleep, he had a nightmare that became the turning point of his life.

Standing in the darkness of hell, he was surrounded by hideous creatures of the night. They had no form and moved like shadows against the walls. Amy was steadily calling him: "Daddy, where are you? I love you." As he ran desperately trying to find her, the shapeless creatures would cling to him, impeding his movements. He called out to Amy as he ran toward her. Every time he heard her voice, it seemed to be fainter than the time before. He struggled with every movement as he continued to run while the hideous creatures sucked his life away. He ran in what seemed a perpetual circle, draining his energy with every step, until he was rendered helpless. He collapsed and fell to his knees with the dark, shadowy creatures fastened tightly against his body, eating away his soul. He heard Amy's voice ring out once more, but far fainter than ever before. He extended his hand as far he could reach as he cried her name.

He leaped forward with sweat pouring down his forehead. He stared into the mirror on the wall across from him. The reflection was not the man he once knew. This man was a total stranger, one with no hope, who had given up on life. The dream was a vivid and realistic portrait; it painted a precise picture of his true reflection. He realized the hideous creatures were not from hell, but instead were his own feelings of guilt, sucking at his life, draining him, leaving him with nothing. "John tried to tell me this three years ago and what did I do? I threw him out of my house," the Drifter mumbled as the memory of that dreadful day returned.

His overwhelming guilt forced him to pick up the phone to call his brother. When the phone rang, John answered. He sat in silence as he tried to get a response from the unknown caller. After several seconds, he placed the phone back on its cradle. *I'm not quite ready yet, I still have a lot to answer for,* he thought. He had to prove his worthiness before he could go home and ask for forgiveness from those he had deserted. Unable to get back to sleep, he decided to take a shower, hoping he would feel better. After the shower, he once again stared at the reflection in the mirror, thinking the soap and water might have washed away the years of pity. As he stared into the mirror, he realized it was the same man, and he knew then it was time for a change. That evening, in his lonely hotel room, he began a new life.

Sitting at the small table in his room he contemplated his next move. What was his future to be? After several hours of exhausted thinking, he decided to travel once more, but not be the vagabond as before, this time with a purpose. *Go north,* he thought, *to Alaska. Find a secluded spot deep in the mountains, design and build my ultimate home. Build it inside of a mountain, in the memory of my beloved wife and daughter.*

A smile broke from his lips, and with an uplifted spirit, once again, he began to feel like a man. A sense of pride surrounded his aura, removing some of the roughness that had scarred his face, caused by the many years of guilt. *One day I'll return home and ask for forgiveness from those I deserted,* he thought, as he prepared for his departure. He used the motel phone to call his accountant, Sam. After a brief conversation of how he was doing, he explained the dream. Sam listened as his friend went on telling him of his intentions and what he was attempting to accomplish. The Drifter explained that it could take several years before he'd be finished, but when it was over, he would be coming home.

Before he would let Sam get off of the phone, he had to give him some last-minute instructions. "Okay Sam, if you should get a phone call from someone you don't know about some purchases made by a man called the Drifter, just pay it and ask no questions. Also, do not reveal my name to anybody, until I have the chance to earn the right to use it again. Sam ... it's important to me that you don't tell anyone about this. I have to do this for myself, before I'm ready to come home. Do you understand?" There was a moment of silence before Sam reluctantly acknowledged the question and was forced into a promise he did not want to keep.

The Drifter checked out of the motel where he had spent the night, in the small town of Buffalo, Texas. He drove around, checking car lots, looking for a vehicle that caught his attention and stood out from all the others. It had to be rugged enough to travel in terrain that you normally dare not take. As he passed by Joe's Used Cars, he saw an old army jeep that looked like it had been customized. It was a light shade of blue with a custom-made white hardtop. He decided to stop and check the vehicle.

Joe, the owner of the lot, approached him while he was examining the jeep. He was a short, plump man, wearing a blue leisure suit, and from the sleazy way he looked, the Drifter figured he would do anything to make a sale. With that in mind, he decided to spend some time talking with Joe, just to see how far he would go. With some smooth political talking, the Drifter convinced Joe into trading the jeep for his Lincoln Town Car. With a handful of cash, he had Joe convinced into throwing in a small trailer.

When they went back to his small office to sign the paperwork, the Drifter handed Joe Sam's phone number. "I want you to call this number. He will work with you on our agreement; just tell him the Drifter is with you." Joe took the number as he reluctantly called Sam. After a brief conversation, Joe filled out the owner on the title as Sam Pitts.

Joe stared at the title, shaking his head for a moment, before he spoke. "He said he would take care of this, and to let you know that the insurance will be covered. I don't like this at all ... but for some reason I feel like I can trust you. Here's the keys to the jeep ... also, Sam told me to tell you to call him right away." The Drifter agreed to call Sam and grabbed the keys from Joe's hands.

He quickly loaded the trailer and left Joe's before he had a chance to change his mind. The Drifter proceeded to a small convenience store, where he had a brief conversation with Sam on the payphone outside of the store. When he was finished, he went inside to buy a cup of coffee, and saw an automobile trader's magazine. Thinking this might be a good method of finding and purchasing an ATV, he decided to grab a copy before leaving. He knew that the ATV would be needed as a secondary mode of transportation in the event the terrain became too rough for the jeep to travel. As he glanced through the magazine, he found a small four-wheel ATV advertised. He again went to the payphone outside the store and called the number listed for the vehicle.

After a brief conversation with a young-sounding gentleman, he discovered it was still available. The Drifter quickly informed the young man of his interest in the ATV, and that he would pay cash. After receiving the directions, the Drifter jumped in his jeep and headed south on Highway 45.

He found the house in the middle of the country on a small farm. This was a streak of good luck that he needed. The young man, by the name of Tony, showed him the ATV. Satisfied with it, he paid cash and waited for Tony to sign the title. The Drifter loaded the ATV onto the trailer and prepared for his journey north.

Along the way, he stopped in several different cities and purchased camping supplies, groceries, tools, and anything else he thought he might need. In one small city in Nevada, he bought some lanterns, cooking utensils, a hatchet, and a small axe. At a surplus store in Idaho, he found a thick, warm sleeping bag and a small tent. At a small hardware store on a mountain pass in Oregon, he purchased a chainsaw and some climbing gear. He continued to purchase items throughout his travels, as he analyzed all the possible situations he might encounter.

He traveled for days, until he reached the far corner of Washington State. Here he found a private ferry service that could take him to the southern border of Alaska. On his arrival at Homer, Alaska, after several days on the ferry, he decided to spend the night. After a good night's rest and a full tank of gas, he took the Sterling Highway toward Anchorage. When he arrived in Anchorage, he decided to remain there for a few days to gather the last remaining supplies. On his fourth day, he took the Glenn Highway north in search of his dream.

When the Glenn Highway intersected with the Denali Highway, he decided to go further north. After taking the Denali Highway, he drove north for a while, before it took a westerly direction toward the Alaska Mountain Range. After several days of travel, he broke from the main road onto what seemed to be an old logging road. This took him deep into the mountain range, further away from civilization. The more he traveled, the more difficult it became.

The logging road turned into a trail where the shrubs and trees became denser, making it more difficult. It became slow and cumbersome, only covering a few miles a day. The deeper in he went, the more he was forced to clear brush, small trees, and some fairly good-sized rocks that blocked his way. On the fifth day, he arrived at an impasse and could no longer use the jeep. He unloaded his ATV from the trailer, loaded it with camping supplies, food, and fuel. His search was not finished, for he had not found that perfect place to build his memorial home. On the sixth day of his journey, he crested a mountaintop, and below him was the most beautiful valley he had ever seen. In the middle of the valley was a clear blue body of water, surrounded by spruce, cedar, and pine trees. From his observation point, he could see two mountain passages. One passage was to the north end of the valley and the other to the east, close to where he stood. He swelled with excitement when he saw what looked like a cave opening at the base of a mountain on the far west end of the valley. He spent the next few days investigating the valley, getting familiar with it, establishing landmarks and directional bearings. When he was satisfied with his exploration, he headed west toward the cave he had seen. There was an entrance at the base of the mountain, leading into a large cavern. The opening was large enough to drive his vehicle into, and led through a corridorlike entrance about twenty feet before it opened up into a larger room. It was about thirty feet wide and fifty feet deep, then stopped abruptly. There were no other passages that led further inside the mountain. The floor was smooth and looked very level to the naked eye. It had high ceilings with a small three-foot ledge approximately twenty feet from the floor, circling almost the entire cavern. He had walked almost to the end of the cavern, and with his flashlight, he circled the ledge using his light. On this ledge, almost directly overhead of the corridor he came through, he saw what looked to be another cavern, going back toward the outside. Without a visible method of reaching the upper ledge, he went back to the ATV and unpacked his climbing gear.

When he returned with his gear, he climbed up the small ledge and found a small room on the northeast wall. This room covered about two hundred square feet, ten feet by twenty. The ceiling in the small cavern was eight feet high, but the entrance was only six feet, making him bend slightly as he walked in. There was a four-foot hole in the east wall leading outside, giving him a good view of the valley. A vision came to mind as he thought about putting a piece of glass over this crack. *This room would make a great study, a place where I could think and relax,* he thought as he looked around the small room. He left the small cavern and walked back to the ledge, when he decided to explore the rest of the ledge. There was a fourteen-foot gap in the ledge to his left, so he got out his climbing gear once more, and scaled the rock wall to the other section of the ledge. Once he got there, he found a small crack in the southwest wall. The crack was large enough to walk through without any hindrance, so he followed the rock hallway into a larger cavern. This cavern was huge, with ceilings that stretched at least a hundred feet from the floor; the stalagmites were reaching up toward the stalactites as if they were trying to kiss. It was a beautiful sight with all its magnificent colors of glamour. His mind was filled with thoughts of how and where he would build his home. *The house could fit inside this room easily and set up against the south wall,* he thought with excitement.

While searching other parts of the caverns, he found another crack on the west side of the large cavern, leading into a small room. This room stretched up further than the eye could see and had no floor, or at least one that could be seen. The air was constantly moving through this room, flowing from somewhere at the top and downward toward the bottom. His plans were coming together. This room could house a small wind generator. With electricity, he could have hot and cold running water, lights, and with air pumps, he could build a compost bed for trapping natural gas. This would give him a source for heating and cooking.

His first objective was the retrieval of his jeep. He spent many days and fought the wilderness to create a passage into the valley. His jeep fit perfectly through the opening at the base of the mountain leading into the bottom cavern. Through the coming years, this room became his garage, and he built stables in the back half, away from his study. He spent the next few days drawing the plans and building a list of materials required to build his home. His first step was to find a place to order the materials and figure out a way to haul them. He designed a block and tackle configuration for lifting the material into the foyer, leading from the lower cavern to the larger upper cavern. His plans were finally complete and it was time to begin.

He decided to take the north pass to see if he could find a town close enough to order the materials. The pass just took him further into the mountains. The terrain became steeper and rockier, so he decided to turn back and try the east pass. The east pass, after a day of traveling, took him to small town called Cyprus Springs. Cyprus Springs was the closest sign of civilization that he had found for at least hundred miles, and offered a place of refuge if he decided he needed one. Cyprus Springs had very little to offer him. There was a small store where he could buy some camping supplies and food. The only other businesses in Cyprus Springs were the town bar and a small bed-and-breakfast hotel, with only a few rooms. Most of the locals would gather every night at the bar, where they would drink and socialize. He met some of them, after buying a few rounds of drinks. He listened to their tall tales and learned much about the small town. It uses to be a prosperous gold mining town back at the turn of the century. To the Drifter, it now seemed to be a gathering place for all the riffraff living in the surrounding area. He met a few gold miners, who told him their tall stories about panning for gold and how they were going to hit the mother lode. He just smiled at them and let them believe in their dreams.

He saw two scruffy-looking gentlemen sitting alone at a corner table, off to the side of the bar, and asked one of the miners about them. He was told they were brothers, and the two of them were trappers who drifted into town once in a while to buy a few groceries and have a drink before they left. Travis, one of the miners he spoke with, seemed to think the two brothers were not trappers at all. He could not remember ever seeing them with beaver pelts or any other furs to trade.

The Drifter examined them more closely after hearing what Travis had said. It seemed to him by the way they kept their distance that they were trying to remain anonymous. He began to wonder what these brothers were doing here. Their suspicious nature led him to believe that their dealings were somewhat illegal. This would explain why they keep their distance and why they seemed to not associate much with the townspeople.

All the locals were friendly and did not seem too inquisitive about him or his business there. Not once did anyone ask his name; they all minded their own business. The town was a perfect place to work from, without fear of having to reveal his intentions. He talked to Jake, the store owner, one night at the bar about getting some supplies. Even though Jake usually did not carry all of the items he would need, he convinced him to buy these supplies, having them delivered and stored in his barn. The Drifter paid extra for these conveniences, but he needed a place to store the materials until he had a chance to pick them up and haul them into the valley.

He placed his orders with Jake and spent the summers hauling the building materials to his new home inside the caverns. During the winter months, when it was too cold to think about anything else, he would build his dream home. Winters in the mountains were very cold, and the sun barely clipped the horizon. It was like a continuous dusk, just enough light to barely see, but not enough to warm the skies.

Chapter Three
The Rescue

(Present Day)

It was another cold, dark morning in early December. The sun was barely clipping the mountaintops, causing a dark shadow to gloom across the valley. The Drifter sat in his thinking room, peering out over the valley and watching the weather, filled with thoughts of going home. The house was finished and his journey would soon come to an end. His biggest fear was facing his family after being away so long. His thoughts of how to present himself once he was home filled his mind, as he watched the winds blow the treetops, causing them to sway gently, releasing the tightly clenched snow from their branches. The howling winds cut through the valley, putting him in a deep, mesmerized state of mind as he slowly allowed his eyes to close.

Memories began flashing before him, popping in and out in random patterns, like scattered pieces of a puzzle. Places, people, and times in his past presented themselves quickly before disappearing. He sat quietly in his easy chair, allowing these visions to come freely. A smile broke from his lips as some images of his youth flashed before him; back when he was young, full of vibrancy, ambition, and satisfied with his life. Without warning, a vivid and realistic picture of Amy pushed all others out of his mind. The smile was broken as he took a deep breath and sighed. *I miss you, Amy*. Visualizing her loving presence quickly brought tears to his eyes, as he began blaming himself once again. The feelings grew out of proportion, causing his emotions to consume him. Dog, sensing something was wrong, came to sit beside his master. He moaned as he laid his head upon the Drifter's lap.

As the Drifter tried to regain control, he realized it was now too late. The emotions had grown so enormous that the tears began pouring out heavily from his eyes. He finally gave in to these feelings and let the tears try to wash away the years of pain. This was the first time he had really cried in mourning since her death. He had held back the tears for so many years, thinking it was not manly to cry, that now he seemed to have no choice. It had been very hard accepting her death, and for such a long time, he had held back his feelings; now he was unable to break away. The crying became more intense as all his emotions from deep within surfaced at once. His breaking heart vastly overpowered him as these emotions burst out of control. He stood up to pace the room, hoping to regain his senses, but the more he tried to stop crying, the harder he seemed to cry.

He paced about the room for what seemed like hours, unable to control the tears until finally his heart was finally content. Slowly, the tear ducts began to dry as he regained his composure and the strong emotions began to subside. After wiping the last remaining tear from his eye, he walked to his wood-burning stove to pour a fresh cup of coffee. Dog had been pacing the room beside him, but had been completely ignored. Feeling remorse for not giving Dog any attention, and knowing he was worried, the Drifter knelt beside his companion and gave him a loving hug.

"I'm sorry, Dog, I know you were worried," he said as he thanked God for his friend. Dog had become his only friend in the wilderness, and he had come to rely on his companionship. The moment of passion was broken when he felt the soft, wet kisses upon his face. Dog was excited about the loving and was repaying his master with a wet tongue. The Drifter, after having enough, pushed Dog's head aside as he stood up and picked up his cup of coffee.

He went back to his easy chair to relax and have a cigarette. As he lit his cigarette and drank his coffee, he remained calm while enjoying the rest of the morning, feeling better than he had felt in many years. As he puffed on his cigarette, he began to think that now was the time to pay his respects to his beloved wife and daughter. The crying had released some of his pain and grief that he had suffered for so many years. For the first time since their deaths, he had faced its horrible sight. *Their memorial home is finally finished and now I feel I can pay homage to their memories. I can only hope I've earned my forgiveness from them. All I have left to do is go home and pray that those I left will find it in their hearts to also forgive me.*

(A few nights later)

The Drifter was not sure what driving force took him to his thinking room this night. It had a strong, mysterious feeling that surrounded him with a choking grip, holding him very tightly, as if trying to squeeze the life from his body. The air was thick and stale, and weighed heavily against him, as if pushing his head and shoulders toward the ground; he felt imprisoned by his own weight.

All night, he had tossed and turned in a restless sleep and failed to free his mind of all the wondering thoughts. Memories of Amy seemed to engulf his mind once again. He wasn't sure why he was feeling this way; it seemed something or someone was there, urging him on. Compelled and unable to sleep, he had gotten up and come here.

It was a cold, dreary night, but the skies were clear, with the stars glittering off the black background of space. It was a wonderful sight. He sat in his easy chair, staring into the night sky, watching the stars as they sparkled. The memories of Christmases past made their presence known, for soon it would be upon him once again. *Maybe this is why I couldn't sleep,* he pondered. This used to be his favorite time of the year, but until tonight, he had come to dread it. He closed his eyes to allow the memories of the past Christmas seasons with Janelle and Amy to return. *Those were the very best years of my life.* The spirit of Christmas was in the air, bringing back wonderful memories, the ones he had once forced from his life.

Joy filled his heart as he enjoyed this brief memorial moment. It was not long before his thoughts were rudely broken by a draft of cold air across his legs, a phenomenon that had gotten his attention many times before. Opening his eyes and turning his head in the direction of the airflow, he saw it. There it was on the north side of his study wall, the small, forgotten hole. The hole he was going to patch last year, the hole that always seemed to elude him. A small hole which led outside to the east side of the mountain, and every time the east wind blew, his small thinking room turned into a refrigerator.

"I've got to patch that hole, Dog. My memory isn't as good as it use to be, so next time we're in here, you remind me, okay?" He asked this as if he half expected Dog to respond.

He arose from his easy chair and went to the small wood-burning stove on the south wall of the study. With some pine knots — which are easy fire starters — and a few chunks of wood, he loaded up the stove. From a small shelf mounted next to the stove, he grabbed a lighter and a wood chip from one of the pine knots. He lit the pine and placed it inside with the other wood, and in a short time, the fire was blazing, bringing welcome warmth to the small cavern. He stood there enjoying its warmth with a feeling of serenity as the heat from the stove removed the chill from the air. The thought of coffee filled his mind and the smell of that succulent brew forced him to want a cup. Dog watched his master leave, but did not move to follow his friend and companion. He sensed where the Drifter was going, and knew that he would return soon. He turned his head back to the window and stared into the night sky once more.

(Flight 493)

Flight 493, a red-eye flight originating in Seattle, Washington, headed for Anchorage, Alaska on what seemed to be a routine flight. Three hundred miles from Anchorage, they dropped to an altitude of 7,000 feet to prepare for their approach. From the atmospheric conditions that were present, a high-altitude electrical storm had spawned fifty miles southeast of Seldovia, in the Gulf of Alaska. It gained fortitude and began moving northeast toward Anchorage. Its arrival was unexpected and caused a major commotion in the control tower. The air traffic controllers were doing their best to divert planes already on approach, to Fairbanks. To avoid this impending storm, Anchorage control changed their flight heading to 360 degrees, due north. Their flight path was to take them around the storm, safely to Fairbanks until the storm passed; however, they managed to get caught up in its outskirts. Maneuvering the aircraft to an altitude of 10,000 feet in an attempt to get above the storm, the pilot unknowingly flew the plane right through its center!

Lightning struck so close on the port side of the aircraft that the passengers could feel the heat from it as it ripped through the atmosphere toward the ground. The boom of thunder was so loud, it was almost deafening, causing the plane to rattle as though it was going to break apart in midair. The passengers were tossed about in their seats, setting off a domino effect of panic. This magnificent force of nature unleashed itself on the Boeing 747, cracking the fuel line on the port engine. The spewing jet fuel ignited, causing the engine to catch fire. The lightning disrupted the electrical system, taking out the flight computer and most of the navigational equipment. The radio and the transponder were both fried beyond repair. There seemed to be no hope for the passengers and crew, only an impending doom. The aircraft was out of control and plummeting back to Earth.

(Anchorage – Flight Control)

There was a panicked hustle in the control tower, with people scurrying about trying to solve the problem with all the aircraft on approach to Anchorage. Silence fell on all when Dave, a young flight controller, yelled out, "Sir… I lost the transponder signal from Flight 493!"

Everyone stopped in their tracks and looked at each other in horror. After what seemed hours, Anthony the chief controller asked, "Are you still in radio contact with them?"

"No, sir!" Dave stammered.

Anthony let out a long sigh as he sat down in his chair. He looked at one of the supervisors sitting at her control station and advised her to call air rescue and give them the last known coordinates of Flight 493.

Dave spoke up, "I'm already on it, sir."

The chief nodded his head as he propped his elbows on his small desk and placed his head in his hands.

Dave was on the phone with the National Guard, giving them all the information, when his lower jaw slowly dropped. He looked back at the chief with the look of a man who was given the death penalty as he related the words that caused a feeling of helplessness among all in the room: "They're not able to mount a rescue operation right now. The storm is headed their direction and it could be hours before they will be able to get choppers in the air."

The chief lifted his head, solemnly looked at his hands, and mumbled, "I guess they're in God's hands right now. All we can do is pray for them."

(Back on Flight 493)

Even though the plane was on its northerly heading, it was still over the Gulf of Alaska and losing altitude due to the failure of the port engine. The fear of a water landing and sinking to the bottom of the ocean, never be heard from again, caused the captain to reach for the throttle and bring it all the way back, in the hope of gaining altitude. The plane shuddered as the starboard engine began to frantically whine, having all the work forced upon it. The captain was trying his last attempt to push the plane upwards, to give them a chance to make it to Fairbanks. With all the hope in the world, he relaxed, now nurturing a glimmer of hope.

The aircraft gained the altitude needed, giving them time to start repairs of the vital system components. The copilot was trying desperately to flush the port engine to stop the fire, but was unsuccessful. The plane continued to spew out its precious fuel that would be needed to complete its flight to Fairbanks, even with the copilot's valiant attempt to stop it. All looked comparatively better to the passengers and crew of Flight 493.

(The Drifter's Mountain Home)

The Drifter returned to his thinking room, carrying the pot of freshly brewed coffee. He walked over to the small shelf above the wood-burning stove and grabbed a cup to fill. He returned to the comfort of his easy chair while he enjoyed his fresh brew. Dog watched his every move but never once left his spot by the window. The taste of the coffee was satisfying his addiction to caffeine. Relaxing and sipping on his coffee brought to mind another addiction, cigarettes. This need for a cigarette to go with his coffee caused him to once again leave the comfort of his chair. He walked back over to the stove and grabbed a cigarette out of the pack of Marlboros that was lying on the small shelf. "I never could break this habit, although I've slowed down a bit, but I really enjoy a cigarette with my coffee," the Drifter remarked, as if speaking to Dog.

For the first time tonight, he was feeling content; his mind was clear of all thoughts. He returned to his easy chair to enjoy his coffee and cigarette in the serene silence of his thinking room. The peacefulness of the moment began to make him somewhat sleepy, causing his eyelids to droop as he relaxed. This feeling of peace did not last very long, when he was suddenly aroused by loud barking. Slowly he opened his eyes as he gave Dog a look from hell for interrupting his relaxation, and asked, "What's the matter, boy?" Dog was standing on his hind legs with his front paws resting on the window. He glanced at the Drifter and then through the window, before he barked once more.

Not sure why Dog was barking, he put out the rest of his cigarette and walked to the window. At first glance, he did not see anything, but then in the clear sky, he saw it. "What is it boy?" he asked. "It looks like a comet, but I don't really think it is," he said as he continued to talk out loud. "I need my binoculars."

Back at the window, he could make out what looked like a plane, and it was on fire. *What's a plane doing out here?* he wondered. He stared at it with a childlike excitement, for he had never seen a plane this low in the skies around here before.

(Back on Flight 493)

The pilot was using all his strength to hold the nose of the aircraft up, allowing it to glide. He was hoping to find somewhere to land soon, because he knew their time was running out. The copilot was persistent and focused on finding a spot, but the darkness of the night was not cooperating. "I need a place to land!" yelled the captain.

"I'm trying to find a place; it's dark out there, Captain, and all I can see is snow and mountains," replied the copilot.

"I know, Ken, just do your best. We need to land this bucket before it becomes scrap metal," the captain said, slightly calmer.

"There, at 2 o'clock," yelled the copilot.

"I see it," replied the captain.

In the back of the aircraft, there was much confusion and fear among all the passengers. The stewardess's were busy doing their best to calm them down and bring some order to their hysteria. Silence fell upon all the passengers when the loudspeakers boomed with the captain's voice. "Please, everybody, be seated, calm down, it is important that you remain calm. Please buckle your seatbelts and prepare for an uncontrolled landing. Please carefully listen to and follow the instructions from your flight attendants ... God help us all." The flight attendants immediately went to work preparing the passengers for what was sure to be a disastrous landing.

(In a small hunting cabin northeast of the Drifter)

In the cabin, located by a small icy lake in the midst of fir and spruce, three men sat around a table playing a friendly game of poker. Every year, these men would leave their families and travel to this beautiful winter wonderland. They came here to hunt elk and take the much-needed vacation from their mundane lives. They always spent at least a day or two in Cyprus Springs before leaving for the cabin. They would spend their evenings in the small bar, having drinks and telling tall stories of years past. The money these men threw around brought a little prosperity to this desolate, forgotten town. The citizens of Cyprus Springs came to enjoy their visits to their small community and never questioned their stories. Jack had walked to the window, trying to relax and get his mind off of his losing streak. Jack was a very large man with an unpleasant disposition. He was easily angered, which always resulted in violence. He trusted no one and blamed everyone for his life being shaped by the turn of events out of his control. Many times he had been arrested back home, after starting fights in the local bars. He had been charged with disorderly conduct, destruction of private property, and assault. His wife had left him because of his jealousy and unwillingness to control his temper. Ending up in the hospital with a broken jaw, she decided it was time to get out of the marriage. Even now, his anger was raging. He had lost a hundred dollars to Tom playing poker, and felt he had been cheating. Tom was a tall, slender, good-looking man. He was married with two children, but was very bored with life. He always came up with new ideas to add excitement to his life. This trip to Alaska was only one of many. He enjoyed the risky challenges the most. The closer to death he would get, the more pleasure he received from the experience. Though he loved his wife and kids, they could only satisfy part of his needs. His other needs took him to challenges that would completely satisfy him and leave him with the feeling that he was living life to its fullest. Jack stood peering out the window at the lightly lit sky, clenching and unclenching his hands, trying to fight off his anger. He so badly wanted to put his fist through the window or just pick up something and throw it at Tom. His anger was broken when he saw a fiery object off the horizon. "Hey guys, look at this," he said as he pointed to the fireball in the sky. The other two stopped playing cards and came over to see what the excitement was about. All three stared at the approaching fiery object, not quite sure what it was. As the object moved closer to the small cabin, Tom was able to identify it as a plane. Jack and Tom looked at each other with puzzled wonderment.

(The Drifter's Mountain Home)

The plane was bright against the dark night sky. The normal running lights and even the bright landing lights could not compare the brightness of the flames. As he watched the plane, it seemed to be dropping closer to the ground, dropping fast, as if it was out of control. He looked down at Dog, who was staring at the plane just as hard as he had been. "Hey, Dog, what do you think of it?" the Drifter asked inquisitively. Dog looked up and let out a whining noise, the one he used when he felt troubled. Both of them knew this was not a good sign. They stood and stared into the heavens, watching the plane as it dropped. The Drifter knew they were in trouble, and out here, he and Dog were their only hope.

It did not take a very long before the plane dropped behind the mountains to the northeast side of the valley. He looked down at Dog and then toward the mountain where he had last seen the plane. There was a tremendous flash of light that lit up the sky behind a mountain crest, like a halo on top of an angel's head. "Oh shit! Did you see that?" he asked Dog. Dog cocked his head to one side and groaned as if he didn't understand the question. The Drifter was not sure what caused the crash or why it happened, but it was obvious they were going to need some help. "Hey, let's take a hike, Dog," he said as he backed away from the window and headed toward the door. Dog had dropped to all fours and begun barking wildly, before darting for the opening to join his master and friend.

(The Hunting Cabin)

The plane came to a rest several miles northeast of the cabin and burst into flames as it crashed into the thick forest, lighting up the sky for a brief moment before darkness was able to regain its supremacy of the night. Tom slapped Jack on the back of the shoulder and said, "Hey, let's go see if there's anybody alive." Tom winked at Jack as he nodded his head in a sadistic manner. Jack knew where Tom was coming from and nodded in agreement. They left the window and began packing for the trip. Peter, who Tom and Jack called Peety for fun, stood there totally confused and unaware of what the other two were planning. Peter was a small, slender man, an entrepreneur and self-made millionaire. He was unlucky in love and in friendships. Tom used to work for Peter, and introduced him to Jack. He liked Tom and Jack and truly believed they were his friends. Even though the two of them picked on him and showed him very little respect, he still loved them. Tom usually called the shots, and Peter would dish out for all of the expenses. Peter was the one who always sponsored these trips and any other adventure Tom desired. It was a great relationship for Tom, but Peter, being so desperate to have a friend, had fallen into the cataclysms we all fall into at least once in our life. The three men packed up food, extra clothes, and firearms and left the safety of the small cabin, headed northeast toward the crash site. Tom and Jack were in front, leading the small expedition, leaving Peter to trail behind. The two of them were busy discussing their plans once they reached the plane. Some of that discussion was how to convince Peter to join them. They were planning on having some fun with the survivors, and Peter would probably have a hard time dealing with it.

Tom was very excited about their plans, for this was the opportunity of a lifetime. He could do whatever he desired out in the remote wilderness of Alaska, without fear of any retribution for his actions. Peter, not sure what they were discussing, asked, "Hey, what's going on up there? What are you two talking about?"

The two of them looked back and shook their heads in disappointment. Tom answered, "When we've finished our discussion and feel it's time to let you know, I'll tell you. Until then, be quiet and don't interrupt us again, *capisci?*"

(Back at the Drifter's Home)

The Drifter was forced to lower Dog into the stables with a harness. He had not yet completed the installation of the lift that would leave from the stables up to the ledge in front of his study. Before he could reach the bottom of the ladder, Dog had already run to the elevator lift on the opposite side of the stables and was patiently waiting. He smiled as he walked across the stable floor toward the lift. He had not seen Dog this excited since the last time they had gone hunting together. He entered the lift where Dog was waiting, and they rode the elevator up to the ledge leading to the rock hallway. They scurried back to the house to gather supplies needed for the trip. When the Drifter reached the living room, he picked up a pencil and a piece of paper from a small table sitting close to the fireplace inside the den. He walked to the dining room table and began writing down items he might need.

Blankets, food, water, lanterns, flashlights, and the list went on. When he finished, he proceeded to gather all the items accessible in the house and laid them on the dining room table. Some of the items were in the stables, and he would have to gather them later. When he was finished, he laid all the items in one of the blankets spread across the table. He tied off the ends, giving him a way to carry the supplies to the stables. He turned around and glanced toward Dog. He was being very patient, wagging his tail with his tongue hanging out of his mouth as he panted. The Drifter could see the excitement in his eyes, so without further ado, he said, "Hang in there, boy; we're almost ready to leave." Dog barked once as he understood and remained sitting with his tail wagging. The Drifter grabbed the ends of the blanket and swung the bundle over his right shoulder. It was heavier than he expected, causing his legs to buckle slightly from the weight. He limped through the living room to the front doors leading outside, with Dog close behind. He clambered through the rock hallway to the elevator, before he could relieve his burden of weight. Laying the bundle down in the lift, he motioned for Dog to join him, who had been clinging to his heels since they left. They rode the lift down to the stables, and once there, he again threw the bundle over his shoulder. Inside his workbench, on the lower shelves were some lanterns, and the oil for them was on the upper shelf above him.

He took the oil from the shelf and placed it next to the bundle of supplies. He then grabbed two lanterns from behind the sliding doors on the bottom shelf, when he saw some ropes lying there. *Will I need rope?* he wondered as he contemplated the idea. After a few seconds, he decided against it and finished closing the door. He then took Horse, a gelding, from his stall and put a bridle and saddle on him. He finished by tightening the girth cinch and then led Horse to the east side of the stable to get the travois — a primitive sled. He had it stored against the east wall, and it was the only thing he had for carrying a large load, at least during the winter.

When he was finished laying the travois across the hindquarters of the horse, he then secured the ends to the saddle. After leading the horse to the workbench, he was able to load the bundle of supplies on the travois. Grabbing some leather straps hanging on the wall next to the workbench, he secured the supplies.

"Let's go, Dog," the Drifter said with excitement. Dog jumped up and headed toward the east door. The door was hydraulic and operated by an electric pump. It opened out toward the valley and was disguised like the rocky wall of the mountain. From the outside, you would think it was a part of the mountain and not an entrance to a cave. It was purposely disguised for his privacy, and to keep unwanted guests at bay. This gave the Drifter an added sense of security.

He led the horse to the door and pressed the green button. The familiar sound of the hydraulic arm echoed though the stables as it strained, pushing against the heavy rock. The door slowly opened, and now they were officially on their way. "Hey, Horse, I hope you're ready for this!" the Drifter said as he led him outside. When Horse gave no response to the Drifter's question, he shook his head and murmured, "Sometimes I wonder why I even bother talking to a stupid horse." Once he was outside, he reached inside a small crevice in the mountain wall, next to the entrance and pressed another button, concealed within.

The heavy rock door began crackling as it concealed his dwelling once more. Dog darted in the direction they needed to go. He started barking and running in circles, excited and impatient. The Drifter nodded his head and without hesitation said, "Go find them, Dog." The wolf took off running while the Drifter, leading Horse, followed.

(The Crash Site)

The plane was a total wreck. The tail section was completely gone, lost before the plane came to rest. It had clipped the edge of a rocky cliff and broken from the plane before it crashed into a ravine at the cliff's edge. The rest of the plane glided uncontrollably through the small plateau and came to rest in a small clearing. The cockpit broke off during impact and was flung more than a hundred feet from the body of the aircraft, and came to rest when it collided with a large spruce. Several of the passengers from the front of the plane were thrown out. Some large cedar trees had ripped off the wings as it passed through the densely packed forest, causing the one with the flaming engine to explode on impact. The ground around the craft was covered with bodies, luggage, and other debris.Rachael had regained consciousness from being thrown against the wall and hitting her head. She slowly opened her eyes and stared at the top of the plane. There was warm blood running from her forehead down the side of her face. She wiped the blood away with her hand and carefully picked herself up from the floor. Still dazed, she staggered toward the rear of the plane. Suddenly, she gasped and grabbed her mouth. The rear section of the plane was completely gone. She was puzzled and bewildered by its disappearance. She stood there horrified as she wondered about the condition of the rest of the plane.

She was still trying to regain her senses and was thinking hard about the missing section, which made it hard to believe that she was standing there. All she could think about was the poor passengers who were sitting back there, and how anyone was going to find them. She was totally engrossed in thought when she felt a hand touch her on the back of her shoulder. It startled her, causing her to jump and lose her breath. She was paralyzed and unable to move. It was a nightmare, and the fear had overtaken her reality. "Rachael, it's me, Jennifer," came a voice from behind. Rachael slowly turned and saw Jennifer with the same look of horror in her eyes.

Jennifer yelled, "You scared me!" Rachael stood there with her heart still pounding against her chest as she thought *I scared you?*

They each stared at the other without glancing away. They were both faced with this horrific tragedy that neither of them had ever experienced before. Rachael and Jennifer were the best of friends, and each was glad to see that the other had survived. Relieved after the shock of their first encounter, Rachael embraced Jennifer as she softly said, "I'm so glad you're okay!" There were tears of joy and sorrow running down both of their cheeks.

"What happened?" Jennifer asked in a stuttering, frightened voice.

"I'm not sure. The last thing I remember was that Captain Joe asked me to go back to my seat and buckle up. I was on my way back when the plane took a hard dip, and that's the last thing I remember, until now."

Rachael stepped back from their embrace, and with a gentle touch, she held Jennifer by the arms. In a motherly and sympathetic voice, she said, "We need to see if anybody is still alive, and take care of them, so both of us need to pull it together and do our jobs, okay?"

Jennifer nodded as she wiped the tears from her face and began looking about the airplane. She must have noticed the rear section missing, because she yelled, "Where is the rest of the plane?"

Rachael looked toward the rear, as if hoping to get a glimpse of the tail section, even though she knew it was nowhere to be found. "There were people sitting there and it's completely gone," Jennifer said with a frightened look in her eyes.

Rachael sighed, "Okay, I know we lost a few back here, but we still need to check the rest of the plane. I'm sure there has to be a few more of us still alive. Now get a hold of yourself and go to the front and check. I'll stay back here and look around. We are both still in shock over the crash, and helping the others will make us both feel better." Rachael watched Jennifer as she stepped over the bodies and luggage. She was really worried about her, but knew she was strong and would make it through this. As Rachael watched her movements, she noticed Jennifer was limping on her right leg. "Jennifer, what's wrong with your leg?" Rachael asked. When Jennifer turned back toward her, she could see the rip in Jennifer's dress, exposing a large laceration. The cut was bleeding heavily, and ran from above the knee to the ankle of her right leg. "You're hurt," Rachael said sympathetically.

Jennifer looked back at Rachael and smiled, "I'll be okay. It doesn't seem to bother me right now."

"Are you sure you'll be okay?" Rachael said in a soft, concerned voice. Jennifer nodded with a smile, turned back toward the front of the plane, and limped off into the darkness. Both women began checking the bodies for a pulse or any sign of life. Jennifer was walking back toward the front when she heard a small voice say, "Help me." She walked toward the sound and found Amy sitting over her mother. She had met Amy and her mother earlier in the flight. Jessica, Amy's mother, had told her about the divorce and how she had caught her husband sexually abusing their daughter. Jessica was on her way to visit an old college friend, in the hopes of getting Amy away from the court proceedings. Jennifer approached the two of them and saw that Amy was crying. She could tell Amy was frightened and worried about her mother. She knelt down beside Amy, putting her arms around her for comfort. She then gently whispered, "Everything will be all right …I promise."Jennifer, afraid Jessica was dead, carefully checked her pulse. There was a great sense of relief when she felt a strong beating of the heart. Jessica was alive, but before Jennifer would say anything to Amy, she had to thoroughly check her mother. She looked for any major cuts or bruises on Jessica's body. Not finding anything she gently felt for any broken bones. After a few minutes and a thorough examination, she only found a few minor cuts. She gently shook Jessica as she called out her name. In a very short time, Jessica opened her eyes.

"Are you all right, Jessica?" Jennifer asked.

Jessica shook her head briefly and as she regained complete consciousness she yelled, "Amy! ... Where's my Amy?"

Amy quickly brushed past Jennifer and grabbed her mother, crying, "I thought you were dead, Mommy."

Jessica held her daughter very tightly and began crying herself, knowing her little girl was okay. Jennifer stood up and watched them briefly. She did feel better after helping them, and she no longer had that feeling of remorse or self-pity. Jennifer, with a slight movement of her hand, indicated that she needed to leave. She was rewarded with a smile and thank-you from Jessica.Rachael was checking the bodies, in the rear of the aircraft when she came across Alice. She was holding her husband George in her lap as she swayed back and forth in a rocking motion. She was mumbling some words that Rachael could not understand.

When she approached Alice, she looked up and said, "George is alive. I think his arm is broken, but I'm not really sure." Rachael knelt down next to Alice and checked George's arm.

After a few seconds, she glanced at Alice. "It may not be broken; I'm not sure either. It might just be dislocated and could easily be reset." Alice was a very beautiful woman and younger than George. Earlier in the flight, she told Rachael about their trip to Hawaii for their eighth wedding anniversary. Rachael had congratulated them on their anniversary, but now felt sorry for them having to spend this happy moment surrounded by tragedy and death. Several hours passed as the surviving passengers slowly gathered outside of the fuselage. Rachael was self-chosen to be the organizer and strength for all them in the midst of this crisis. She had to pull the group of survivors together and bring some order to the chaos. She hand-picked some men, ones who seemed to be in better shape than others, to gather wood for a fire. Some of the women were given instructions by Rachael to help the injured, by cleaning and bandaging their wounds. Rachael laid out some blankets for Jennifer to lie on, taking the weight off her leg.

The men returned, dragging some large logs. They placed the dead logs in a circular shape about ten feet in diameter. They returned to the woods and later came back with smaller branches. They dug a small hole in the middle of the larger logs and placed the branches inside. With napkins and dry clothes, they were able to start a small fire. It was not long before the fire was blazing, giving warmth and light to offset the darkness. Twenty-five survivors gathered around the fire, sitting on the larger logs, enjoying the warmth it had delivered. There was silence among them; not a word was spoken. Rachael and Jennifer had checked the entire plane, and these were all who had survived. Rachael sat in silence, as if she was stuck in nightmare, one she could not awaken from. She glanced at each of the passengers, only spending a moment on each. They all seemed to have the same blank stare in their eyes, with the look of melancholy across their faces. They were all stuck together in the same bad dream. It did not feel real, and yet, deep inside, they all knew it too well. As hard as it was to accept, Rachael knew she had to remain strong; their lives were in her hands. She was drowning in self-pity about a responsibility that was thrown upon her, and she never noticed the movement in the woods to her left. A loud cracking sound, which echoed through camp, brought Rachael to her feet. Shaking with fear, she turned toward the sound. She could see three shadowy figures moving through the darkness of the forest. Jimmy, one of the passengers, after seeing the figures, got up and ran to Rachael's side, stepping in front of her, as if he was there to protect Rachael. He yelled out, "Who's there?"

Chapter Four
The Survivors

(The Crash Site)

There was a moment of silence before they heard a deep booming voice say, "Hello." Jimmy and Rachael stood there, waiting for the shadows to move closer, into the light of the campfire.

The one leading the group looked much like Captain Joe, but Rachael could not be sure. She was filled with excitement, followed by fear. There were no signs of the front of the aircraft, and she assumed they were lost, just like the ones sitting in the rear. When the shadows moved close enough to the light, Rachael recognized Joe and Kenny. Kenny was not their normal copilot. Paul was sick and Kenny was his replacement. Rachael ran toward the three figures and threw her arms around Captain Joe. "I'm so glad you're okay; I was scared we had lost you," Rachael said, feeling better knowing the burden of decision had been lifted off of her. Joe returned her hug and they embraced for a brief moment.

He then pulled away from Rachael, and in his deep, authoritative voice said, "You've done well, Rachael. I'm proud of you. Who do we have here and what's been done so far?" Rachael was very relieved by the captain's presence. Captain Joe was a smart man and a good leader. She knew with his guidance that they were in good hands. She started pointing out what they had completed. She introduced the captain to the passengers she remembered. "Over there is Alice and George Stickler. His shoulder is dislocated or maybe even broken, I'm not sure. Down on that end is Jimmy and Janice Aaron; they're newlyweds. Jessica and Amy Anderson are over there in the middle. They seem to be only bruised and scared a little, kind of like the rest of us. Jennifer is lying down over there, close to the fire, on the blankets. She has a really nasty cut on her right leg."

Rachael continued until she had Captain Joe completely updated with most of the passengers' current conditions. After hearing everything from Rachael, Captain Joe immediately went to work. He appointed a small force of men to take the only three flashlights and search the area for any bodies. He went on to instruct them to pile the bodies as close the fuselage as possible. He asked Mi'chelle, a young French student, and Rachael to gather all the supplies from the plane and pile them next to the fire. He wanted blankets, food, water, and any spare clothing they could find. "Get the emergency first aid kit if you can find it," he said as Mi'chelle and Rachael were walking away. Rachael could hear Captain Joe barking out orders behind her as they crossed the opening into the remnants of the plane. They both searched the scattered luggage on the ground and throughout the plane for anything that could be used. Mi'chelle gathered all the blankets she could carry. Rachael gathered all the food and water she could find. They both were carrying all they could as they left the plane heading back to the campfire. Neither of them could find the first aid kit.

(The Drifter)

He had walked for hours in the deep, loosely packed snow. In the rush of getting ready, he had forgotten his snowshoes, and now was feeling the pain for rushing. The snow was so deep and thick that walking became more difficult with each step. He would sometimes sink in the snow above the top of his boots, forcing him to lift his legs higher to take the next step. His back was aching, as his legs stiffened more with every step. His feet were freezing and he knew if conditions did not change, he would not be able to keep his current pace. He figured that he had covered most of the distance, but still had another hour or so before arriving at the crash site. Since he started this mission of mercy, he had mixed feelings of excitement and distress, fearing he would find no survivors.

Shivering with anticipation of finding nothing, he forced the thoughts completely from his mind. Throughout the trip, these feelings would always return, making the pain of suffering less forgiving. He continued to ascertain how and what he was going to do once he arrived. Suddenly and without warning, a very sharp pain shot through his chest and continued down his left arm. All rational thoughts ceased as he grabbed his chest and fell to his knees. He realized he was far too weak to continue without a rest. He sat in the snow as he waited for the pain to subside. After a few minutes, he was able to regain some of his strength when the sharp pain became a trivial numbness in his chest, allowing him to stand. He walked to his horse and took a bearskin rug from the travois. He placed it on the ground next to a small tree. He sat down and leaned back against the tree, which provided some support for his aching back. "Ahhh, this feels good." Dog had traveled several hundred feet in front of him, as he always did, before noticing his companion was nowhere to be seen. With concern, he doubled back to find the Drifter sitting by the tree. He approached his master and sat down beside him, giving his concerned whine.

The Drifter glanced at Dog, smiled, and said, "Look at you, you're not even panting or breathing hard." Sometimes he envied Dog's youth and endurance; it made him feel very old. "You know, when I was younger, I could have kept up with you, but I'm getting older and my limitations have changed." Dog's head cocked to one side as if he understood every word. The Drifter knew his wolf companion was very patient with him and loved him unconditionally. He laid his head back against the tree, closed his eyes, and pulled Dog close to his chest. Dog sat there, wagging his tail, gently brushing it across the snow, as his master scratched and rubbed him under the neck, which was his favorite spot. "I thank my lucky stars for the day that we came together, Dog. You're my best and only friend in this godforsaken country," the Drifter said as he rested his weary body.

(The Hunters)

The three hunters were keeping a fast pace. Tom was in the lead and very excited about his plans. There were no intentions of him slowing down for the other two. Jack, the big one, was out of breath and struggling to keep up with Tom. "Slow down, Tom," Jack yelled out. Pete, who was having no trouble keeping the pace, looked back at Jack and started laughing.

This angered Jack even more. "Wait until I get my hands on your scrawny little ass!" Pete laughed even harder; he knew Jack would never catch him, because he was too fat. Tom stopped and turned around as he listened to Jack and Pete's conversation. Pete was walking backwards as he laughed and tormented Jack. He unknowingly backed into Tom, who was waiting for him. When Pete turned around and saw the angry eyes of Tom, he immediately apologized. "Excuse me, Tom, I'm sorry."

By this time, Jack had caught up with the other two and immediately grabbed Pete by the shoulders and flung him into the snow. "Don't you ever laugh at me again, you little piece of shit!" Jack yelled, as he stood over Pete, shaking his fist. Tom grabbed Jack's left shoulder and pushed him away from Pete. "You two stop it," he said in a very low voice. "We will be there soon, so the both of you shut up and keep quiet," he whispered as he pressed his right index finger against his lips. "Shhhh." Pete had picked himself up from the snow and was brushing the loose snow from his clothing when Jack approached him. Jack, still angry, put his fist into Pete's face and shook it heavily, without speaking or making a sound.

(The Drifter)

The pain in his legs began to subside, just leaving them slightly stiff. He took off his boots and gently rubbed his feet, allowing the warmth of his hands to help the blood circulation. His toes began tingling, releasing the numbness and bringing the feeling back into them. He then wrapped his feet in the bearskin rug and washed his hands, using the loose snow. Reaching into his leather backpack, he pulled out a bag of jerky. He took out two slices, one for him and the other for Dog. He gently sucked on the piece of jerky, chewing very lightly, allowing the salt from the jerky to soothe his throat, which had become very dry and itchy.

Dog began nudging him gently against his chest with his nose. The Drifter stared at him, slightly confused, before realizing he had not given Dog the other piece. He knew Dog could have taken it from his hand, but he was trained never to take anything, unless it was given willingly. He raised his hand from the ground and gave Dog his piece of jerky. As soon as it was close enough, Dog grabbed it from his hand, and within seconds had it devoured. The Drifter looked at him with a smile. "You're hungry, aren't you, boy?" He reached up to the piece in his mouth, removed it, and gave it to Dog. He rested while Dog finished eating the other piece.

The Drifter, thirsty after sucking on the piece of jerky, could only imagine the thirst Dog must have felt. He grabbed his canteen, took a swallow of fresh cold water, and then poured some in his hand for Dog to drink. Dog lapped up the water until it was gone and then gave him a begging look. Sensing his thirst, the Drifter continued pouring water into his hand until Dog had drunk his fill and backed away. "Okay, boy, let's go," the Drifter said as he stood up. Dog again darted into the woods, taking the lead as the Drifter followed, leading the horse.

(The Hunters)

The small group of survivors from Flight 493 was totally unaware of the three hunters closing in on their location. Tom's intention was not that of help; instead it was to have them partake in a new game he and Jack had brewed up along the way. Pete followed his friends blindly, unaware of their motives. With their rifles drawn and cocked, they approached the small plateau where the plane had crashed. They moved quietly through the trees, like a cat stalking its prey, until they reached the outskirts of the crash site. Tom stopped short of the plateau while he observed the small group of people surrounding the fire.Pete, out of curiosity, asked Tom why they had stopped. Tom quickly indicated to Pete to be quiet. "We're making sure they don't have any weapons. You don't want to get killed trying to help them…do you?" Tom whispered. Pete acknowledged Tom with a thank-you for being so smart and thinking ahead. Pete always admired how Tom was able to handle dangerous situations with calmness and intuitiveness. The three hunters stood behind a small clump of trees as they watched every movement made by the survivors, and checked for any sign of weapons.

(The Drifter)

Two hours had passed since he had stopped to take a brief rest, before he saw the first flicker of light through the dense forest of pine and spruce. He slowed his approach toward the light and moved very carefully, trying to be as quiet as possible. Dog sensed his caution and began moving slowly and quietly, like a mountain lion, sleek and sure of every step. The Drifter, not being sure how his presence was going to be accepted, decided caution should be his first concern. Many years had passed since he associated with a crowd of people, and his mannerisms had become stale. He was unsure of the conditions that awaited him, as he moved closer to the light. When he was close enough, he could see a small campfire and several people standing and sitting around it. He was still too far away to hear the conversations clearly, but from the sound of it, there seemed to be something wrong. He tied the reins of Horse to a nearby tree and moved in for a closer observation. As he approached the opening in the woods, he decided to drop to his belly to help conceal his presence. As he slithered through the snow, he became one with it, camouflaged in the darkness. He slowly moved up a small embankment, where he could get a clear view. Dog, seeing his movements, also dropped to his belly and was mimicking the Drifter.

Looking through the binoculars, he could see several bodies lying in the snow close to the fuselage. *Those are the poor bastards who didn't make it,* he figured. As he searched the area, he saw what possibly looked like the front of the plane buried deep in the forest about a hundred feet from the main body. The wings and tail section were missing, so he assumed they were lost before the plane came to rest. He stared back into the woods toward the direction of the plane's flight path, looking for the missing pieces, but he could not see any trace of them. There was extensive damage to the body of the plane, and it was a miracle that any survived the crash.

Letting his binoculars fall back against the snow, he placed his hand on Dog's neck. With a slight gesture, he placed his finger against his lips, and gave a gentle *"shhh,"* indicating for him to be very quiet. Before he finished with his silence gesture, a loud voice broke the silence: "What are we going to do?" The Drifter quickly picked up his binoculars and glanced toward the sound next to the campfire. He could see a very lovely blonde dressed in a light blue dress suit, standing over a man sitting down on a log. From the man's hat, he figured him to be the captain of this flight. From her dress, she could possibly be the head stewardess.

The man stood up and shrugged his shoulders, followed by a sigh. "I'm not sure exactly what to do right now, except wait here patiently until we get rescued. We have some food and blankets; we'll be okay for a while," the man said. Apparently, this was not what she wanted to hear, because her next move was to get right back into his face, bellowing, "What about Jennifer and Mr. Stickler, what about them?"

His response was a simple one: "We have to be patient … everything will work out, I'm sure of it." The stewardess just waved her arms in the air frantically as she turned back toward the campfire.

The Drifter, after hearing the confrontation, knew this was his cue to move in and introduce himself. He stood up and started to approach the group of survivors, when he saw movement out of the corner of his eye. When he glanced to the opposite side of the campfire, he saw three men standing alone, away from the rest of the group. He decided to wait, and immediately dropped back on his stomach so he could observe these men more closely. As he watched, he began thinking, *Who are these men and why are they dressed in white? I need to do something, 'cause time is running out. I figure within the next eight to nine hours, a heavy snowstorm is going to hit and this rescue will be disastrous. Why am I waiting?* Paralyzed by some unknown fear, he was forced to lie there and watch.

After a short time, the Drifter decided on a different approach. He motioned for Dog to follow him as he backed down the small incline, still on his stomach. When he reached the bottom, he stood up and moved around the outskirts of the campsite, being very careful everywhere he stepped. He wanted to get closer while still keeping his presence unknown, but not too close in case he needed a quick retreat.

He was able to find a safe refuge behind a small clump of trees slightly behind the campfire. From here, he could watch and hear everything, even the faintest of whispers. His major problem was getting there undetected. He again dropped to his belly and slithered up the embankment to reach the small group of trees. He moved very quietly until he reached the last one that stood between him and the clearing, giving him the visibility of the entire plateau. From here, he could see and hear their every whisper. He lay behind the tree as he carefully watched the three strangers he saw earlier approaching the camp.

The three men were dressed in white camouflage suits, and each was carrying a rifle. They were heavily dressed, wearing a large overcoat over their suits. He could not tell if they were carrying any other weapons under their coat. He assumed them to be hunters, from their attire. One of the hunters had stepped in front of the young blonde stewardess who had caused the commotion earlier. "Can we help?" the man asked. The other two men had stopped behind him, and were standing poised as if they were expecting some kind of trouble. The whole scene looked suspicious, and he could not ascertain their intentions.

The young stewardess stood up and faced the lead hunter. "Yes, we could use your help. There are several injured and many dead. We are being led by a captain … who seems to have lost his balls. 'Just sit here and wait for a rescue,' he says. Well … I believe in action, and the best thing we can do is try to find a way to get the hell out of here."

The hunter crouched down as he started drawing something in the snow. When he glanced up toward the stewardess, he said, "Here is the closest town which may have a phone to use. This time of year, the lines are usually down; however, there is a possibility they can radio in some help. There is a small medical clinic there that can take care of the wounded."

The young stewardess turned toward the one who looked to be the captain with a questionable look in her eyes. He remained with his head bowed and said nothing. The young lady again spoke. "Well …don't you think that's better than just sitting here and waiting?"

The captain stood up, looking very angry, when he faced the two of them and asked in a sarcastic tone, "How are we going to carry the injured and how long will it take to get to this so-called town?"

The lead hunter stepped backward as he faced the captain. "It's going to take a few days to get there, and as far as the injured are concerned, well … they'll have to remain here until we can get a rescue team back to pick 'em up." The statement caused a hellish commotion among the survivors. The mumblings could be heard about the campfire as they spoke among themselves. Their conversations were garbled, as if mixed in a blender, and the Drifter was unable to make out most of what was being said. He did know from some of the words he was able to understand that these people did not like the comment this hunter made.

He saw the young stewardess turn around and face the group of passengers. The Drifter could tell she was not comfortable with her command position, but she seemed to be handling it quite well. "Let me assure all of you — we all go or we all stay. We are not going to leave anyone behind to die, so please … calm down." Red-faced with anger, she turned to face the hunter. "Why can't we build some sort of stretcher and carry the wounded to town?" The next sound that was made had the eeriness of your worst nightmare, when the lead hunter began a sadistic laugh.

The Drifter could hear the mumblings begin again. The sounds had more stress and anger embedded in the words, as these people could not believe the actions of this man. The young stewardess shook her head, trying to grasp the meaning of his laugh. "What's so damn funny?"

The lead hunter stopped his laughing to take a long, cold, hard look at the young stewardess. "You people are really stupid. Do you think I would waste my time dragging you assholes anywhere? The reasons I came here are far better than that, and will be so much more satisfying to me."

The Drifter saw the other two hunters lift their rifles from their sides, as they stood poised with guns at the waist. He heard the rifle hammers, as they were cocked and ready to be fired at a moment's notice. The other two hunters stood steadfast, rifles ready for action, as the lead hunter boastfully spoke. "If you do as I say, some of you may live to see your future, others … well, some of you will be stalked and hunted, just like we would any other animal. Those of you who are fortunate to be selected for this great thrill must realize you are participating in a very exciting sport, and there is some slim chance you may survive. If you can evade your capture for longer than an hour, we will let you live. However, if we find you before the hour has ended, well … consider it as part of the hunt. Does everybody understand these rules?"

The Drifter was struck by fear, as if paralyzed and unable to move. He could not believe what he just heard, or why these hunters were doing this. His only thought was to run away and leave these people to their own fate. With a quick glance toward Dog, and a slight motion of his hand to follow, he began moving back away from the camp. He slithered out of the clump of trees and down the slope, like a snake scurrying away from a fight. When he reached the woods and out of sight of the hunters, he stood up and walked quickly and quietly, not making a sound, back to where he had tied Horse.

(The Campsite)

Tom walked to a young lady sitting on a log next to her daughter. He found her to be a very attractive woman with long, light brown hair and green eyes. She stood about five foot six with a slim, nicely shaped body. Her clothes were torn in a few places, but he could tell from her attire that she was a respectable woman. He leaned over her and asked in a very strong voice, "What's your name?"

The young lady raised her head so she could see the hunter's face. In a very nervous and scratchy voice she said, "My name is Jessica and this is my daughter, Amy."

This angered Tom. "I don't give a shit what your daughter's name is—I only wanted yours. If I wanted your daughter's name, I would have asked for it. It's important for me to know your name, since you're the one I'm going to be hunting. It's for personal reasons—I'm sure you can understand that, you stupid bitch!"

Jessica began crying as she lowered her head from the shock caused by his words. "Please, Mister … please don't do this. My daughter doesn't have anybody to take care of her but me … Please, I beg you … don't do this." Rachael, now getting tired of Tom's attitude, took her turn as she lashed out at him. "Leave her alone, you sadistic asshole."

Tom, surprised by her lack of fear, cocked his head and gave her a crooked smile. "Shut up, bitch, your turn is coming … just be a little more patient, okay?" He quickly turned back to Jessica and grabbed her by the arm, forcing her to her feet.

The copilot, Kenny, who had been watching the ludicrous actions of Tom, launched his body from the log and ran swiftly toward him, shouting, "I'll kill you … you bastard." Jack pivoted his rifle toward the unsuspecting copilot and from the hip he pulled the trigger. The shot echoed through the woods as the bullet sank deep into Kenny's chest. The small group of survivors felt all their hopes and dreams fade like the echoes of the shot as it lost its hold over the silence. Kenny was thrown off his feet from the power of the bullet as it struck under his arm and into his chest, propelling his body into the crowd of survivors. He struck Alice and George Stickler, knocking them both off the log. He was knocked back from the force and fell to the ground, next to Amy's feet. In fear, Amy jumped away from the log and began screaming at the top of her lungs. Tom lashed out in a backhanded motion, smacking her across the forehead, knocking her to the ground. "Shut the little bitch up, Jessica, before I take the pleasure myself!" Tom said, as he released his grip on her arm. Jessica went to her daughter's rescue, picking Amy up from the ground. With all the strength she could force from her lips, she reassured Amy that everything would be fine. Before Jessica could finish easing Amy's worries, she felt the pressure on her arm as Tom grabbed her, pulling her away from her daughter's hold. "You have a ten-minute head start; after that, you're in God's hands. Remember, you only have to last for one hour and I'll let you live." Jessica glanced toward Amy and gave her a comforting smile as she slowly walked across the plateau and disappeared in the darkness. "Maybe you'll get a chance to see this little bitch of yours again—huh?" Tom scoffed, laughing. Jessica was now running for her life, but her greatest fear was for Amy. She was all that stood between her and the father who had been molesting her. She began to fear she would never see her little girl again.

(The Drifter)

He stood still as the gunshot echoed through trees and off the surrounding mountains. He glanced down at Dog. "That sounded like a gunshot. From the sound of the echo, I would say that it struck its target very hard and very solid." He heard Dog's whine as he bowed his head toward the snow-covered ground. With a frown on his face, he remained still. *I've been running for the last nine years … and now I'm running again. If I'm going to help these people, I need to do it now. I have the advantage; they don't know I'm here. One of the passengers is either dead or seriously wounded because I've taken no action. I have to decide quickly what I'm going to do and do it. I can't live with myself if I turn my back on these people; if I stay and help, there's a good chance I could die.*

Without further thought, he grabbed his holster and pistol from the saddle. He strapped the holster to his waist, tying off the straps holding the pistol tight against his leg. He pulled his rifle from its sheath mounted on the saddle, and made sure it was fully loaded. He slung the rifle around his neck and shoulder before opening his saddlebag to retrieve his large hunting knife. He tied the knife around his lower right leg between his knee and ankle. He stood straight and proud as he took in a deep breath, turned toward Dog, and quietly said, "Let's go get 'em, boy." The two of them headed back toward the camp fully dressed, ready to kill or be killed. Of course he had no intentions of being killed; this was just a figure of speech and the last thing on his mind. His thoughts were not about failure, but how he was going to handle each situation as it presented itself. He continued to analyze and project possibilities, but without collecting more data, he could possibly fail in stopping the hunters. He was short of the tree line leading up to the small incline before he stopped. From here he could observe them with his binoculars at a safer distance and hopefully gain an advantage. He had to stay anonymous to keep the hunters from discovering him. If this should happen, his element of surprise would fade, and that would likely be a fatal mistake. He lifted his binoculars and placed them over his eyes. Peering through them, he saw a handful of people sitting around the campfire. Fear engulfed him as he scanned the entire area and could only find two of the hunters. The one he had considered to be the leader of the three was nowhere in sight. Trying to keep his panic under control, he continued scanning the area in hopes of finding the last hunter. The more he looked, the more afraid he became. He removed the binoculars and began searching everywhere, including the area behind him. Not being able to find the last hunter caused his fear of discovery to be overwhelming. He dropped down to a sitting position as he continued his search of the area.

As he sat motionless in the snow, his mind began to wander. *What if he should walk up on me? Should I shoot him and expose my presence? Maybe he is just out gathering some firewood. Yeah, that's it. No, if he were the leader, then he would send someone else to get the wood. Why was he not in the camp? What is he doing and where the hell is he?*

Dog sensed the disturbance in his master and came to lie down next to him. The Drifter placed his hand on Dog's warm coat and gently rubbed the back of his neck. He opened his ears to the silence, listening for soft crunching of snow being packed by the weight of one's step, or the cracking of a twig as it broke off from a tree, but the only sounds he heard were the distant mumblings of the survivors sitting around the fire.

As he continued to listen for any unusual sounds, he began to wonder why he was so afraid. He was carrying weapons and was very capable of defending himself. Besides, Dog would have picked up on their presence long before he ever knew it. He glanced toward his wolf companion lying beside him, and saw no signs from him that might suggest the hunter was anywhere close to their location. Feeling more calm and self-assured, he pushed himself back to his feet and continued observing the campsite. Moments later, a frightful scream tore through the night sky, ripping its way through the silence. Then there was another scream, followed by a third. The Drifter carefully listened to the sounds, trying to get a bearing on the direction and distance. The screams were coming from the north and sounded much like a woman, a woman who was possibly fighting for her life. From the echo, he ascertained it was approximately two hundred yards from his position. Without further thought, he began moving toward the screams as fast and as quietly as he could. Time was important, but his invisibility to the hunters was his only ace in the hole. The wolf dog was hot on his master's trail, as they moved like shadows through the trees, neither making a sound. Too much time had passed before the Drifter arrived at the spot he had last heard the screams. He stopped and stood behind a large tree, staying undetected where he could search the area very carefully. He could see something lying in the snow about fifty feet from where he stood, but was unsure of what it was. He carefully scoured the area for any movement as he listened for footsteps. When he felt it was safe, he began moving slowly toward the object, keeping close to the trees to hide his ascent.

He was within thirty feet of the object when Dog darted out from the cover of the trees with a sudden burst of speed. The shadow in the snow had the shape and form of a body. It was lying next to a trunk of a small pine tree. Dog had stopped next to it and sat poised over the shadow. He once again searched the area very carefully, looking and listening, for he could not afford to fail. There was no movement to be seen nor sound to be heard, so he stepped away from the cover of the tree and walked toward Dog.

He stood over a limp and motionless body. Dog was licking her face as if trying to wake her, but it was too late, she never moved. To the Drifter, she was a very beautiful woman, at least from what he could tell. Her face was covered with blood and bruises. Her clothes had been ripped off, leaving her soft and tender body exposed to the cold. The snow was red from her precious blood seeping out of what looked to be hundreds of wounds. As he examined her more closely, he found cuts across her breast and down her stomach. There were lacerations all over her legs and even in the genital area. He estimated not one inch of her body was untouched by this blade of death. She had been raped and slaughtered for fun, and the bastard who did it was a very sick individual. He could not understand how one's mind could be so twisted and perverted enough to do this to another human being.

He dropped to his knees as he stared at her lovely face, wondering what kind of woman she was. Was she a good person or was she some sort of bitch who used men for her own gains? At this point in time, its importance had no bearing on the effect. It did not matter what kind of person she had been; nobody deserved to die like this. He began to feel sick, staring at her savagely beaten and tattered body. He slowly removed his warm fur coat and covered her with it, leaving only her face exposed. "I don't know your name, but I'm really sorry for not being here to help you ... there is no excuse—please forgive me." Tears filled his eyes as he began covering her face so no one could see the hideous condition the bastard had left her in.

He was placing his coat over her face and had it almost covered when her hands came up from the ground, pushing his hands away. He was so startled by her movement that he fell backward into the snow. He saw a God-awful fear glowing from her eyes as if she was ready to scream; he quickly moved toward her, clamping her mouth with his hand. "Shhhhhh," he whispered, "I've come to help. So please don't scream. I'm not going to hurt you." He released his grip when he felt her body starting to relax.

The moment of triumph was broken when he heard a loud voice directly from behind his position. "What the hell happened out there, you bastard? And where is Jessica?" Startled by the question, he turned quickly toward the voice, expecting to see someone standing there, and let out a deep sigh after seeing no one.

The voice sounded like the stewardess he had heard earlier, and it was not very far away. This meant the camp was closer than he originally realized. He turned back to the battered woman and stared into her pitiful eyes when he heard a soft trembling voice say, "Sir ... sir, please help my daughter." She stared into his eyes when she asked, "Promise me you'll protect my daughter from those hunters ... Please promise me."

He nodded his head in acknowledgment of the promise as she took her last breath. Sadness filled his heart as he laid the coat over her face and picked up his rifle, lying in the snow. He bowed his head and said a short prayer before leaving. He again moved among the trees for protection and camouflage.

He walked very slowly toward the sounds of voices. Within twenty steps after he left the body, he could see the campfire flickering through the trees. He heard a man's voice bellow, "Don't worry about that bitch. Your turn will come soon enough. Jack, Pete — it's your turn, one of you pick someone and let's get on with the fun."

The Drifter could tell by the authority in his voice that this had to be the leader. He was the one missing earlier and now he was back in camp. He must have been the one who butchered that poor woman. *I'm going to take that bastard down or else ... or else what? It was them against me, and the odds where in their favor. But if the opportunity should arise, I'll make sure that son of a bitch does not leave these woods alive!*

The Drifter reached the edge of the tree line, about twenty feet from the small incline leading up to the campsite. He monitored every movement the hunters made. He did not want to make any sudden decisions and end up doing something stupid, causing more hardships for these people. He had to think this out thoroughly, before he could make his next move. Dog had stopped next to him and sat down in the snow, wagging his tail, still full of excitement. The Drifter was just as anxious to tear into these hunters as Dog was, but the time was not quite right. He lifted his binoculars once more as he carefully combed the entire area, looking to gain an advantage.

He could see two of the hunters standing in front of the campfire, facing the small group of survivors. He figured they were checking out the group, and the reason seemed to be apparent. The first of the two was a very heavyset man who stood about six feet or better; the other was smaller, medium build, and had a full beard. The smaller one of the two seemed to be somewhat nervous or just sickly; his right hand was shaking, with sweat pouring from his forehead.

The larger, heavily shaped hunter had walked to a bed made from blankets and was standing over someone lying on the ground. He watched as he saw the hunter kneel down and softly speak to the individual on the blankets. "What's your name, lady?" There was no response from the lady, so the hunter asked again, slightly more angered. This female still did not answer the hunter, which must have pushed him over the edge. He saw this large man reach down, and with one hand, grabbed the female, lifting her off her bed by her neck. He noticed she was wearing the same outfit as the outspoken female stewardess. This stewardess was a head and shoulder shorter than the hunter, and had long black hair that reached to the middle of her back.

The big hunter threw the small petite female forward, like a feather in the wind, causing her to fall backward onto the ground. "I don't give a shit what your name is, bitch. I'm not like Tom who cares to know the name of the person he hunts. Me, I'm going to hunt you anyway, and to hell with your name." The Drifter knew then it was time to make a decision, before one more passenger was killed. He slowly lifted his rifle, putting the crosshairs of the scope on the hunter's head. He was about to squeeze the trigger when he heard the hunter say, "You have ten minutes to get away before I come after you, and from the looks of your leg, you'll need every minute. So get the fuck out of here, bitch … the game is on."

The Drifter moved the scope of the rifle toward the stewardess as he watched her limp very slowly into the woods, heading across the plateau going west. A sudden fear entered his thoughts: *Oh shit! She's headed toward Horse!* He lowered his rifle and by the time he had it back around his shoulder, he had already turned and was headed back into the woods. Moving as quietly and quickly as he could, he created a semi-circle beeline back toward his horse. He had only a few minutes to catch up to the stewardess and head her off. He still could not afford for them to find out he was here, at least not yet.

"Five more minutes, my love, then I'll come rescue you," came the sick, twisted voice of the hunter from behind and to the left of the Drifter. The sound was far too distant. *That's not right. I should be closer than that.* He looked around the dark forest, searching for some of his previously established landmarks, and could not find any of them. *Great, in my panic to get back, I seem to have lost my cool sense of direction and headed deeper into the woods,* he thought. With a quick movement, he knelt onto the snow next to Dog. "Okay, boy, I'll let you lead; go find Horse … time is running out." Dog dashed into the woods, moving much faster than him. His only fear was Dog finding that poor stewardess, and he was not there to stop him from ripping her to pieces. The thought of Dog barking for his attention, like when they would go hunting, brought even greater fear into his already-panicked behavior.

He followed Dog's pawprints, which was the only thing left of him, for he was now completely out of sight. The Drifter was moving slightly faster than before; his fear of not reaching Dog in time kept his momentum. He was dodging limbs as he moved in and around the trees, trying to catch up, when he caught a glimpse of movement off to his left about 10:00. He quickly stepped behind a tree trunk to conceal his presence as he peered around the tree, checking to see if he had been detected. He used his binoculars to scan the area, panning in a 180-degree radius, covering his field of vision. He could not see any movements in the area he had previously seen. Thinking it was his imagination, he let his binoculars fall back onto his chest and stepped away from the tree. Again he saw the movement, except this time, he could make out a dark figure.

Not sure of whom he was getting ready to stalk, he reached down his right leg and unlatched the strap holding his hunting knife. He moved very slowly, so as not to attract any attention to himself, as he watched the figure, not letting it out of his sight. Slowly he approached the shadow, keeping the trees between them. He had moved within twenty feet of the figure before he was able to determine that the shadow was a female. It had to be the stewardess by the way she was limping. He entrenched his body up against a tree trunk, as if he became one with the tree. She was headed in his direction, and all he had to do was patiently wait for her to pass.

He waited as he stared down at the snow slightly behind the tree to his right. He could hear her panting and the crunching of snow as she moved closer to his position. A few minutes had passed before he caught a glimpse of her foot, when she stepped next to the tree. He patiently waited for her to pass, but the foot remained in the same position. *What the hell is she doing? Is she resting on the same tree?* He closed his ears to the softly blowing wind and opened them to other sounds as he listened intuitively. He could hear the steady sound of heavy breathing behind him. She had stopped to rest against the same tree he was standing under. Slowly he moved to his left, keeping the tree as close to his body as possible, trying not making a sound. His plan was to come around the tree and hopefully be able to subdue her before she had an opportunity to scream and bring the hunters down on both of them.

He was moving around the tree when a sliver of bark caught his shoulder and was peeled from the trunk, revealing his presence. "Who's there?" came a frightened voice. He now had to move fast before she became too frightened and did something stupid. He launched his body around the tree, grabbing her from the rear in a very quick movement. He slung his left arm around her shoulder, pulling her close, and at the same time grasped her mouth, cupping it with his right hand. He held her very tightly against his body, trying to keep this frightened woman from getting away or making any noise. She was kicking him, hitting his shins from time to time, along with some scratches to the face. She was very strong and it took all his strength to hold her still.

"Calm down, lady," he whispered. "I'm not going to hurt you. I'm here to help, so please … calm down." He continued repeating his phrase until he felt her body loosen and the fighting ceased. "I'll take my hand off of your mouth if you promise not to scream." She nodded her head, acknowledging his request. Still unsure of her intentions, he added, "Now listen, if you scream or do something stupid, you risk losing the chance of saving your friends and yourself. You'll lessen my chances of overpowering these idiots and get this situation back under control. Now I'm going to let you go … so don't be stupid!"

He slowly loosened his grip on the young stewardess with the anticipation of her bolting and running away. To his surprise, she did not show any signs of being crazy or doing anything stupid, so he completely released his hold on her. As soon as she was released, she immediately turned toward him with the look of an angry woman. He had seen this look before and knew she was about to raise her voice to scorn him on his method of getting her attention. Quickly he lifted his finger and placed it in front of her mouth as he gave her a long "Shahhhhh." She immediately closed her mouth, fighting back her urge to yell.

"What's your name?" the Drifter inquired. She gave him a frightened look, taking a step backward as if she wanted to run away. He was not sure what brought about the scared look. Confused and not wanting to frighten her anymore, he lowered his voice as he gently spoke. "Fine, if you don't want to tell your name, that's okay. I'll just call you Lady for now. I want you to sit here by this tree and wait for that fat-ass hunter."

She looked at him with a crazed look in her eyes, saying in a whisper. "Are you fucking crazy or what? That bastard wants to kill me. Is that your plan? Because if it is, we're in big trouble."

The Drifter knew it sounded somewhat ludicrous, but it was the only way he knew of overpowering the large hunter, to catch him off guard. The only way to catch him off guard was to make him think everything was normal, and still going as planned.

"Okay, I know it sounds crazy, but as long as he thinks everything is normal and he's unaware of my presence, this plan will work. Now sit there and pretend you're scared for your life or something like that." She shook her head in disappointment, still not believing she was listening to this man, especially since she had never seen him before.

Finally, without further hesitation, she sat down next to the tree trunk. "Jennifer," was the soft-spoken voice he heard next. He looked slightly puzzled, so she repeated her statement. "My name is Jennifer; what's yours?"

He knelt in the snow next to her as he reached to shake her hand. "It's a real pleasure to meet you Jennifer, call me the Drifter; everybody else does." Seconds later, he left her to hide behind a large tree approximately five steps from her location as he waited for the hunter to arrive.

He was there for a short time when he heard footsteps approaching. The sounds were close, steadily moving toward the trap that awaited him. He could hear the soft, sadistic voice of the hunter as he called Jennifer. "Where are you, bitch? Come to Daddy, don't be afraid." The Drifter thought how wonderfully he used the English language, and from his speech, he had the intelligence of a worm. *What a real dumbass this guy must be if he really expects Jennifer to come running to him like some poor little schoolgirl afraid of the dark.*

"There you are, bitch," came the hunter's voice. He found Jennifer and now it was up to him to stop this guy, dead in his tracks.

"Go ahead and do whatever you want. I'm too tired and hurting way too much. I really don't give a shit what you do. I hope you choke on it and die, you stupid bastard," Jennifer said in a miserable tone of defeat.

"Oh, don't worry about that, my sweet pretty. I plan on fucking you first, and if I feel like it, I'll do it again," he said as he bellowed out a hideous laugh.

The Drifter peered around the tree to view the two of them, waiting for his moment to strike. The hunter was kneeling down beside Jennifer with his back to him. He saw the hunter as he grabbed Jennifer's blouse and completely ripped it off her of her body, exposing her breasts. Her breasts were small, but very luscious with small pink nipples. He watched the man as he began rubbing the breast very gently at first and then progressively getting rougher with each stroke. Jennifer noticed his stares and began to wonder why he was doing nothing.

He caught her glance and could see the fear in her eyes. With a quick movement of his hand he indicated for her to stop staring at him and be patient. The time was not right, for the attacker was not fully engrossed in his pleasure and could possibly notice his approach. After what seemed a very long time to Jennifer, the Drifter finally decided it was time to make his move. He knew the large hunter's attention was now fully focused on her, and he would be unsuspecting of an attack.

He slowly stepped away from the tree and moved very quietly toward his victim, not making a sound, with his knife poised, ready to strike. He knew that he needed to penetrate the man's kidney; that was the best place to strike. If he managed to hit his target, it would kill the hunter instantly, not giving him a chance to scream. He was three feet away when the large hunter apparently sensed his presence and began turning his head. It was it now or never. The Drifter lurched forward and grabbed the hunter's mouth with his left hand while he plunged the knife into his side. He then twisted and lifted the knife upward, making it cut deep into his kidney; the result was a quick death. Very shortly after the attack, the hunter's body became limp as the Drifter let him fall onto the snow.

He suddenly felt sick to his stomach; this was the first time he had ever killed another human being. He did not like the feelings it gave him, but he knew there was no other way it could have been accomplished.

Jennifer grabbed her blouse and pulled it back over her chest as she whispered in an angry, but low voice, "What took you so damn long? That bastard stunk and I didn't enjoy his hands all over me. I bet you really enjoyed him ripping my blouse off, huh?"

He stood still, looking confused by her remark, as he thought, *What a bitch! I saved her life and this is my thanks.* He felt the rapport between them was being built on quicksand. In his defense, and in a sarcastic tone, he answered, "I had to wait for his attention to be fully focused on you so he would not sense my approach. As to your other question, well I think your tits are too small and to be honest, I've seen and had better."

Jennifer let out a sigh followed by, "Humph." He knew his comment created more anger in her, but he felt a warm, satisfying sensation from deep within. With a calmer and more collected outlook on the turn of events, he looked deep into her beautiful brown eyes. "Now I want you to scream at top of your lungs."

"Why?" she responded.

"Because they are expecting to hear you scream," was his answer.

She nodded as she let out a very loud and awful scream, one that would send shivers down anybody's spine.

He nodded is head, as if applauding her for her spectacular performance, "Very good." He reached out his right hand to offer help. She hesitated for a moment before taking his hand, allowing him to help her to her feet. He placed her arm around his neck, and glanced around, looking for a landmark. After finding one, he helped support her weight as the two of them walked back to his horse.

Chapter Five
The Hunt

(The Drifter)

By the time the Drifter and Jennifer reached the area where Horse was tied, Dog was patiently waiting. When the wolf saw Jennifer, he immediately came running toward them, snarling, with his sharp, white teeth showing.

"Sit," the Drifter said, causing Dog to immediately sit down without moving another inch. He was a very well-minded wolf, and his master only had to speak once. He was still snarling at Jennifer but patiently waited for the approval to move. The Drifter helped Jennifer to the trunk of a small tree and sat her beside it, before giving Dog permission to join them. Dog came over but was growling with his disapproval of their newfound friend.

"Friend," the Drifter said as he grabbed Jennifer's hand and placed it into his. He lifted her hand to Dog's nose, allowing him to get a sniff of her scent. After Dog had picked up her smell, he finally calmed down and stopped his growling.

"Thanks, I really thought the reason you saved me was so you could feed your dog," Jennifer grumbled.

The more Jennifer spoke, the more the Drifter seemed to regret his decision in helping her. Her personality was very displeasing, and he could not help his mannerism when he responded to any of her comments.

"It's a wolf, not a dog. And yes he's hungry, but I would hate to see him choking as he tried to eat you. So why don't you just shut up and be grateful you're still alive?" He spoke a finial few words to her before he left the campsite. "Now just sit there and be quiet. I'm going back to help the others, and I will be back for you later."

With Dog walking by his side, they headed back toward the crash site. He moved very quickly before anyone suspected there was something wrong, since the fat hunter was not going home. He once again stopped when he reached the edge of the forest leading up to the small plateau, where the group of survivors still remained. With his hands, he gestured for Dog to circle the campsite. Dog cocked his head, not understanding what was being asked of him. Seeing the response, the Drifter grabbed Dog's head and pointed toward the opposite side of the plateau. He again moved his hand in a circular motion. This time, Dog got the picture, and without hesitation, darted for the other side of the plateau, keeping to the tree line.

The Drifter raised his rifle, placed the scope to his eye, and began searching the camp for the last two remaining hunters. The smaller one was standing by the fire, and from where he stood, he had a very clear shot. His biggest concern was for the lead hunter, for this was the bastard he wanted to kill the most. He continued searching the area, looking for him, only to find him sitting on a log behind a child who was sitting in his lap. The child was a pretty young lady with long, dark hair and resembled his daughter Amy. He steadily observed the lead hunter before realizing the bastard was holding this child against her will, and this angered him more.

He lowered his rifle as he waited for Dog to reach the other side of the plateau. Minutes ticked by as his anger heightened thinking about the bastard and what he had done. After what he thought was plenty of time for Dog to reach the other side, he stepped away from the tree line walking very slowly across the small plateau staying in the shadows of the forest.

When he was within 150 feet of the campfire he again raised his rifle planting the butt against his shoulder. He aligned the crosshairs of the scope on the lead hunter's head, as he thought. *I could take a chance and put a bullet between his eyes.* He stood fast with the rifle pointed at the hunter's forehead, as he contemplated on squeezing the trigger. The longer he stood the less steady his aim became. With the fear of accidentally missing and killing the young girl, he moved the rifle away from him and toward the smaller hunter.

I could take him out and even the odds, the Drifter thought. *Maybe if I move closer, I could get a better shot on the other hunter.* He lowered his rifle after this last thought. He began circling the plateau, keeping in the shadows, and had not traveled very far when his time ran out.

"Jack — where are you?" the lead hunter yelled. "Get back here now! It's Peety's turn."

The Drifter now feared his presence would soon be discovered. He stopped in his tracks and again raised his rifle. The lead hunter had not moved from the log and still held the young lady against her will. Not sure what the small guy would do, he was forced with the only decision left open. He slowly lined up the crosshairs of his rifle on the unsuspecting fate that awaited this hunter.

He took in a deep breath and held it as he steadied his aim. "God forgive me," he said, as the crosshairs aligned with the small hunter's heart and he squeezed the trigger. The bullet made a whistling sound as it left the barrel, headed for its target, warming the cold air as it cut its way through. The sound from the rifle had pierced the silence, awakening all, and instilling fear in the bullet's wake. It reached its target, penetrating through bone and tissue as it ripped a hole through the small man's chest. From the scope, the Drifter watched him as he fell to the ground and never moved, while his life slowly drained from his body.

Startled from the shot, the last hunter jumped from the log, firmly holding on to the frightened girl. Using the child's body as a shield, he yelled out, "Who's out there?" The Drifter could see the man searching the area where he now stood, but the dark shadow of night made him invisible to the hunter. Again the hunter yelled as he pulled the young girl tighter against his body. "I don't know who you are, but if you don't come out now, I'm going to blow this little bitch's head off!" The Drifter stood fast without saying a word as he tried to evaluate his choices.

It's possible I could get a shot off before he could do anything about it. His chest and head are clear of the girl, but at this distance, I could miss. If I give up, he'll probably kill both of us anyway. If I don't, he'll kill the child. His thoughts continued to pour in as the sense of helplessness settled in his heart.

Ah shit ... I guess I better give myself up. If I don't, I'm sure I will regret it the rest of my life. With a deep sigh for his failure, he responded, "Okay, I'm coming in, so don't get nervous and shoot the little girl."

He walked very slowly toward the hunter, not making any sudden moves, trying to calm his burst of anxieties. He was within thirty feet of the campfire when he heard him yell, "Stop there!" He stopped as he waited for his next set of instructions.

"I want you to very slowly raise your rifle straight out from your body and throw it toward me."

The Drifter cooperated without hesitation. He very slowly raised his rifle and tossed it in the direction of his captor. The rifle dropped close to the hunter's boots, throwing a clump of snow on top of them.

"Very good. Now very slowly move closer. Any sudden moves and the little bitch gets it."

The Drifter again walked very slowly toward the hunter, not making any sudden moves. With every step, he was able to see the young girl more clearly. She reeked with fear, making him want to reach out to comfort her. As he moved in closer, he began wondering, *Where's Dog? What's keeping him?*

His thoughts were quickly interrupted when he heard, "Stop!" He stopped once again and took in a deep breath. He was now close enough to see into the man's eyes. There was a crazed look of hysteria, which made him unsure of his next move. He returned the stare, with a hard look of strength in his own face, for he could not afford to show his fear.

The Drifter waited patiently until Tom told him what he expected next. "I want you to slowly, with your left hand, unbuckle your holster and hold it out straight in front of you. Remember, any sudden moves and this little bitch gets it." There was desperation in the man's eyes, and the Drifter knew he could not afford to provoke him. Slowly reaching down his right leg with his left hand, he untied the leather strap holding the holster to his leg. Then slowly he unbuckled the holster until it fell away from his hips. He raised it straight into the air away from his body. As it dangled in midair, he gave the hunter a cold, calculated stare. The man released the child as he quickly stepped forward and grabbed the holster out of his grip.

Each of them stared into the eyes of the other. Cold is the only word to express the feelings each had, for neither was able to gain superiority. The hunter searched the rest of the Drifter's body, looking for other weapons, when he saw the large hunting knife strapped to his right leg. Minutes passed before the silence was broken when the hunter spoke. "I want you to pull the knife from its sheath and toss it into the woods." Without losing eye contact, the Drifter slowly reached down and removed the knife. He flipped the knife in the air and caught it by the blade, never breaking eye contact. Without further hesitation, he turned completely around, leaving his back exposed to the hunter, and with a hearty toss from his right arm, he threw the knife. There was a loud thud, followed by a slight vibrating sound as the knife cut its way into a tree twenty-five yards away and came to complete rest.

The Drifter slowly turned back to face the hunter once more. The hunter lowered his rifle as he said, "I'm really going to enjoy hunting you ... that was a great display of skill." There was a brief moment of silence before the hunter asked, "I suppose Jack isn't coming back ... huh?"

The Drifter hardened his stare, and without blinking an eyelid he quietly said, "No ... I guess not."

Tom slowly nodded his head before he continued, "You know, you shouldn't have killed Peety. That was cold-blooded; he didn't want any part of this, the poor bastard."

The Drifter bowed his head, feeling deep regret for his decision. "If it makes you feel better, I really wanted to shoot you, not him," the Drifter said sadly.

Tom began an eerie laugh, sending chills through the Drifter. Shortly after it had begun, he stopped his laughing as his face turned cold. "My name is Tom. I want you to know who's going to kill you. You look like a man who knows his way around the woods, and hopefully will present a real challenge for me. Now that you know my name, I want to know yours." The Drifter stood steadfast, still looking into his eyes, and remained silent. He could see the anger rising in his eyes just before his face exploded into a rage.

"What is your fucking name, you son of a bitch?!"

A sense of pride swelled in the Drifter, for now he knew the hunter's weakness. He was a proud man, full of self-confidence, but easily provoked to anger. The Drifter was not quite sure how, but it should be easy to use his pride and self-confidence against him. Momentarily, the Drifter took his glance away from Tom to check on the other survivors of the plane crash. He saw the young girl in the arms of the bold stewardess, and knew she was safe for now. The others were scared and uncertain about the turn of events. Without showing them weakness, he turned his eyes back to Tom, who was now showing signs of his impatience.

He was still at the hunter's mercy, but with a feeling of confidence, he answered Tom's question. "I lost the right to use my name many years ago. I haven't earned the right to use it yet, but someday I will. For now you can call me the Drifter."

His response was not taken well, and caused turmoil in the hunter's manner, as he shook with anger. "I guess it's really not that important to know your name. After the wolves have stripped the flesh from your body, nobody's going to know or care who the fuck you were. I'm going to enjoy hunting you down like an animal and taking my time and pleasure in killing you. My first shot will be the shoulder or maybe the leg. My second shot will be somewhere else that only wounds you. I will kill you very slowly, and when I think you suffered enough, I'll field dress you while there's still a little life left in you." The Drifter remained expressionless, not giving in to fear from the words he was forced to hear.

"You have ten minutes to run and hide before I start the hunt. Oh, before you leave, thanks for the handgun. It's a nice piece to add to my collection. Who knows, maybe I'll shoot you with it. That would make it very ironic to be killed by your own gun. Now get going before I change my mind and decide to shoot you now." Tom said just before he fouled the air with his sadistic laughter. The Drifter took his suggestion and began his trek across the plateau toward the northeast.

Without any weapons, his task seemed hopeless. He had managed to take out two of the hunters, but left the worst standing. Tom was a lunatic and the craziest of them all. To beat him at his own game would not be an easy accomplishment. After he was out of sight, Tom picked up the Drifter's rifle and unloaded the shells. He tossed it as far as he could into the dark forest, knowing that without the shells, he remained in control.

Tom turned toward the woods where he had last seen the Drifter and yelled, "You have eight minutes, Mr. Drifter."

(The Hunt – The Drifter)

He knew he needed an edge if he was to defeat Tom, and Dog was that edge. He walked down the small incline toward the edge of the woods, making him invisible to the others, before he stopped to look around. He saw a large pine tree, with a knot protruding from it, about twenty feet off the ground. It looked like a very large nose, so he burned the image into his brain. He ventured deeper into the woods as he searched for other markers that he would need to guide his way back. For without them, he could get lost in the forest and freeze to death before finding his way home.

Sixty paces inside of the woods, he stopped once more to listen. He could barely hear anything from the campsite, little murmurs, but nothing distinguished. It was time to call Dog. He whistled, but not very loud, only loud enough for Dog to hear and not the others. A few minutes passed, and there were no sounds to break the silence around him. Again he let out a short whistle, slightly louder than before. Off in the distance, coming from the north, he could hear a faint rustling noise, as if something or someone was heading his direction. He turned quickly toward the sound, only to catch a short glimpse of movement among the trees.

Dog suddenly appeared between two pine trees, running toward him, very excited. Without any warning, he jumped up and landed his front paws onto the Drifter's chest, knocking him off his feet. While his master was down and helpless, he began licking his face, as if that act gave him power over the Drifter. Both were excited at seeing the other, but he was more excited at seeing his ace in the hole. The two of them shared their simple loving for a few seconds, wrestling in the snow. He finally pushed the wolf off of his chest. "Good boy." His time was running out, and there was a great need to get serious about his current affairs.

As he brushed the snow away from his clothing, he began searching the surrounding area. This time it was for something different than finding a marker. He could clearly see Dog's prints in the snow. He immediately began evaluating methods of covering up the tracks and any other signs that might lead Tom to believe he was not alone. This would be the end of his edge and possible success in defeating his adversary. Without further ado, he motioned for Dog to return in the same direction that he had originally come from, while he walked in Dog's prints, concealing them with his own footprints. They headed north with the hope of getting far enough ahead so he could circle back and wait for Tom to pass. If he could get close enough, he figured he could overpower Tom and take his weapons.

"Two minutes, asshole, and I'm coming to get you," came Tom's next warning. The sound of his voice seemed to be loud, meaning he was still very close to the crash site. He had wasted too much time finding Dog, and now his time was running out. He softly whistled to Dog, as he picked up his pace. Dog, noticing his movements, responded by extending his stride. They were now gliding through the snow, putting more distance between them and Tom.

Their travel brought them upon a small rock quarry. The Drifter stopped and softly whistled for Dog to stop, while he examined the area. Not noticing Dog's tracks in the snow, he surmised that he must have walked through the quarry. He quickly followed Dog's lead. When he reached the other side and looked back, he was pleased with the results. There were no signs for Tom to follow, and this he hoped would buy him some more time. When he caught up to Dog, he pointed northwest, and Dog took the lead once more. The Drifter followed, moving erratically as he tried to cover Dog's tracks. He was now skating through the snow, leaving no chance of missing any prints.

He kept running as fast as his legs would scuttle through the deep snow, trying to put some distance between him and his captor.

"Time's up," he heard Tom say, but this time, the sound was far more distant. Felling somewhat relieved, he continued moving further northwest until he caught a glimpse of a large shadow off to his left. He softly whistled, pointed toward the direction of the shadow, and Dog immediately turned west without breaking stride. The closer to the shadow they moved, the more distinct and larger it became, until the forest opened into a small clearing, exposing a large rock formation protruding from the ground.

Trees lined up, forming a wall of wood on both sides, as if they were perfectly planted. Small brush was scattered among the trees and surrounded the large rock. He stopped as he admired the area, for this was a perfect place to ambush Tom. Thinking quickly, knowing time was running out, he whistled for Dog as he patted his leg. Dog came running to his side, stopped, and sat next to him. His plans had slightly changed in light of his new situation. *If I can get back to that small rock quarry, I could circle around and approach the rock from the rear. This might confuse him, and by the time he was able to figure out what I was doing, it would be too late.*

Feeling strongly satisfied with his decision, he began heading northeast, back into the forest, creating a diversion. After putting 100 feet between him and the large rock formation, he began stepping backward, planting his feet perfectly into the footprints previously made. When he was back in the clearing, he picked up Dog and walked backward as fast as he could, back toward the small rock quarry. With a crooked smile lifting his lips, he thought, *This plan is perfect and there's no way it can fail. I'll make that bastard pay for what he has done to these people.*

(The Campsite - Rachael)

Rachael could see Tom standing proud and defiant. He was constantly glancing at his watch as his patience ran out. She could see the frustration strengthen in his eyes as the minutes slowly ticked by.

"What are you going to do to us when you finish hunting and killing this guy?" she asked. Tom took a moment from staring at his watch to give her a cold stare, one that made her feel creepy.

"I was thinking, maybe I'll drag your beautiful little ass with me. After I kill and field dress that son of a bitch, I could have you as my treat. What do you think about that?" His voice was cold, with a sadistic tone to go along with the look in his eyes. He began laughing with that cynical voice, "Yes, that's sounds like a perfect finish."

Rachael was not sure who the stranger was, but he had risked his life to help them. She felt very sorry for him, if this bastard should manage to find him. Tom began walking toward Rachael as she shivered at the thought of his plans.

"Time's up," he yelled, but in a lower voice, "it's time to go, lady." He grabbed Rachael's arm very firmly, shoving her in front of him. "Follow the tracks, bitch," he said as he pushed her toward the woods. They reached the other edge of the plateau leading down the small incline. At the bottom of the incline, they followed the tracks into the woods. They had traveled a very short distance when Tom forced her to stop by grabbing her hair. Rachael watched him as he squatted down and searched the entire area.

Tom's hands swept across the loosely packed snow, never disturbing one snowflake. He began talking out loud, as if he was speaking to her. "It looks like he fell down right here. He wasn't running, so what tripped him and why did he fall backwards toward the south when he was headed northeast?"

Rachael wondered why Tom was telling her anything, unless he was just trying to impress her with his skills. He stood up and walked back toward Rachael, shaking his head in confusion. The scene was puzzling, and he looked troubled by the markings.

She could see the disturbance in his face. Curious, she asked, "What's wrong?"

Tom was still shaking his head when he responded to her question. "Something's wrong. Maybe this Drifter guy is hiding something or just trying to buy some time by confusing the hell out of me." She turned her head away just before a large smile forced its way onto her lips.

Rachael decided to work on Tom as a decoy to stall for time. "Do you have a family?" she asked.

Tom's look of confusion turned into a softer expression when he answered. "Yes I do. I have a wife and two kids. My boy is nine and my daughter is twelve." Tom's response was softly spoken.

This made Rachael feel that she was getting through to him for the first time since the three of them had arrived. "You look like a respectable man and a proud father. I don't understand why you are doing this to us," she said, hoping to get him to change his mind about their disposition.

Tom's loving look turned back into his original cold stare. "Because it's fun, you stupid bitch. I know what you're trying to do and it won't work."

He firmly grabbed Rachael's hair, pulling her face close to his. "I want you in front of me so I can keep my eye on you. If you try to run, I'll kill you. I'll just have to come back later for my treat. It doesn't matter to me; either way will work." He pushed her backward with a strong shove, causing her to stumble and fall. "Now get up and follow those tracks," he said as he pointed to the Drifter's footprints below her feet. He seemed to be a very short-tempered individual, and she decided not to provoke him again. She stepped out about four feet in front of Tom and started following the tracks in the snow.

The tracks stopped at a rock quarry. She stopped to wait for Tom to catch up, before she went any further. Soon Tom joined her and stood by her side as he searched the area.

"Well, what do we do now?" she asked.

"Shut up, bitch, I'm thinking," he snapped. *The Drifter was heading north. Chances are, he still is, unless he's trying to confuse me again.* His thoughts were broken when Rachael tapped his shoulder. She had her arm pointing out to the northwest. Tom acknowledged her gesture as he walked past her and around the edge of the rocks toward the northwest.

Seconds later, she heard, "Over here." She walked to where Tom was standing, and the Drifter's tracks were embedded in the deep snow.

Her heart sank for this was not her intention at all. She was hoping to delay Tom, giving the stranger more time to get away. "Thanks ... you've got a sharp eye," Tom said, making her feel even worse about helping him. He grabbed her arm and pushed her in the direction of the tracks. She gave him a brief, "Go to hell" look before she continued with the hunt.

They had not traveled very far when she heard Tom bellow, "Stop!" Turning around, she once again saw him squat in the snow, moving his hand slightly above the prints.

Her curiosity was aroused once more, forcing her to ask, "What is it this time?"

Tom's response was somewhat puzzling to her. "Something isn't right. He's skating through the snow. It takes a lot of energy and strength to do that, and it's slowing him down. There are a couple of places here where he stopped and backstepped as if he missed something. Now what is he missing, and why is he skating like this?" The more Tom spoke, the more confused he seemed to look.

Rachael was doing everything in her power to hold back her laughter. She was enjoying watching Tom scratch his head, trying to figure out what the stranger was thinking. Her face straightened up when she noticed Tom looking up at her.

In his low, sadistic voice, he said, "You seem to be having too much fun with this, bitch. Just remember, I have the guns, and as long as I do, I've got the upper hand. I know he's trying to hide something. Nobody would go to this effort if there wasn't a reason for it." He stood up and motioned for her to follow the tracks once more.

Once again the hunt was on, as Rachael followed the tracks, being careful not to step in them. She did not want to bring down his wrath by accidentally destroying any evidence. The thought, however, had entered her mind on several different occasions.

Tom's last words warmed her hopes as she thought to herself, *Whoever he was, he is giving that bastard a run for his money. This guy we're hunting may be smart enough to save us from this lunatic. He seems to be very intelligent and clever, the way he's baffled Tom. I sure hope he has something up his sleeve. I'm getting desperate, even desperate enough to try to overpower the bastard myself. Someone has to stop him or all of us are doomed.*

Her thoughts were broken by the harshness of Tom's word when he yelled, "Stop!"

What now? This stopping shit is really getting old, Rachael thought as she waited with her arms crossed against her chest.

The air was very still and silent. Tom's silence spiked her curiosity. She turned to face him, and again saw that puzzled look along with fear. "It's a perfect place for an ambush," he said as he was squatting down for a closer look. Rachael was no longer impressed with his tracking skills, but she patiently waited for his stupid explanation.

"Now I know the stranger is not as clever as I originally hoped he would be. If he were a good hunter, he would have stopped here and checked this area out. He would also know this place was a good place for an ambush. I would expect he's in the area somewhere."

Rachael, with a worried look, searched the area with Tom. They were standing in a clearing with a large rock protruding from the ground. There were trees surrounding it, but she could not understand why this bothered Tom. She was hoping the stranger was here and would soon show himself.

"Dumb bastard looks as if he's not smart at all. Damn ... I was really hoping for a good hunt." Rachael looked at Tom very inquisitively. He was already standing and no longer looking at the tracks, but was searching the area very closely.

"What did you mean by that?" Rachael inquired.

"Looking at these prints in the snow, he only stopped here briefly before he turned northeast. I guess he's too scared to think."

(The Drifter)

The Drifter had heard every word that Tom had spoken. He smiled. *My plan is working.* He was not sure why Tom brought the stewardess, unless it was an attempt to subdue him or use her as protection. It wasn't going to work. There was more at stake than just her and him. He slowly peered around the tree trunk to get a better view. Tom was standing in the clearing in front of the boulder, scanning the area. The Drifter could not see his face, so he was not sure if he suspected treachery from an attack. Tom began moving closer to the large boulder, as he searched the area in all directions. His actions were very suspicious, causing the grin on the Drifter's face to widen.

As Tom approached the rock, he pulled his rifle away from his shoulder. He placed it against his hip with it pointed toward the rock. The Drifter heard a click as Tom cocked the hammer back, as if preparing for an attack. He was now glad he had changed his mind about hiding behind the rock and chose a different approach. Tom was ten feet from the boulder with his back to him when he raised his rifle and put the crosshairs on his adversary's back.

He took a deep breath and with the voice of defiance spoke. "Freeze, you bastard. I have a rifle pointed at you. One false move and you will feel the sting of lead as it scrambles your insides and leaves a big hole in your chest on exit."

Tom stood there without moving as he spoke. "Why should I believe that you really have a rifle?"

Tom heard the whistle of a bullet as it passed close to his head, followed by a loud boom. "Do you believe me now?" the Drifter remarked as he casually stepped away from the tree that was hiding his presence.

"So where did you get the rifle?" Tom asked.

"You remember your fat buddy? The one who went hunting for Jennifer, the stewardess with the bad leg?"

Tom sighed. "There's no way you could have his rifle. He left camp heading south and you headed northeast. I've been following your tracks and checking them carefully. I would have seen the signs telling me that you doubled back. And besides, you wouldn't have had enough time to get there and back here, before me."

The Drifter smiled while he held the crosshairs of the scope on Tom's back. "I'll tell you the entire story, after you toss your rifle to the ground. If you don't, I'll squeeze the trigger and the story ends here."

Tom, in his anger, threw the rifle forward, striking it against the boulder, causing it to fire. The bullet whistled through the thick air, shattering a piece of bark from a nearby pine tree.

"That was really stupid," the Drifter said as he walked into the clearing where Rachael stood. He was next to Rachael before he allowed Tom to turn and face him.

"Jennifer is alive?" Rachael asked. The Drifter nodded, never taking his eyes off of Tom.

He lowered his rifle, leaving it cocked, as he looked hard into the eyes of Tom. "Before I tell my story, I first want to introduce you to a very good friend of mine. Tom, this is Dog. Any false moves and you're his dinner."

Tom shook his head in compliance, for he now knew why this man had been skating through the snow. He was covering up the dog's tracks with his own. Proud of his assessment for clearing up part of the puzzle, Tom was now ready to hear the rest of the story. "Go on," he said.

Tom and Rachael were both eager to find out how the Drifter managed to retrieve the rifle and get back before they arrived. The Drifter stood proud, in outfoxing the hunter; he gloated over his success as he told his story.

"When I arrived here, I stopped to look around. It was a great place for an ambush, but I had to figure out a way to surprise you without you suspecting it. My first thought was to find a way to get behind the boulder. I was going to climb it and perch on top to await your arrival. Dog was to wait on the ground, lying between the rock and the tree. When the time was right, I would jump you from the top while Dog attacked from the ground.

"While I was figuring out how I would get behind the rock, I also had to add hiding Dog's tracks to the equation, or my plan would fail. I decided to head northeast for about 100 feet. I backstepped all the way back to the clearing, being very careful to step into the same prints I had made earlier. I picked up Dog and then backstepped all the way back to the rock quarry. When we arrived, I was exhausted from carrying Dog, so we sat down behind one of the larger rocks to rest. I had only been resting for a few minutes when I heard you coming up the path toward us.

"My first fear was that you would search through the rocks, trying to pick up my tracks. After a few minutes of waiting, I peered around the rock, but I could not see you anymore. I glanced over the top of the rock and saw the two of you heading northwest.

"I sat back down and started formulating a new plan. I knew there was no way I could get back to the boulder and get situated before you arrived at the clearing. As my mind relaxed thinking, I remembered your fat friend had laid his rifle against a tree before he attempted to rape Jennifer. When you were far enough out of sight, I took off toward camp, following my original steps.

"Once we were there, I sent Dog for my horse, while I circled the plateau looking for your hunting buddy. I stayed concealed from the others to avoid any delays, because I knew my time was limited. I found the rifle leaning against the tree where he had left it. I grabbed it, checked to see if it was loaded and headed toward my horse. It was not long after when I caught up with Dog leading my horse to me.

"I jumped into the saddle and rode like a bolt of lightning. We crossed the plateau, frightening a few of the survivors as we streaked through the woods following my original steps. We passed the rocks in a blinding flash as I headed due west to come up south of this clearing. You were here long before we arrived. You were just too busy being cautious to notice our approach from the south woods. The rest you already know."

Tom stood fast looking into the eyes of his captor. "Pretty ingenious. I guess you were smarter than I expected. Huh ... so what now?"

The Drifter took his eyes off of Tom briefly to give Rachael a glance. When he returned his stare back toward Tom, he started his speech. "Let's see, I believe you have a ten-minute head start and an hour to evade capture. That's how it went ... right?"

Tom looked into his eyes, hoping to find some sort of a sign to indicate that he was not serious about the game.

The Drifter stood steadfast without blinking an eyelid as he continued. "Before we start, I need for you to slowly unbuckle my holster and toss it to me. Remember ... Dog's hungry. I would really hate for you to lose the opportunity you gave me." Tom slowly and with his left hand unbuckled the holster. When he was finished he dangled it in the air for a few seconds before he tossed it toward the Drifter.

"You can't be serious about this," Rachael said in a nervous voice.

The Drifter stared straight into her eyes, allowing him to see her expressions before he spoke again. "When you're out there, Tom, trying to find a place to hide or figure out how you're going to beat me at your own game, I want you to remember the woman you left lying in the snow. The one with cuts on every part of her body caused by your hunting knife. The one you enjoyed butchering. She looked really nasty by the time I found her. I'm leaving you with your knife to give you a better chance to survive than what you gave me ... So get going; the clock is ticking." Rachael's eyes displayed sadness and rage all at the same time. The Drifter could tell she was very angry with Tom for what he had done, and she also felt pity for the young woman. He was not expecting her actions when she blurted, "Fuck him, don't give that bastard anything. Jessica was a good woman and he left her daughter Amy alone, with no one to take care of her." The Drifter's heart sank into his stomach when he heard the young girl's name. His anger rose to its highest level, now hating Tom with all the passion that hate could deliver. Rachael continued as tears filled his eyes. "When this man catches up to you, he's going to fuck you up and I'll have the pleasure of watching you die, you son of a bitch." Tom stood expressionless with no sympathy for the young woman. He had no shame at what he did, and Rachael's words rolled off of him, like water off a duck's back. He gave them both a cold stare as he turned toward the northeast to walk away.

"Wait!" the Drifter yelled. "There's one more thing I want you to think about before you leave. If my memory serves me right, I believe you said this to me. My first shot will be the shoulder or maybe the leg. My second shot will be somewhere else that only wounds you. I will kill you very slowly, and when I think you suffered enough, I'll field dress you while there's still a little life left in you. ... Now you have ten minutes. I suggest you use it wisely."

Tom sighed as he turned back northeast and left the small clearing. Rachael and the Drifter watched as he departed. They stood fast as the minutes ticked away. Neither of them spoke until the ten minutes had expired, when the Drifter yelled, "Time's up!"

Rachael looked deep into his blue eyes before she stepped away, walking toward the northeast. The Drifter never moved as he watched her walk off. "You're going the wrong direction. We need to head south back to my horse."

She looked at him puzzled, as he turned and walked in the opposite direction. "What about Tom? Aren't we going after him?" she asked, not understanding his actions. The Drifter turned back toward Rachael, as he spoke. "Tom's not going anywhere. He thinks we're coming for him, which will keep him on the run. We don't have enough time to waste chasing him." He again turned his back to her and began walking away. Rachael, still confused, ran up and grabbed him on the shoulder. Dog, seeing her actions, began snapping and barking furiously.

"Sit," the Drifter said as he slowly explained his actions. "There's a storm approaching and it'll be here very soon. By the time Tom realizes I'm not hunting him, the storm will hit. He will either freeze to death or the wolves will have dinner tonight."

His statement astonished Rachael, as she asked, "What if he survives? He deserves to be punished for what he did to Jessica. You shouldn't let him get away with it. We need to find him and hold him for the authorities." The Drifter shook his head in disapproval and once again he and Dog began walking toward Horse.

"If you want him that bad, go get him. I'm going to camp to help those who might need it. Bye," the Drifter said in a cold voice, as he walked away. Rachael threw her arms in the air to acknowledge her defeat. She lined up behind the Drifter and followed him back to his horse. A smile cracked across Tom's face as he watched them leave. Perched on top of the large boulder, he had heard everything. He waited until they were out of sight before he dropped to the ground. *This is not over yet, you son of a bitch,* he thought, as he followed them back to camp.

Chapter Six
The Drifter's Home

When they reached the area south of the clearing where the Drifter had left his horse, he stopped briefly when he asked, "Would you like to ride?"

Rachael shook her head no, before she thanked him for saving her life. "My name is Rachael. I didn't give it you earlier because it scared me. Tom wanted to know our name before he killed us, so I was apprehensive about giving you mine. I want to thank you for everything … I sure hope you're right about the weather taking out Tom."

The Drifter smiled as he lifted the reins and headed back to the campsite. Rachael and Dog fell in behind and followed in silence. The only sounds heard in the forest were the soft crunching noises from each step they took.

At the foot of the small incline leading onto the plateau, he stopped. With a quick glance and a motion of his hand, she also stopped.

"Wait here," he whispered as he and Dog continued alone. They walked across the plateau toward the campfire and stopped about fifty feet from it, still hidden by the shadows of the forest. He stood there with Dog sitting by his side, waiting to see if anybody had noticed their approach. Out of the corner of his left eye, he could see a shadow of a man entering the plateau from the south.

Before he could determine who this shadowy figure was, he heard a deep harsh voice yell, "Don't move … I have a gun and it's pointed at you!"

Dog began his soft growl, as the Drifter stood motionless against the darkness. The seconds moved slowly as he awaited the arrival of the shadowy figure.

"Move forward with your arms in the air," the voice ordered.

As he moved closer to the figure, it began to take form until he recognized the captain's uniform. The emotions depicted on the captain's face ranged from fear to betrayal, with fear standing out the strongest. His hands were shaking wildly and the Drifter feared the rifle would accidentally fire. Dog, who had not followed his master because he was told not to, had increased his softer growl to a much more distinct sound followed by short barks.

"I think you should stop there," the captain yelled.

He heard a cold resistance in the captain's voice, as he stood there with the rifle steadily shaking in his hands. He understood the captain's responsibility for the survival of his passengers, but somehow he had to gain this man's trust. His first priority was to get him to lower his rifle so they could talk in a more civilized manner, instead of like enemies trying to gain a strategic advantage over the other. The Drifter asked the captain to lower his rifle to show a sign of truce, but there was no response to his request. He tried once more to get the captain to lower the rifle, explaining that he was there to help them, not to hurt anybody. The captain still did not respond to his requests, and not having any patience, he decided to use a more persuasive tactic.

"My wolf does not take kindly to strangers, unless I tell him you're a friend. If you accidentally or on purpose should happen to shoot and kill me, he will most likely tear you to shreds. Unfortunately for you and the other survivors, he may not stop until he has hurt several other people. So I would suggest that you put that rifle down before he takes action on his own and gives you the benefit of a new asshole."

In the meantime, Rachael had walked up the incline and was approaching the two of them. She had overheard their conversation and knew the captain was not the trusting type, so she called out for him to lower his rifle. There was a great sigh of relief when he finally lowered the rifle at Rachael's request. Dog's growling and barking was getting quite loud by this time. Fearing what he might do, the Drifter motioned for Dog to come sit by his side. He dropped to one knee and rubbed Dog's neck, pacifying him, while they waited for Rachael's arrival.

Dog's growling had softened by the time Rachael was standing by the Drifter's side. The captain could see the scornful look in her eyes as she stared back into his. He was not comfortable with the stranger, but could tell Rachael was very angry, so he decided not to provoke her any further.

"I'm sorry, but too much has happened tonight and I'm not sure who you are or why you're here. ... It's good to see you, Rachael. I was afraid that hunter was going to kill you." Rachael's head slightly tilted backwards as she responded in an unpleasant tone.

"If it hadn't been for this man, he might have killed me. He saved my life and he saved yours too." The captain regretfully acknowledged her, but was still unwilling to trust the stranger.

"My name is Joe. I'm the captain of Flight 493, out of Seattle. Thanks for helping us and thanks for taking care of Rachael. Now could you please call off your dog?"

The Drifter, without standing or releasing Dog, extended his left hand as if to shake. "I'll take my rifle now, if you don't mind."

The captain did not move until he saw the look in Rachael's eyes. Deploring the idea of having to give up the rifle, he glanced at Rachael in the hopes she had changed her mind. She motioned again, for him to give up the rifle before he finally decided to relinquish it by placing it in the hands of the Drifter. "Here … take it. It wasn't loaded anyway."

With a deep sigh of relief, the Drifter took his rifle. The four of them remained still for a few minutes, before the Drifter stood up and walked toward the campfire. As he stood in front of the fire, he looked upon all the faces of the survivors, only to see fear and apprehension in their eyes.

To help ease their fear, and in the hope of instilling some trust, he slowly removed the hunter's rifle from his shoulder. By the time the captain and Rachael had reached his side, he had the rifle extended toward them.

"Here, you can have this rifle … I prefer keeping mine. This one is loaded, though," he laughed almost inaudibly. "So be very careful. I have a few things I need to do. I'll return shortly, but I'm leaving Dog here to protect you and guard my return." The Drifter knelt down and whispered into Dog's ear. He barked once, indicating he understood his task. He gave Rachael a quick glance before heading south across the plateau, leading Horse. Dog sat patiently eyeing the passengers, as if he was hoping they would give him a reason to attack.

Shortly after his departure, the Drifter returned with Jennifer and the supplies he had brought with him. The captain's eyes sparkled, as a large smile lifted across his face when he saw Jennifer sitting on the horse.

"I was afraid you were dead!" he yelled as he ran to her side.

"I'm fine, thanks to our mysterious friend, who refuses to give me his name," she replied.

The Drifter was busy unloading the travois to pay any attention to her comment. The captain helped her from the saddle and walked her back to the campfire, sitting her on a log, still smiling at the thought of her being alive. After unloading the supplies, the Drifter crossed the plateau and headed back into the forest once more, leaving Dog to guard his return.

They watched as he left the campsite and was almost to the tree line before Rachael shouted, "Where are you going?" He stopped and gave her a quick glance before he stepped into the trees without saying a word.

The captain had approached Rachael as the Drifter entered the forest. Shaking his head in doubt of the Drifter's intentions, he whispered, "I'm not sure if we should trust this guy. He doesn't seem to be very sociable, and we really don't know who the hell he is."

She gave him a discernible look before responding to his comment. "He saved our lives from those sadistic hunters. He had Tom dead to rights, and yet he did not kill him. You had to be there to understand, and that's not the mark of a killer."

The captain sighed, and as he walked away, said, "But he shot that small hunter, the one they called Peety, in cold blood and let the worst one live."

Rachael became angry at the captain's comment, but said no more. The captain sat next to Jennifer and began whispering in her ear the same concerns, and she seemed to listen very intently nodding her head, as if she agreed with every word.

(The Drifter)

When the Drifter reached the tree where Jessica still lay, he knelt down beside her. Tears filled his eyes as he pledged a solemn oath. "I gave you my word that I would protect your daughter from the hunters, and this I have accomplished. I now give you my solemn oath that I'll do everything in my power to make sure your daughter is well cared for. I make this promise to you and pledge my life as collateral. ... Please forgive me for not being here, when you needed my help the most."

He kept her covered with his heavy bearskin coat so no one could see the horrific circumstances of her death. He gently picked her up from the snow-covered ground and headed back to the campsite. As he walked past the others, he could feel their blank stares, for none of them had any idea who lay cradled in his arms. Very softly, he laid her body next to the fuselage of battered aircraft, making sure it was fully covered before returning to the others.

He stopped and knelt in the snow by Dog, as he looked into the eyes of the captain. Slowly his glance moved from his eyes toward Amy, who was sitting by Jennifer. She had not suspected that it was her mother he carried, and for a moment, that was good. With a deep breath and a short sigh of relief, he began barking orders. "Captain, you need to gather a few men and dig a large hole over by the fuselage. Dig it deep. There are many bodies that need to be buried."

A few of the men stood up, as if they trusted his judgment and were heading for the aircraft when the captain yelled, "You men stop where you are! I'm giving the orders around here."

He turned his attention back to the Drifter, and with an angry face, he harshly asked, "Why do we need to bury the bodies?" The Drifter stared into his eyes with great patience, but not a word was spoken while they all waited for his answer. Once again the captain bellowed even louder, "Why do we need to bury the bodies?"

Resentment began unfolding in the Drifter's attitude when he finally gave in and answered the question. "To protect them from the wolves, so when the time comes, their bodies can be gathered and returned to their loved ones for a proper funeral."

The captain thought about his comment for quite some time before he responded in a slightly less angry voice. "I figure we'll be rescued anytime now. It would be futile to bury them. I know you came to help us and we appreciate you taking care of the hunters. I'm a little disappointed about you leaving Tom alive, but with this rifle, I think we can take care of ourselves now."

The cold air was thick with murmurs from the crowd of survivors when they heard that Tom was still alive. The Drifter released his grip on Dog's neck as he returned to his feet. Rachael could sense his frustration, and being the sensible one, decided to talk with the captain on his behalf.

As the Drifter held back his rage, he decided to give up arguing with the captain and accept his defeat. He took in a deep breath as he walked back where he had left Horse. Dog remained sitting while he waited for his master's return. Holding the reins of Horse, he once again knelt down in the snow and whispered into Dog's ear. He barked once as the Drifter stood up and faced the captain.

Before he was able to say anything, the captain had pushed Rachael aside and asked, "What is Rachael talking about?"

Confused at the question, he shrugged his shoulders with a disturbed look on his face. "She said there's a storm approaching. The only storm I was aware of was the one we went through. It was headed away from us."

The Drifter sighed, still disappointed in the captain; he chose to ignore his remark as he approached Amy.

Stopping in front of Amy, he gave pause before kneeling down in the snow to face the child. He looked into Amy's eyes, hoping she would return his stare, even though her eyes were pointed toward the ground. Softly and with a heavy heart, he said, "I made a promise to someone that I would take care of you. I know you don't know me, but please try to trust me. I'm not going to hurt you. ... But you need to come with me."

Jennifer furiously pulled her away from him when she screamed, "She's staying with me ... I appreciate you saving my life from that smelly fat bastard, but we don't know what kind of person you are."

His temperature began rising as he tried to hold back his rage and remain in control of his patience. Once more he tried to get Amy's attention. "Amy, look into my eyes."

She began to raise her head, and just before eye contact was made, the captain yelled, "That's enough. She's going nowhere with you. We need to get ready for the rescue, and it's time for you to leave."

The Drifter stared off into space, trying very hard to hold back his temper, but his attempt was futile. With a very quick movement of his right hand, he had drawn his pistol, cocked the hammer, and had stood up with it pointed at the captain's head. In a very deep, agitated voice, he spoke clearly and precisely so no one would misinterpret what he had to say next.

"Let's get one thing straight, I came here to help you. I brought food, blankets, clothing, and anything else I thought you might need. If you wish to stay here and die, that's your choice. I don't give a shit one way or the other, but I'm not going to let your incompetence kill this young girl. She is going with me if I have to kill every one of you to accomplish that. ... Dog ... protect."

(Tom)

Tom was standing in the tree line north of the plateau, silently laughing. He laughed so hard, he felt that for a moment he might have been heard. In his present state, they had the advantage and he had no weapons. It would be totally hopeless for him to try to regain his superiority. Hearing the conflict between the captain and the Drifter, he knew they were going nowhere. He watched them stand in peril as he thought of the Drifter's comments. *If this guy is right about the approaching storm, then most of these assholes will freeze to death, making my job easier.* With a crooked smile splitting his disgusting face, he headed back toward the cabin to wait for the storm to pass.

As he followed the tree line around the plateau being very quiet, his thoughts continued to rage. *I'll be back for the rest of you later. You're going to wish you decided to follow that Drifter fellow before I'm through with you. After I've killed the lot of you, I'm going to find him and finish what I started.*

(The Drifter)

Dog stood up on all fours barking savagely as his sharp white teeth glistened against the moonlight. Rachael, now feeling her own frustration rise to its boiling point, yelled, "That's enough, both of you calm down … right now!" For some unknown reason, the wolf silenced his barking and sat back down in the snow. The Drifter, with a surprised look caused by Dog's reaction, held fast with his intentions without giving an inch, as she approached the captain. Rachael had her arm extended as she asked the captain to give up his rifle. Slowly and reluctantly, he surrendered it to her. She walked toward the Drifter with the rifle extended as she said, "Take this before someone gets hurt."

The captain yelled, "What the hell are you doing, Rachael?"

She quickly turned her head and gave him a hateful look. "I'm saving your life. Now shut up and let's hear what this man has to say."

He stood, pistol in hand, pointing it at the captain, ready to fire if necessary. Without flinching or taking his eyes off of him, he grabbed the rifle from Rachael's hands. He slung it over his shoulder as he slowly released the hammer and returned the pistol to its holster.

Rachael softly spoke, not knowing how to handle the Drifter's temper. "Please … tell us what we need to do."

He gave her a quick glace before turning to face the others. The crowd of survivors, feeling more placid after he had released the pistol, waited patiently to hear what he had to say. "You have a problem, and I believe you should be aware of it. There is a storm approaching. My best guess is it will be here within the next few hours."

Before the Drifter could finish his statement, Captain Joe interrupted him. "I don't see that as a problem."

Rachael, very quickly and with complete disrespect in her voice, told Joe to shut up. She then turned back to the Drifter and motioned for him to continue.

"In light of all that's happened here tonight, I could understand why you have a problem trusting me. I want to apologize for my temper. I've been on my own for the last few years, with very little interaction with people. I know that's not a good excuse, but I am trying. I came here only to help you and had no intentions on taking you into my home, but I feel this is our only choice. The storm may be light or heavy. It could last a few hours or a few days. I don't honestly know the strength of it; however, this time of year, the storms are usually gruesome.

"If you stay here, most of you could die. You are welcome to come with me and I will take you into my home where it's warm and there's plenty of food. We'll care for the injured and wait for the storm to pass. When I feel it's safe enough, I'll take you to Cyprus Springs, where they can find you a way home. I'm taking a chance in not getting back before the storm hits by extending this offer. So if you want to live, be ready to go or be ready to stay. Whatever your choice may be, Amy is coming with me. You have thirty minutes to decide."

Silence fell upon all the passengers as they attentively listened. With all the patience he could muster, he turned from them and walked away into the darkness. He led his horse across the plateau to where he had unloaded the supplies. He removed a blanket, laid it on the ground, and sat down to wait for the commotion to begin.

Rachael spoke first: "We all go or none of us will go."

He could hear the little murmurs coming from the crowd, but he knew he was victorious. All he could do was smile while he patiently waited for their decision. He hoped his anger did not lose him the opportunity to gain their trust, but if it did, then the tribulation of the journey would be long and hard.

Ten minutes had passed before Rachael left the circle of survivors and approached him with their decision. "We're going with you. All of us, and this includes Captain Joe."

The Drifter looked at her, and with all the strength of his character, he could not hold back the smile that broke the harshness of his face. "You drive a hard bargain, Rachael. Okay … we all go, but we need to get moving very quickly; time is running out for us all."

Rachael nodded with acceptance and asked what preparation needed to be accomplished before they could leave. The Drifter spent the next few minutes giving her instructions before she left and headed toward the captain. Moments later, he heard the captain barking out his orders. It was not long after when he saw some able-bodied men gathering around the body of the aircraft. After a few short words from one of the taller gentlemen, they began digging a hole with whatever they could find to use as a shovel. Some of the women were gathering blankets and extra clothing, from some of the luggage that had been scattered across the plateau.

From his position, he could see Rachael standing close to a fairly large man sitting on a log close to the campfire. There was a blonde, younger-looking woman sitting beside him with her arm around his waist. His curiosity took a stronger hold as he tried to figure out what was happening, before he finally gave in and decided to help. By the time he arrived, Rachael was standing over the gentleman, poking around his shoulder, and from the gritting of his teeth, it was easy to tell that this man was in tremendous pain.

As the Drifter moved around Rachael to get a better look, the young blonde approached him. "Can you help him? ... I'm sorry, that was rude. My name is Alice and this is my husband George. He is really hurting bad ... could you please help him?"

He gave her a quick smile as he offered his assistance to Rachael, who quickly gave up her position as a nurse. She stepped away from George, as the Drifter took her place in front. After a few minutes of his examination, he knelt down in front of George to give him the diagnosis.

"You appear to have a dislocated shoulder. The tissue around it is very tender and to set it would cause unbearable pain, even to the point of causing unconsciousness. If we have to carry you, it would slow us down. With time running out, we can't afford to waste it. I'm going to suspend your arm until we reach my place, then we'll set your shoulder. The sling will help some, but you'll have to deal with the pain, until I have a chance to set it."

George accepted his fate as the Drifter slowly tied a sling, made from ripped pieces of cloth, around his neck. With help from Rachael, he carefully lifted his arm and secured it inside the sling. The Drifter removed his scarf from around his neck, crouched down, and filled it with snow. He placed the scarf on George's shoulder and took Alice's hand. He placed her hand on the scarf and instructed her to keep the snow pack on his shoulder to help the swelling.

After they were finished with George, and before he had the opportunity to walk away, Rachael had stepped in front, pushing herself close to his body. She lifted her arms and placed them around his neck and gently pulled him closer, thanking him for his help. His body stiffened when he felt a sensual kiss on his cheek. His heart began to race when more sensual kissing followed the first. The closer she moved toward his lips, the weaker he became.

It had been such a long time since he felt the passion of a beautiful woman and the sensuality of being loved, that he felt defenseless to resist. He could feel the warmth of her body forcing him to pull her closer, while he enjoyed the affection she was offering. He glanced into Alice's eyes and could tell by the smile slowly lifting the corners of her mouth that she approved. It was like a crack of thunder that broke his attention when Rachael's lips touched his. Unable to control himself any longer, he gently pulled away from her grip and slowly walked back into the darkness.

Rachael stood there, confused, feeling his rejection. Alice had come to her side to give comfort, as the two of them watched the Drifter slowly blend into the darkness of the plateau.

His legs were weak and shaky as he coaxed himself along, feeling them get heavier with each step. All the while, he was thinking of what he had left behind and regretting the chance he may never have again. He headed to the area where he had last discarded the travois. When he arrived, he was still feeling shaky, so he dropped to his knees as he took in a deep breath. Moments later, he grabbed the travois and dragged it back to Horse, securing it to the saddle. Slowly, he led Horse back to Jennifer as he pushed the strong feelings aside.

As he knelt in front of Jennifer, he lifted her dress, trying to move it away from her injury. She quickly slapped his hand as she pulled her dress back to cover her exposed leg. He sighed, looked at her, already feeling disgusted, and said, "I just wanted to check the condition of your leg. Do you mind?"

Jennifer, in her sarcastic attitude, replied, "You might as well see the rest of me. You've already seen my tits, huh?"

The Drifter shook is head, disappointed, as he replied with a sarcastic remark of his own. "Look, lady, I'm sure you've had some bad relationships in your life and that explains your attitude toward men. But ... could you just shut up and not be a bitch for a while?"

Jennifer's eyes widened, not believing he just called her a bitch. She threw her head back, giving out an expressive "humph," after she impetuously opened her dress, exposing herself.

He carefully examined the laceration on her leg. It was a large cut beginning approximately four inches above the knee and ran the length of the leg. It was on the inside, cutting deep into the muscle, but from his inspection, he could not see any major damage to arteries, tendons, or ligaments. From the redness around the cut, it looked as if the beginnings of an infection were a possibility. He was not sure how deep the infection, so he said nothing, to avoid alerting her. He knew she would be unable to walk, and told her she would have to ride on the travois for the journey home. She opened her mouth to speak, when the Drifter quickly responded, "This is not an option; you will ride, so keep quiet."

He gently picked her up from the log and carefully carried her to the travois without any further trouble from Jennifer. While he was covering her with the blankets, she asked, "How do you know a storm is coming?" The Drifter gave her a quaint smile as he knelt beside the travois to explain his reasoning.

"It was four years ago. I was out hunting, when an unexpected snowstorm brewed up from nowhere. It didn't take long before the winds and snow made it impossible to see. I ended up getting lost and passed out due to hypothermia and almost died. An old trapper found me half-frozen and carried me back to his cabin. He cared for me until I was well, and then sent me on my way. As time passed, we became close friends and he taught me how to hunt and survive in the wilderness.

"His name was John, so I always called him Old Trapper John. He taught me how to listen to the sounds of the forest to help predict the weather, or the silence and what it meant. On my trip here, I could hear the hustle and bustle of small creatures gathering food. I haven't heard a sound, not even a wolf howl in the last three hours. I can smell and sense its presence, so believe me when I tell you it's coming. I'm not exactly sure when it's going to get here, but the longer we delay, the less our chances of survival. It could be a blizzard causing visibility to be greatly diminished, making it very easy to get lost and freeze to death."

He gave Jennifer a fake smile as he turned his attention back to the log where Amy had been sitting. She was not there or anywhere by the campfire; a streak of panic rushed him as he scoured the area. Amy could not be found anywhere in camp. He glanced toward Jennifer when he asked, "Where's Amy?"

Jennifer began looking for Amy about the camp when the Drifter interrupted her and told her Amy was nowhere to be seen. Jennifer gasped, "She did this once before, right after Tom and Rachael went looking for you. The captain found her wandering in the woods, looking for her mother. ... Speaking of her mother, where is she?"

The Drifter turned his head in the direction where he had laid Jessica's body, bowed his head, and no more had to be said. Jennifer gasped and placed her hand over her mouth. "Oh my God!" The Drifter immediately stood up and headed across the plateau in the direction where he had found Jessica's tormented body.

Dog sensed where his master was going and took the lead. Dog stopped short at the edge of the plateau and waited for the Drifter. Amy was crouched down next to a tree at the bottom of the incline. When the Drifter arrived, he casually walked down the incline until he was standing directly over her. He knelt in front of her to gain eye contact, when he saw tears running down her cheeks. She looked up from the ground, when she saw him kneel and asked in a trembling voice, "Will you help me find my mommy?"

You could have stuck a knife through his heart and he would have felt less pain than what he was feeling now. Her request burned deep, but he was unprepared to tell her about the hideous nature of her mother's death. He sat there thinking long and hard before he finally spoke. "I will do what I can to help you, but first I want to introduce you to someone. A few years ago, an old friend of mine, one I call Old Trapper John, gave me Dog. He found him caught in one of his traps one morning. Dog's mother was there trying to help her pup when Old Trapper John ran her off. I'm kind of glad he got there shortly after the wolf pup was trapped. You know, a wolf will gnaw off its leg just to escape. Anyway, John told me that if I was going to stay out here in the wilderness, I needed a companion. Dog is my companion and my best friend. I think right now you could use a companion, and Dog is willing to be just that. ... That is if you want him to be your friend."

Amy's tears slowly dried from her eyes, as the two of them broke eye contact and she moved her eyes toward Dog. He felt so much pain and was not sure how he would ever tell her about her mother, but for now, Dog seemed to be gaining her attention. He raised his hand up, trying to get her to place her hand into his. There was a slight hesitation before the two hands joined. He smiled as he raised her hand to Dog's nose for him to smell her scent. Softly, he said "Friend," allowing Dog to sniff her hand. He sat there for a while as the two of them became closely acquainted, before he asked Amy to take Dog back to the camp and check on Jennifer. Dog had softly whined the entire time, as if he understood Amy's pain at being separated from her mother. The two of them left heading back to camp, as the Drifter remained kneeling in the snow, trying to regain his composure.

Worried that Amy would accidentally find her mother, he decided to get her buried soon. He quickly headed back across the plateau toward Jessica's body. She was still covered with his coat, and he sighed in relief when he saw Amy still talking with Jennifer. He gently picked her up and carried her into the pit, next to the fuselage. He very carefully laid her on the ground, keeping her fully covered until he could fetch a blanket from the supplies. When he returned, he removed the coat and completely wrapped Jessica's body, concealing the horror. Feeling a sense of relief, he returned to Jennifer, carrying his coat over his shoulder. He gently covered Jennifer with the coat and began securing her to the travois for the long journey home. He yelled out to the captain to start gathering the bodies and get them buried, for it was now time to leave.

The camp was busy like a swarm of bees leaving the hive to find a new home. Time was very critical but seemed not to get any shorter, as the survivors prepared for the journey. There was a great focus, as the surviving passengers of Flight 493 gathered the bodies of the dead. He could see them being carried with care as the bodies were gently laid into their snowy grave.

The captain had come to inquire about the missing hunter, which set off a flare of resentment. The Drifter, now impatient and ready to leave, showed his anger once again. "Let their bodies rot where they lie! The wolves need to feed, and besides, we don't have time to waste. After what they've done, I can't understand why you're so concerned." The captain, being discouraged by his comment, held his anger to avoid another clash. He too was not pleased with burying the hunters, but did not feel right about leaving them to the wolves.

The Drifter, feeling uneasy about losing his temper again, still held strongly to his decision. To help him subdue his anger, he decided to check on Amy and Dog. The two of them seemed to be getting along very well, and Amy even had a smile for him as he approached. He smiled back as he knelt beside them. "I'm glad the two of you are getting along. We'll be leaving soon, and I wanted to see if you wanted to ride Horse or ride on the travois with Jennifer."

Amy was disappointed with his suggestions and asked, "May I walk with Dog instead?"

The Drifter smiled as he agreed to her request. Before he had a chance to leave, Amy unexpectedly threw her arms around his neck. Shocked by the action, he pulled his head and shoulders back, but this did not stop Amy. Slowly, the shock turned into a long-lost feeling, bringing back good memories. He returned her hug and before he departed he said, "Thank you, Amy … you have no idea how much I needed that."

When the Drifter checked with the captain on their progress, he was disappointed to find out they were still gathering the dead. He expressed the urgency of leaving once more, and felt the guilt when the captain requested they have a graveside prayer before they left. With a restless sigh of guilt, he agreed to the prayer, but still emphasized the time restraint they were under.

As he turned away to go prepare Horse for the journey home, he heard the captain say, "I know I was hard on you earlier. It's just really been crazy around here tonight. Too many things happening, too many dead..."

The Drifter interrupted him in the middle of his apology as he said, "If an apology is warranted, then I'm the one who needs to apologize. Let's start all over and begin working together. We have a long trip ahead of us and I will desperately need your help." The captain nodded as the Drifter left to prepare.

He rummaged through the luggage as he looked for anything he could use to build a lifeline. He regretted not bringing the rope, for now he was forced to improvise. Finding some shirts and trousers, he tied them together, creating a long rope, resembling a kite's tail. When it was completed, he tied one end of the line to the saddle horn and laid the rest of it across the snow behind Horse. He called out to the captain, telling him it was time to leave and for everybody to line up by the snow-covered grave.

As the group of remaining survivors gathered together, the men who were assigned to the burial detail were covering the grave with the last remaining shovels of snow. The Drifter stood there as he motioned for the captain to say a small prayer. They all bowed their heads, as Captain Joe gave a short prayer of remembrance to the lives lost in this tragedy and a word of gratitude for those who had survived.

(The Captain's Prayer)

"Heavenly Father, We now entrust these beloved bodies and souls to you. Each one of them were daughters and sons, many were mothers and fathers, as well as sisters, brothers, and friends. Please give their families and loved ones the strength they will need as they are confronted with their losses and are forced to deal with them. Help them to focus on the memories of the good times they shared, instead of focusing on the time that has been taken from them. Father, we will try not to question you, for you are our Savior. We do not understand, but surely You must have special plans for each of them as they enter heaven's gate.

"Father, please let us, as the remaining survivors, be grateful for the life that we have left, and also give us strength and guidance; not only for this loss, but the journey that lies ahead of us now and throughout our lives. Father, I would also like to thank you for bringing this man we call the Drifter to us and forgive those of us who doubted his intentions. Let him know we are grateful for all he has done and continues to do. Father, please alleviate the pain and suffering that he may feel, for he truly is a man who deserves no less. With this, Dear Lord, we will dry our eyes and absorb strength from you, for our journey now awaits us. Amen."

After the prayer, they all remained with their heads bowed as each of them gave their final respect to the dead. Shortly afterward, the Drifter requested for all of them to line up behind his horse. Captain Joe motioned for everyone to follow him as they walked to the lifeline the Drifter had laid across the snow. The Drifter asked them to form a single line and wait until all were present. It seemed a lifetime passed before the last person joined the small group.

He quickly and very precisely gave them instructions for the journey home. "I know it might not be apparent right now why I have this line strung out behind the horse, but soon you'll understand. I want you to hold on to the line, because your life may depend on it. It's your job to help those around you. I am asking each and every one of you to keep an eye on the other, so that no one gets left behind. Take a few moments to look around and get to know the person in front and behind you."

The Drifter allowed a few minutes for them to get familiar with each other before he motioned for Dog to take the lead.

"Home," he said.

Dog barked once and darted toward the front of the line. Once he arrived, he picked up the reins with his teeth and began leading Horse home. Amy ran to Dog's side as the caravan slowly began to move. The Drifter and the captain remained behind, watching the small group cross the plateau, marking the beginning of a long and tedious journey. Rachael approached them as they watched and inquired about Amy's safety at the front, with the wolf. The Drifter assured Rachael that Amy would be fine when he answered her question. "Dog will take care of Amy, and if necessary, give his life to protect her."

The trip back was going to be more difficult with the responsibility of the lives he had taken upon himself to protect. The loosely packed snow was deep, making it difficult to walk; wearing at their strength, draining precious energy needed for the long journey. It was not long after the trip began before the mumbling started among the survivors. They had only traveled a couple of miles and there was already a request to stop and rest. The Drifter disapproved of the rest and forced the captain to comply. The captain gracefully accepted his demise as he walked among the crowd, tying to explain the rationality of not taking the rest.

The Drifter went to the front of the line to check on Amy. She was walking by Dog's side, holding his collar and talking to him as if he could understand her every word. He smiled as he turned his attention to Jennifer.

Jennifer was still cuddled up in his heavy fur coat, and acted as if she was doing fine. He could tell by her voice that she was in tremendous pain, but was trying not to show it. He placed his hand on her forehead, and the heat of her fever began to worry him, but there was little he could do for her right now. He gave her a big smile and self-assured blessing, trying not to worry her. He left her side as he walked the line checking on everybody's condition. When he approached George, he could tell from his clenching eyes that he was struggling with every step. He thought about the possibility of letting him ride Horse, but he knew this would slow down the caravan, lessening their chances to make it to shelter.

With regret, he placed his hand on George's good shoulder, and with a sympathetic gesture, asked him to remain strong. George motioned for him to lean over as he whispered into the Drifter's ear, "You may not remember me, but I remember you!"

The Drifter straightened his body with a bewildered look as he tried to place where he and George had crossed paths before. Alice stood by patiently, wondering what her husband had said that made this man stare at him so strongly. She glanced between the two of them, hoping one would explain their actions, but neither offered her an explanation.

Without further thought, Alice asked the Drifter the expected but dreaded question, "Can you offer my husband some help to relieve some of his pain?" Her gaze was so strong that the Drifter could not return her stare. He sympathized with them but his hands were tied, and the safety of the others was at stake. The captain had stopped next to him while he was trying to find a suitable answer for Alice's question. Taking advantage of the captain's arrival, he turned his attention toward him, allowing him to avoid the answer and break away from the uneasy feeling of Alice's stare.

The captain informed him that all the passengers had been visited and they were all tired but doing fine. The Drifter acknowledged Captain Joe and took the opportunity to leave the company of George and Alice. Alice looked down at her suffering husband and knew there was nothing more she could do. She remembered the Drifter's reaction to what her husband had said and questioned George about the comment.

"It's not that important. I will tell you that he has been through hell. Unless you have been there, you wouldn't understand. I'm giving him the respect that he has earned." George said this with defiance in his voice. Realizing that George was not going to answer her question, she dropped the subject and went back to trying to comfort him as much as she could.

(Hours later)

They had traveled about eight miles before the Drifter decided to allow them a short break. Snowflakes were falling lightly and he felt that they had a good chance of beating the storm, but he did want them to know this. He whistled for Dog to stop as he spoke loudly.

"Okay everyone! We are going to take a fifteen-minute break. Get you some water and chew on a piece of jerky. As you can already tell by the falling snow, the storm is close. Take this time to relax and conserve your strength. We only have about three miles left." He knew the rest was desperately needed, for the falling snow would make the journey of the last few miles even more difficult.

There were sighs throughout the caravan, as they stopped and each of them found a place to sit. The Drifter decided to check on Jennifer, before he retired to rest his own sore muscles. He found her fever was getting worse. Perspiration was saturating the blanket she was wrapped in. He offered her some cold water from his canteen to help chill her fever. She could only take in a few small swallows before spitting the rest back up. He wished there was more he could do for her, but for the moment, this was the best he could do, so he decided to retire to an old stump to rest his weary legs.

He reached into his bag of jerky and began sucking on a small piece, when he saw Dog and Amy approaching. He offered both of them a piece, and Dog devoured the jerky as he always did. Smiling, he took his piece and handed it to Dog, only to see it disappear in seconds. Amy smiled at the Drifter's action and followed suit with her own piece of jerky. After Dog finished licking his lips, the three of them had a drink from his canteen.

As he sat there on the old stump, he saw the snowflakes increasing in size and thickness. Visibility was already beginning to diminish. They had only been there for ten minutes when he began to fear the storm would arrive sooner than he first anticipated. Alice approached him and asked for his attention, before he had the opportunity to finish analyzing the weather conditions. She told him that George wished to speak with him, and emphasized the urgency. He agreed and followed Alice back to her husband George. George looked as if had been severely drained; his face was pale white with slightly blue lips. Before he could check on his condition, George spoke in a low, shaky voice. "If I don't make it out of this alive, you have to promise me you'll make sure my wife gets home safely." The Drifter felt the strain on his emotions once more, for again he was being forced into a promise he could not escape.

As he knelt down and bowed his head in respect, he gave George his promise to take care of Alice. After much deliberation, he decided to let George ride his horse during the last leg of the journey. George refused to be babied, as he scolded the Drifter for even considering endangering the lives of the others for his sake. The Drifter sighed and apologized.

A few seconds later, George surprised him when he yelled, "This man we call the Drifter ... is a good man. He has taken on a lot of responsibility, something most men would balk at. We owe him our debt of gratitude. I'm no expert, but even I can see that this weather is getting worse and I think its time to get up and start moving." The Drifter smiled as he extended his hand to assist George to his feet. With a motion from his other hand, Dog took the lead once more.

The Drifter heard no complaining or mumbling from the survivors as they prepared for the last leg of the trip home. Before they began their journey, he again warned them about the dangers of a furious snowstorm and how it was imperative to keep a tight line. He thanked George for his confidence he shared with the others and the strength of his endurance. The Drifter assured Alice that her husband would live, even if he were forced to carry him the rest of the distance. She smiled as the Drifter motioned for the caravan of survivors to start moving forward.

Slowly, one by one, they fell in behind Horse as the small caravan began their race against time. The Drifter was concerned about the hardships they might suffer, being in the midst of a horrendous snowstorm. Their confidence would weaken as the cold winds began cutting fear into their hearts. The more the storm intensified, the greater the risk that hypothermia would become a threat when their body temperatures began to decrease from the freezing winds. He was confident that Dog would find his way home, even if the visibility dropped to zero. He shook the fear from his mind as he took his position in the middle of the small caravan, with the captain bringing up the rear.

Thinking all was under control, the small group of survivors marched through the snow-covered forest, not suspecting the next turn of events. Their progress was slowed as the falling snowflakes thickened with each passing minute. They were thirty minutes into the trip when the winds began to pick up, blowing loose snow across their path. The Drifter motioned for them to tighten up the line, getting even closer, leaving no chance of someone falling without another knowing it.

Without a warning, the downy hairs on the back of his neck stood up as an eerie feeling of being watched wrenched through his mind. He slowly scoured the area, looking for a reason why he sensed a presence, but nothing could be seen that would explain it.

He stepped away from his position in the middle of the caravan, so he could view them from a distance, giving him a better opportunity to focus on this unknown presence. He slowly turned in a complete circle as he looked through the trees, trying to see any shadowy movement. His first thought was that Tom had been following them, and feared what he might do. *What if he follows us home? What if he was able to get his hands on a weapon? Why doesn't Dog sense his presence, or am I just overreacting?* Not seeing any reactions from Dog or movements among the trees, he dismissed the feeling and determined it was a deception of his imagination.

He turned his attention once again to the small caravan as he watched their progress. The storm was beginning to turn into a light blizzard, thickening by the raging winds. Their journey would end soon, but the remaining miles would feel like the longest part of the entire trip. The cold winds were freezing the clothing, causing snow to settle and stick, adding weight to every step. Exposed flesh was turning light shades of blue as the warm blood rushed away from the skin. The air was so thick, it was making it hard to see the entire caravan, forcing him to leave his outpost and return to his original position in the middle.

When the Drifter reached line, he again motioned for the group to tighten the ranks even further. The minutes began to pass like hours as they slowly trudged through the snow, straining with every step. Visibility was now down to a minimum, as the storm unleashed its fury upon the small group of survivors. He could sense that some of them deplored the idea of being here, after walking all this way unprotected for nothing, just to die. He too felt helpless, but knew death would be the consequence of giving up. He walked the line, encouraging each of them with the hope of arriving soon. Before he reached the end,, he noticed the caravan began to slow down until it came to a complete halt.

As he ran to the front of the line to see why they had stopped, he passed Rachael, who looked even more confused than he. She fell in behind and followed him in close pursuit to the front of the line. When they arrived, they found the reins of Horse lying in the snow, with Amy and Dog missing. The Drifter's eerie feeling returned, sensing Tom's presence, and somehow feeling he was involved in their disappearance. He searched the entire area, but could only find the remnants of a few prints heading south. Not wanting to instill fear in Rachael with his feelings about Tom, he decided to act stupid and confused. He was concerned about the possibility of Tom kidnapping Amy, but confused why Dog would allow it.

He took a long, deep breath, then looked at Rachael before he confidently asked her to lead the caravan. He pointed to the west and instructed her to continue until they reached the mountain's edge. He then turned away to follow the prints when Rachael yelled, "Where are you going?"

He stopped and softly spoke these simple words of encouragement: "You'll be fine. Keep heading west until you reach the mountain's edge. I have to find them while I can still follow their tracks. I will catch up to you. Now get going before these people start worrying." The Drifter followed the tracks heading south while Rachael took the reins of Horse and moved west.

The further south he traveled, the lighter the tracks became, as the wind and snow slowly erased their memories. He could not see any indication that Tom was traveling beside or behind them. The only prints in the snow were from Amy and Dog. Even though he still had the feeling of being followed, his greatest fear about Tom faded. He still could not understand why they had left this close to home, if Tom was not the reason. Nightmarish thoughts plagued his mind as he continued calling their names. All he could hope was that they did not travel too far south to the raging river canyon. It was sixty feet deep, and he feared if they stumbled, they would slide down the steep incline, smashing their bodies against the rocks below.

He had traveled approximately a quarter mile when the tracks just disappeared. The storm had reached its full glory, erasing all signs of any existence in the valley. Even his tracks were slowly disappearing behind him. He scoured the area, trying to find any sign that would give him their direction of travel, but he was unable to get a bearing. He circled the area, starting from where he last saw their tracks, wandering aimlessly, hoping to find any sign. Every pass discouraged him even more as the heaviness of his heart increased. It was as if they were lifted into the heavens, leaving him no hope of finding them. He screamed their names, only to have his voice silenced by the howling winds, which added to his frustration.

Thoughts of his promises to Jessica and George came back to haunt him. Once again, he had failed to protect the ones he loved, and the guilt of years past returned like a wall of water crashing against the cliffs. He stood there in conflict, being torn between his desire to find Amy and his promise to George, as the two emotions waged war. Not willing to give in to his defeat, he once again circled the clearing. All he needed was some small sign that would help him settle the raging dispute that was tearing at his heart.

Chapter Seven
The Search for Amy

(The Drifter)

His trance was broken when a cold blast of wind slapped his face with ice, stinging it like a barrage of needles. All hope of finding them was now gone, forcing him to return to the others. Slowly and reluctantly, he turned back north, forcing his legs to walk away, even though he felt compelled to stay. He knew Dog was smart enough to survive in this weather, and could only hope he was able to protect Amy from a fate worse than death. He dragged himself back to the caravan with an empty and guilty heart. Rachael and the others needed his help if they were ever to find the entrance into the caverns.

His fears of survivors' panic and disorder were laid to rest when he reached the caravan, for Rachael had kept the small group functioning in an orderly fashion. As he walked among the ranks, checking on their condition, his heart hung heavy with guilt. He could sense the concern from the survivors, but no one said a word until he reached the captain at the end of the caravan.

"Did you find Amy?" the captain asked.

He quickly turned his back to the captain in an attempt to hide his shame. As he tried to flee, he was stopped when he felt the touch of Joe's hand upon his shoulder. He slowly turned to face the captain and saw reassurance in his eyes that all would be fine, but he still could not shake his failure. He cleared his emotions of failure by focusing his attentions toward helping Rachael.

(Amy and Dog)

Amy was crouched behind the trunk of a large spruce tree, trying to block the wind. Her head was lying on her arms, which were wrapped around her legs in a sitting position. Her eyes were closed and the snow was beginning to cover her small, frail body. Dog lay in the snow next to her, using his body as a blanket to help keep her warm. His head was perked and very attentive to the surrounding area. He glanced around the tree, looking for movement while he sniffed at the air to detect any scents. Satisfied that they were alone, he wedged his head back under Amy's arms and rested on her legs. The warmth of Dog's head caused Amy to open her eyes as she unfolded her arms and looked at him. She lifted her head, exposing the half-frozen tears that were stuck to her cheeks. With a pouting expression on her face, she whined as she asked, "Dog, where's my mommy? Why did she leave me?" Dog lifted his head and gave her a gentle nudge under her cheek with his nose. Amy could not understand why her mom never returned. She was missing her and desperately in need of finding her. With the exception of Dog, her new friend, she was feeling very much alone. "I love you, Dog." He whined once more, as if he understood her grief and the pain of loneliness. He laid his head back down on her lap as the winds continued to blow with great fury, slowly covering both of them with a light blanket of snow. His instincts told him their peril was growing with every minute. If he did nothing, he would lose his newfound friend.

(The Drifter)

It seemed hours had passed before he finally saw the shadows of the mountain. When they reached the edge of the rocky side, he realized they had traveled too far south. He took in a deep breath, shook his head, and with a sigh, he increased the pace once more. His frustration grew deeper, knowing this delay would only lessen his chances of ever finding Amy.

They followed the mountainside north for thirty minutes, until they reached the cave door leading into the stables. He opened the door with the hidden switch inside a crack of the rocky wall. The door rumbled and creaked, as it swung open, exposing a corridor leading to the stables. He instructed Rachael to lead Horse into the corridor while the others followed.

When everyone had entered the stables, he pushed the green switch on the inside, and once again the stables rumbled as the huge door closed, blocking off the cold winds. There was a great sigh of relief from all the survivors as they began to feel the warmth of the caverns extinguishing the colder air. The Drifter quickly walked into the stables with the captain hot on his heels.

When they reached Rachael, he gave them the following instructions: "We need to get these people settled in as quickly as possible. There is an elevator over against the south wall. Take it up to the small hallway on the left, which leads to a larger cavern. It's easy to see my house from there. Go on in, it's not locked."

Rachael nodded as she corralled the passengers into a small circle. The Drifter left them to prepare Jennifer, knowing Rachael and the captain had the situation well under control.

As he removed the restraints from Jennifer, he could hear the lift constantly in motion. Every once in a while, he would glance toward it. The captain stood at the bottom of the lift while Rachael remained at the top. He could hear faint sounds as both of them gave instructions to the passengers as they stepped on and off the lift. After they had all been lifted to the upper ledge and the elevator returned to the floor, the Drifter gently lifted Jennifer out of the travois and carried her to the lift. The captain joined him, and they both rose to the ledge where Rachael was waiting. With Rachael's help, they carried Jennifer through the small corridor, across the cavern, up the stairs, and into the house.

Once inside, they carried Jennifer into the living room and laid her gently on the soft cushions of the sofa. He instructed Rachael to get some gauze and hydrogen peroxide from the main bathroom on the west wall. While she was retrieving the supplies, he removed his fur coat. Jennifer was unconscious and burning with fever, but all the Drifter could do was try to make her comfortable. When Rachael returned with the supplies, he instructed her to clean the wound as much as she could and keep Jennifer cool to help break her fever.

Rachael laid the gauze and peroxide on the floor before she turned toward the Drifter. "This place is magnificent. I would've never dreamed this was even possible. Did you do all this?"

He nodded his head. "We have plenty of time to talk about this later. My first obligation is complete; now I must go back to find Amy and Dog. There is a stew in the refrigerator inside the kitchen. You and the captain know what you need to do, so I suggest you get to it."

While he was putting on his fur coat, Jennifer slowly opened her eyes. She saw the Drifter as he was walking away. "Where are you going?" she inquired in a soft, gentle voice.

He glanced back with a smile, seeing she was now conscious. "I have something I need to do. You lay there and rest; Rachael will take care of you. I will be back soon and we'll take care of that leg."

As he turned away and was heading for the door, he heard her soft, trembling voice from behind. "I can't feel my leg; it's numb."

He felt very uncomfortable about leaving, since he felt it was his responsibility, but his first priority was Amy and Dog. He headed for the front door as he motioned for Captain Joe to join him. "I need someone to feed, water, and brush down Horse." Joe acknowledged his request while the Drifter was walking out of the front door toward the small corridor.

(Moments later, in the stables)

The worst of the storm was upon, them making the search next to impossible. He grabbed a handful of fluorescent streamers and placed them in his coat pocket. He picked up a flashlight from his workbench and placed it in his pocket with the streamers. As he was getting prepared, he heard the elevator rumbling and echoing through the cavern. He was sitting down and strapping on his snowshoes, when he heard the lift once more. Staring back toward it, he saw the captain riding it to the bottom of the stables.

After he had finished lacing up the snowshoes, he heard the captain say, "Good luck. I'll take care of your horse and make sure the passengers are taken care of. You find that young girl, and that dog of yours."

The Drifter thanked him as he walked the passage leading to the stable doors. The creaking and rumbling of the door as it opened sounded throughout the stables once more. A blast of cold wind hit him, sending cold chills throughout his body. Even fully dressed, he felt the cold, and only the thought of Amy being out there unprotected gave him the strength to continue.

He walked through the doorway into the blinding blizzard and closed the door behind him. He wrapped his scarf around his neck to protect his mouth and nose. He felt the wind blowing through the small opening around his collar, so he closed the gap. The air was cold and his lungs felt like they were freezing with every breath he took. The trees were swaying furiously in the strong winds. Quickly and without further hesitation, he headed south along the mountain edge, until he reached the pathway they had traveled. This is where he tied his first streamer for retracing his steps. About twenty feet into the woods, he turned the flashlight on and pointed it back toward the streamer. It glistened in the light as the winds blew, causing the branch with the streamer to sway. Satisfied with the radiant sign that marked his return, he continued his journey. Approximately every twenty to thirty feet, he would hang another streamer. The journey was long and hard as he retraced his path back to the location where Amy and Dog had disappeared. The air was so thick with snow, his clothes began to freeze, causing the snow to stick. After a while, he began to look like a walking snowman, weighed down with an icy covering.In a short time, he was forced to stop and remove the tightly packed snow from his clothing. With a brushing motion, he was able to knock some of the looser snow away. He pulled off his scarf and shook it in the air, releasing the thickly packed snow. With his hunting knife, he scraped away the rest of the snow.

By the time he arrived back in the area where Amy and Dog's prints were last seen, all was erased by the blizzard. There was little hope of finding new signs, and he sincerely doubted he would find them now. His only hope of ever finding them lay in his tracking skills and intuition. His first move was to go south, because that was the direction of the tracks that he had last seen. From there, he would begin his search. He followed the small trail south until he reached the spot where he was forced to leave and go back to help the others. He tied his last remaining streamer on a small branch and began circling the area, keeping the streamer in view at all times. His trip back here seemed to take less time than he expected, even though the snow was thicker. His walking was easier with the snowshoes, and his only obstacle was when the snow had packed against his clothing. The Drifter, in his hurry to begin his search, had forgotten to bring some food, and was reminded when his stomach began to growl. His strength was draining by the minute, but his passion to find them drove him onward. It had been a couple of hours since they disappeared, and his only hope of Amy being alive was in Dog's instinct.

He started his search by moving in a clockwise direction, circling the area and expanding the circle as he walked. He continued to yell their names as loud as he could. This plan of expanding his circular pattern was his only hope of finding some sign. It was not the best idea, but it was the only one that offered any hope. Keeping visibility on the last streamer for guidance helped him keep his bearing and not get lost in the blizzard.

(Amy and Dog)

They were sitting by the spruce tree, almost totally covered by snow before Dog decided to take action. In desperation, to protect Amy, he grabbed her coat sleeve between his teeth and gave it a slight tug. There was no response from Amy, so he continued tugging at her coat, but she still did not budge. Dog darted away from the tree, barking very loudly. He stopped and turned back as he continued to bark, trying to get her to follow.

She rested her head against her knees as she looked at Dog, before she asked, "Dog, do you know where my mommy is?"

Dog barked once before returning to her side and gently nudged her on the cheek. He then darted out away from her once more barking for her to follow. Amy, finally understanding Dog's intentions, stood up from the tree and walked to his side. With her hand tightly clasped around his collar, Dog led her toward home. They had not traveled very far before Amy could feel herself getting tired and sleepy. She held on to Dog's collar as he dragged her weary feet through the snow. The winds were blowing so hard, it was causing some of the smaller limbs to be ripped from the trees. At times, the winds were so blustery that some of the smaller trees were torn from the ground and flung into the heavens. Dog held fast as the winds resisted his forward thrust, making it difficult to walk. Amy held up her arm, covering her face to keep the stinging ice away from her eyes. They fought the fury of the storm until Amy stumbled and fell face-first into the snow. Dog barked, trying to get her attention, but she lay motionless. He nudged her with his nose as he whined, but still no response. With his teeth embedded in her coat, he managed to turn her face-up in the snow. He licked her face with his warm tongue, trying to get her to open her eyes. She lay there with her eyes closed, not responding to his actions. He reverted back to his instincts, as he began howling like a wolf that had lost his mate.

(The Drifter)

The wind was blowing against him, draining his strength more with each step. As he leaned into the wind, all he could see were faint shadows from the trees. He called out their names as loudly as he could yell, and then waited for a response, but the winds only silenced his words. He decided to expand his search even more so he could cover a larger area. He walked in a circular pattern in search of any clues that might indicate they had been here. He continued to look for fresh tracks or snow-packed indentions in the ground, where they might have rested. The harder he searched, the more skeptical he became of ever finding them alive. He turned his flashlight on and pointed it in the direction of the last streamer. There was no reflection, and his heart sank into the pit of his stomach.

His heart began racing as panic rushed at him. In his hurry to find them, he had lost track of his own movements and was clueless which direction was home. He held the flashlight over his head and slowly turned clockwise hoping to see the reflection from the streamer. When he completed the cycle and no streamer was found, he shook his head disgustedly, while he retraced his steps before the winds erased his only hope. As he followed his tracks backward, he held the flashlight high and toward the center of the circle, where he presumed the streamer to be.

(Amy and Dog)

With no protection from the freezing snow, Amy's lungs were beginning to freeze. Dog was now dragging her by the collar of her coat as he continued toward home. They came upon a small clearing when he caught the scent of another wolf. He released her collar and began searching the area for the presence. It was not long before it perked its ugly head out from a nearby bush, with its teeth flashing and eyes glowing with a green haze. Poised over Amy's limp body, Dog ferociously growled as the wolf slowly approached. Soon after the first wolf arrived, several others began coming from the trees surrounding them. Dog feared for Amy and continued barking savagely, trying to dominate the pack.

The wolves stopped short of them as they continued to snarl and snap their teeth. Dog returned the ferocious growls and snapped his own teeth. After a brief hesitation, the wolves once again slowly surrounded them. In a desperate, last-ditch attempt, Dog lifted his head and howled fearlessly, penetrating the cold air and silencing the winds. The dominant female of the pack heard the howl. She slowly perked her head out from a small hole burrowed through a snow- and ice-packed mound. The other wolves stopped their growling as the female wolf slowly circled Amy. Dog continued to snap his teeth and growl at the approaching she-wolf.

(The Drifter)

The Drifter could not find the streamer as he circled back. He knew now that he was lost. Landmarks were impossible to see in the flurry of the blinding snow. Visibility was only a few feet, and his tracks were being erased within minutes of making them. His hope of finding them slowly diminished. He began to enter a condition of self-preservation, as he had been severely weakened from hunger. His survival was important and now first in his thoughts. He could dig in and cover his body with snow to keep warm, but with no food, he would slowly die. This storm would last longer than he could survive. He turned off the flashlight and decided to rest for a few minutes to regain his thoughts. He hoped getting his mind off the current affairs would allow him to focus more clearly. He stopped by a large tree and sat down between two large roots to help protect him from the cold winds. There was a slight depression between the roots. The snow had been trapped around the roots, making a small wall on both sides. With the winds cut off, he began to feel the warmth of his own body. The cozy alcove allowed him time to rationalize a way out. He retraced his steps over and over in his mind until he concluded, *Let's see ... I'm lost, hungry, cold, and tired. I think that sums it up, I'm screwed. If I'm to die out here, it would be nice to know why Amy left.* He knew his walking had become erratic as he circled the area, but he could not figure out how he had managed to get lost. *How could I have lost the streamer?* He knew it had to be out there somewhere, and feeling somewhat more confident, he stood up to look. He turned on the flashlight once more and pointed it in the direction of where he thought the streamer might be. As he was looking, he heard a familiar sound from behind him, the sound of a wolf howl. He turned his ear in the direction of the sound, but the winds had carried it past him.

(Amy and Dog)

The she-wolf moved closer as the two wolves faced off, ready for mortal combat. Both wolves continued to flash their teeth and growl in defiance of the other. As Dog was perched over Amy, he caught a sniff of the she-wolf's scent, one that had been long forgotten. He silenced his growling and slowly stepped away from Amy's limp body and sat down in the snow beside her. As the she-wolf approached them, he offered no signs of resistance. The dominant female's snarl became more ferocious as she approached. Dog sat patiently in the snow, whining and whimpering as she moved in for the kill. The she-wolf was ready to pounce on its prey when some great force, beyond our understanding, silenced her growl. There was a moment of silence as a miraculous event unfolded this night. For a brief moment, the two wolves remained quiet as if frozen in time. Dog was the first to make his move as he slowly rose to all fours. He gracefully moved toward the female wolf that remained perfectly still.

Once he was beside her, he sniffed again, as she turned her head and repeated his gesture. Suddenly, the dominant female wolf lifted her head and muffled the winds from her eerie howl. Dog barked once, now knowing this was his mother. He walked back to Amy's side and patiently waited for his mother's approach. When she stopped her howling, she slowly walked closer to Dog. Gently, Dog lifted Amy's sleeve with his teeth, putting her hand in front of his mother's nose. She sniffed Amy's scent, lifted her head, and turned toward the other wolves, as she barked loudly. She then turned away from Dog and Amy and slowly walked back toward the wolf den. Dog grabbed Amy's collar with his teeth and dragged her limp body into the den behind his mother. The other wolves held fast to their positions until Dog was inside. Slowly, each of the wolves took its turn entering the den, keeping their distance from two intruders. Dog dragged Amy to the end of the den and laid his body against the young girl in an attempt to keep her warm. His heat and the heat coming from the bodies of the other wolves made the den warm and cozy for Amy. This was all he could do for the moment, so he laid his head on her chest and closed his eyes.

(The Drifter)

Thinking it might have been Dog's howl, the Drifter quickly headed in the direction of the sound, forgetting his own troubles. This had been the first sign of life since he started the search, and his hopes were revived. He was no longer concerned about finding the streamer, since it would not matter, if he were able to find Dog and Amy. He knew the winds could have played tricks on his hearing, and it was possible he was headed in the wrong direction, but this did not stop him. He ran as fast as his snowshoes would allow, dodging low-hanging branches and shrubs, his heart racing from excitement. He had traveled several hundred feet without finding any signs of them, when he decided to stop and yell their names. He did not hear a response from his calling, and he feared the winds could have carried his cries away. In desperation, he turned the flashlight on once more and lifted it high into the air. He pointed it in the direction he was traveling, hoping if Dog was out there somewhere, he would see the light. Again, hopelessness overtook him, as he realized that he was just as lost as he was before. He slowly and aimlessly walked in the same direction, as he steadily yelled their names. Some time had passed before he came upon a small clearing. In this clearing, there was a large mound of snow and ice that was packed against some rocks, with a small cavelike hole. His thoughts of using it as a shelter were broken when a large wolf exited the small hole. His first instinct was to grab his pistol, but before he had a chance to raise it, other wolves had appeared. They began circling him as they growled and flashed their teeth. His first thought was to find the leader of the pack, the dominant one. If he could kill the leader, the others would disperse. With his pistol focused on the closest wolf, he waited for the sign of its attack. Possessed by an eerie feeling and the desire to pull the trigger, the Drifter held fast as the wolf moved closer. He was about to unload his pistol into the approaching wolf when he noticed, out of the corner of his eye, another wolf leaving the den. He took his glance from the approaching wolf as he watched the new one enter the clearing. When the wolf was clear of the others, it raised its head and howled against the winds. This caused the other wolves to stop their barking and back away from him. *This has to be the leader,* the Drifter thought, as he slowly moved his pistol, aligning the sight with the wolf's front shoulder. He stood shaking from the cold as he waited for the dominant wolf to approach, but noticed it was not moving toward him. His shaking had become so erratic, he feared missing the wolf and not having a second chance. He forced his hands to steady and when he was finally ready to pull the trigger, he decided not to. It seemed this wolf was not going to attack, but instead sat still with its eyes fixed on him. He slowly lowered his pistol as he began to back away, trying to escape the peril. He noticed there had been no attempt from the other wolves to attack him, which to him seemed very odd. As he walked backward out of the clearing, the wolves opened a path, allowing him to leave. He was almost clear of the opening before he turned his back to them to escape into the forest. When he reached the edge of the forest, he felt a blow against his back, knocking him to the ground. With the great weight of his body, the wolf had the Drifter pinned against the snow. His greatest fear of being mauled seemed to be coming true as he wrestled to retrieve his knife. With all his strength and a powerful thrust, the Drifter was able to roll over to face his adversary. With his knife poised, ready to plunge into the heart of the wolf, he was taken by surprise when he felt a warm tongue licking all over his face. He could not focus clearly on the animal's face, so he placed his hands into the throat of the wolf and pushed its head back.

As his eyes began to focus, he saw the face of Dog. His emotions grew like a weed out of control when he grabbed Dog by the neck and wrestled with him in the snow. He was so glad to see him that both of them played for a few moments before he realized Amy was not with him. He stopped and yelled Amy's name. The Drifter looked around the clearing, noticing the other wolves were staring at them but were not trying to attack. His curiosity grew as he tried to understand what was happening and where Amy might be.

"Dog, where's Amy?" the Drifter asked.

Dog barked once and headed for the small opening in the snow bank where he disappeared. Within a few seconds, he returned, dragging the limp body of Amy. When he cleared the opening of the wolf den, he stopped, sat down next to Amy, and waited for his master. The Drifter began moving toward Amy when the dominant female wolf stood up and also approached them. Before he could get close enough to check Amy's condition, the she-wolf had stopped next to Dog and sat in the snow. The Drifter hesitated for a brief moment while he examined the situation more closely.

Uncertain of what transpired with the wolf, he cautiously moved toward the three of them. He slowly knelt down next to Amy, only taking his eyes of the wolf long enough to examine the young girl. His guilt of failure passed after discovering she was still alive. From what he could see, she showed minor signs of frostbite and hypothermia. Still somewhat apprehensive of the wolves, he gently lifted her head into his arms. He carefully shook her gently, trying to wake her, until she finally opened her eyes.

She looked into the Drifter's face, and in a surprising flash, reached up with her arms to pull herself against his body. They were tightly embraced while he lifted her from the ground and covered her with his fur coat. With a quick glance toward Dog and the she-wolf, he said, "Let's go home, Dog." There was a moment of silence before Dog let out a soft whine. He looked at his mother, then toward his master, before standing up to leave. Dog's mother remained still as she watched them leave the clearing. After they had cleared the woods, the Drifter asked Amy if she could walk or if she needed him to carry her. She indicated that she could walk, so he placed her on the ground beside him. He removed his bearskin coat and wrapped her in it to keep her warm. He then took her hand as they both walked slowly toward home.

As they proceeded, the Drifter took a moment to glance around the surrounding area. His sense of direction indicated that they were going the wrong way, but he trusted Dog's instincts more than his own. The winds began to affect him more since he gave his coat to Amy, chilling his body thoroughly. His only recourse was to keep moving to stay warm.

As the journey progressed, he began feeling Amy dragging behind, forcing him to pull her, putting a strain on his arm. When he glanced toward her, he noticed she was struggling with every step. He yelled for Dog to stop as he knelt beside her and asked if she was all right. She nodded as if she was, but from the strained look on her face, he could tell she was exhausted. He knew she would not be able to keep the pace at which they were traveling, so he decided to carry her the rest of the journey.

He removed his fur coat from her and put it back on. The warmth could be felt throughout his body and made his chills subside. He picked Amy up, placing her against his chest, and wrapped her frail body with the coat. The warmth of her body added comfort to his. The memories of his daughter returned as he reminisced about the many nights they had watched TV, while she slept in his arms wrapped in her blanket. He smiled at the ironic thought of finding a beautiful child like this in the middle of nowhere who resembled his daughter. She even had the same name and was the same age at the time of his daughter's death. It seemed next to impossible, but here he was, carrying this child who reminded him so much of his own daughter. His love for her grew even stronger that night as the warmth filled his heart. Once again he felt like a dad, as if God had given him a second chance.

"Let's go home, Dog," he blurted out.

Dog, who had been patiently waiting, took the lead once more. Hours passed as the Drifter, carrying Amy in his arms, blindly followed Dog. Their travel seemed to go on forever, as if they were traveling to a nonexistent land far away. Amy was now asleep, and the Drifter's strength was drained. The wind was freezing his clothes, causing snow to stick once more, adding more weight for him to carry. His legs were weakening after every step, from the weight of his clothes and the hunger in his stomach.

Finally forced to stop, he began searching the area for a suitable resting place. He spotted a large fir tree that would help block the freezing winds. He placed Amy against the trunk as he removed his coat and whipped it into the air, breaking off the snow and ice. He covered Amy with the coat as he scoured his surroundings, trying to get a directional bearing to his mountain home.

The horrendous winds made visibility low and hard to determine his current position. His only hope was Dog and his wonderful sense of direction. Distant barking interrupted his thoughts; as he looked around, he noticed Dog had not stopped with them. He realized that he did not tell Dog to stop, and that he had traveled away from them and was waiting for them to catch up. He picked up Amy and wrapped her inside his bearskin coat. They again undertook their journey, unaware of the next turn of events that lay ahead. Seconds felt like minutes as they slowly walked toward home. Three hours had passed since they encountered the wolves, and the Drifter was now weaker than he had ever been. The journey felt like it was moving in slow motion as his walking became more erratic. His legs were weak from the weight of Amy and the newly packed ice on his clothes. He was again faced with the need to rest.

Unknown to him, they had traveled too far south, and the path they had taken was paralleling the edge of the great river canyon. With the furious winds and dense falling snow, the canyon was invisible to the naked eye. He yelled for Dog to stop as he slowly walked to a large pine, hoping it would block the freezing winds while they rested, when he tripped over a root protruding from the ground.

Before he was able to gain focus on what just occurred, he found himself sliding down a steep slope toward his doom. He looked up to see Amy, sliding slightly above him. He could hear her shouts of terror but there was nothing he could do. He too was rolling and sliding out of control with only precious seconds remaining.

Thump, came the sound, as his back hit the trunk of a small pine. The pain was immense and left him slightly paralyzed, stunned with confusion. He heard a fateful scream from above before he was able to regain his senses to see Amy closing in and about to slide past him. With his right arm fastened to the tree, he pushed his body away as he grabbed Amy by the coat sleeve. The force of catching her caused him to lose his grip, and again both of them were sliding to their doom. The Drifter quickly glanced around, trying to find something to grab that would help stop their fall. All that was available within his view was more snow and a dark ledge quickly approaching. His instincts told him it was time to take action or they would fall into the river canyon, never to be heard from again. Quickly, his thoughts raged as alternatives raced through his mind. Within a second, a brilliant thought overrode all others, and with the speed of light, he reached for his hunting knife. He drove the knife deep into the snow above, and as the knife cut into the loose snow, it began to slow their descent. The weight of their bodies pushed the knife deeper into the snow, slowing them even more, but it was not stopping them. As he glanced up toward the knife, he saw that it was cutting into the snow, not offering enough resistance to stop their fall. He pulled the knife out and turned it sideways, where the width of the blade would offer more resistance. With all his remaining strength, he drove it back into the snow. His arms began to ache from the strain of their weight, as the knife dug deep into snow and ice. Their lives were resting on the strength of his right hand as he desperately struggled to hold on to the knife. His arm ached from the strain as his grip began to loosen. He struggled to hold on with all his strength before he realized their descent had slowed to a complete stop. Relieved from the current burden, he lay there in the snow as he rested to regain his strength.

This rest was interrupted when Amy began kicking and screaming wildly, putting a strain on his left arm. She had slid below him and was dangling over the edge of the cliff, with her coat being her only lifeline. With her constant moving and the weight of their bodies, he was causing the knife to slowly lose its hold on the ice.

"Be still, Amy, I've got you. Everything will be okay," he shouted persuasively. After a few seconds, he felt the relief from his arm as she stopped her wiggling and remained still. He could hear her soft cries and knew she was very scared. He glanced up toward the top of the incline, trying to get a glimpse of Dog. He could hear him barking but was unable to see him through the thick, blinding snow.

Chapter Eight
The Storm

(The Drifter)

The Drifter lay in the snow, resting while he summarized their situation. He was suspended on the edge of the cliff about 150 feet from the top of the ridge, holding on to the only thread preventing their death. Amy was dangling over the edge of the cliff, and it was taking every bit of his strength to keep her from falling. He knew his first priority was to relieve the strain on both of his arms and find a more secure method of anchoring his body.

He slowly pulled Amy up closer to the edge of the cliff, trying to get a secure hold on her coat. "Amy, grab my arm," he said in desperation. There was no attempt from Amy to help, so once more he repeated his demand.

"I'm scared," she cried out.

With a gentle and understanding voice, he replied, "I am too, Amy, but I really need your help right now. If you grab my arm and help me, I can pull you up onto the ledge. You can then climb on my back and hold on. We won't be able to get out of this if you don't try to help me. So please ... grab my arm and pull yourself onto the ledge." Amy stopped her crying as she took a firm grip of his arm. With his help, she was able to climb over the ledge and onto his back. She immediately slung her arms around his neck and squeezed so tightly that it cut off the Drifter's air. His breathing became strained as he gasped for his next breath.

"Loosen up a little, Amy, I can't breathe," came the wheezing sound of his words being squeezed from his throat. Amy slowly began to loosen her grip, allowing him to take a deep breath as he inhaled.

"Thanks … Now hold on tight, but not too tight, okay?" With all his strength, he pulled both of them up until his shoulder was touching the handle of the hunting knife. With his right foot, he plunged it into the snow, creating a foothold. He continued until the snow and ice were packed hard enough to hold their weight.

With his right foot planted in the packed snow, he was able to lift their bodies up about a foot toward the top of the incline. With the weight on his right leg, he was able to remove the hunting knife and plunge it deep into the snow as far above his head as he could reach. With his foot and knife secured, he lifted his left leg and started packing the snow for a second foothold. Again, he created a hole of tightly packed snow, allowing his left foot to help support his weight. With both legs secure, he was able to release his hold on the knife, giving him the opportunity to carefully unbuckle his belt.

With the belt loose, he was able to place it around his neck and left shoulder. He asked Amy to secure it over her back and underneath her arms. Once the belt was in place, he bulked it tightly against his neck and shoulder, holding Amy firmly against his body. He could barely hear Dog's barking over the howling winds, but he knew that he was worried about them.

He yelled toward the top of the incline, "We're okay, boy!" to help comfort Dog's hysteria. He kept his fears to himself, as not to alarm Amy, but he knew that they had fallen into the clutches of death, and his strength was at an all-time low. Releasing his fears, he reached up and secured both hands on the handle of the hunting knife. With Amy fastened tightly to him, he began his slow ascent to safety, with his last remaining strength. His climb was slow due to the creating of the footholds he needed for each step he took. With his feet planted, he would again push his body upwards until he was completely stretched to his full length. Then with the strength of his arms, he would pull his body up to the knife until his shoulders touched the handle. He repeated the process, gaining only three feet for every thrust of the knife. Weary from hunger, he remained calm as he slowly inched his way to the top of the ledge. Hours passed in a blinding flash as he continued to make his way to safety. He was within thirty feet from reaching the top of the incline, when his right leg began to cramp. The muscles were taut, causing him unbearable pain with no way to release the tension. Being forced to remove his feet from the footholds, he stretched his body in an attempt to relax and relieve the cramp. Again the knife was their only support, as he lay stretched with his right leg extended as far as he could. After a few seconds, the pain began to subside, bringing some relief to his leg. "What's wrong, Mister?" he heard Amy say.

"I'm okay. I need to rest for a minute," he replied as he remained calm, not wanting to alarm her. He was beginning to show signs of hypothermia, wanting to sleep, as his eyelids slowly began to droop. Amy's life in his hands and the promise he had made were the only true factors that kept him motivated, but he now needed some rest. He closed his eyes as he lay in a bed of snow. The Drifter was immediately startled when he felt his body slip as the hunting knife begin to lose its grip on the ice. He panicked and began thrashing his legs, trying to dig a foothold before the knife lost its hold and they plummeted down the incline. His efforts were not rewarded when he felt the knife release its hold and once again they were sliding. He dug his knife into the snow in an attempt to slow down their descent. After what seemed a fearful struggle against fate and strength, he was able to regain control and stop their fall. They had slid down the incline close to a hundred feet toward the bottom before they finally came to rest. He dug his feet into the snow to help hold their weight, but now his strength was completely drained.

(Dog)

Dog, sensing the perilous condition of his master's plight, took off in a flash as he dashed through the woods toward home. He traveled as fast his legs would carry him in the deep snow. Time raced by as he headed toward the rocky cliffs of their mountain home. Upon his arrival, he stopped at the stable door, stared at the crack that was hiding the switch, and pondered how he could open the door of rock. His attempts to push the button with his front paws were useless; his paw was too large to fit into the small hole. He barked loudly while jumping on the rock door with his front paws, scratching it, trying to get someone's attention. His efforts were again in vain. No one could hear him from inside of the caverns; the walls of rock were too thick. His front paws began bleeding as he continued to scratch on the rocky door. With a sudden thought, he began running north toward the small hole that led into his master's thinking room. Time was of the essence, and he gave no thought to his bleeding paws. He remembered that the opening had never been closed off and it could offer his only way to gain access into the mountain home. When he reached the opening, he stopped at the bottom and stared at the jagged wall of rock. The snow was packed on the rocks, making the climb more precarious, but his determination to save his master drove him to take the chance.

He began his ascent up the mountain, following small trails at different sections of the climb. This made the journey somewhat easier for the moment, but it was soon to get more difficult, the higher he progressed. The snow-covered rocky wall was steeper by the small opening that led into the small thinking room. There were jagged rocks to hold on to, but the incline was steep and dangerous. Dog struggled with his injured paw until he reached a small ledge four feet from the opening. There was no path to follow or steps making the end of the climb less treacherous. If he wanted to get inside, he was forced to jump the four-foot clearing to a small rock ledge. He was only going to get one try; if he missed, he would surely fall to his death. He paced back and forth on the small ledge, stopping once in a while to look down toward the ground and then to the small opening. After several minutes, he gathered his courage and decided to make the jump. With all the power in his hind legs, he jumped toward the small ledge in front of the opening. It was a perfect jump, as his front paws touched down on the snow-packed ledge. Everything felt perfect until his hind legs cleared the opening and were planted on the rocky ledge. The force of his entire weight against the snow caused it to break and begin sliding away off of the ledge. He lost his footing when a chunk of snow slid off with his paws still attached. He turned toward the hole as he lurched forward with his front paws and planted them inside of the opening. The claws sunk deep into a small crack, providing an anchor that kept him from falling off the mountainside.

With a small portion of his body inside the small opening and his stomach lying on the ledge, he struggled to regain his foothold. His hind legs dangled in midair and were in constant motion, scratching at the rocky ledge. His attempt at getting his hind legs planted in a firm foothold was futile. His legs were too far below the ledge to reach high enough to have any success. Realizing his efforts were not being rewarded, Dog stopped wrestling with his hind legs and lay still for a moment.

With his front paws planted, he pulled his body toward the opening. He released his left front paw and reached deeper into the opening, finding a spot to secure it firmly. Slowly, he inched his way into the small corridor until his hind legs were able to reach the ledge. With his hind legs secured, he was now in complete control. He crawled into the small two-foot opening and inched his way toward his master's thinking room. The deeper into the corridor he went, the narrower it became, forcing him to extend his body to squeeze through the narrow opening.

Through his determination and great efforts, Dog reached the end of his journey when he was outside of his master's thinking room. He had to force his large body though the narrow opening, and was rewarded when his hind legs cleared the hole. He stood up and shook his body, releasing all the snow and dust from his fur. After his quick cleaning, he darted into the stables, where he stopped at the ledge. He glanced into the stables and whined when he found no one present. Unable to reach the stable floors, he found himself helpless. All he could do now was stand by the ledge and bark as loud as he could.

(Inside the Drifter's home)

Rachael was weary from the journey and was desperately in need of some rest. For the past few hours, she added to her weariness by slaving hard, trying to feed and take care of the survivors, and now her body ached beyond her endurance. There was a very small supply of gratitude from the survivors for all her efforts, and sometimes they acted as if it was her fault they were suffering. After she had finished feeding the last survivor, she slowly walked to the captain and softly whispered her despair, hoping for some comfort.

The captain gently laughed as he explained to Rachael that her feelings were normal under the current condition, and not to worry. "We have been through a lot. I'm sure it will pass in time."

Rachael felt somewhat frustrated with his answer and not receiving the comfort she desperately needed. The captain, noticing her sorrowed expression, reached out and gave her a loving hug, with a smile of reassurance. She embraced him even while she wrestled with her volatile emotions. He sensed the tension in her grip and felt compelled to ask why she was still distraught.

Rachael answered, "The stranger, the one that calls himself the Drifter, he should have been back by now with Amy. I'm getting a little worried about them."

The captain nodded, and in a subtle tone replied, "Me too. I hope they're all right." Rachael sighed before she finally exposed her true feelings.

"He is our only ticket to getting out of here. I was hoping to see him long before now." The captain agreed and their conversation ended.

The house fell silent as the survivors searched for a place to lie down and sleep. The captain and Rachael were sitting together on the small sofa, watching the others prepare for the night. The silence of the dwelling was broken by faint sounds of barking. Rachael was the first to pick up the sound as she strained to hear more.

"Shhhh! Does anybody hear that? It sounds like barking," Jennifer cried out. There was complete silence as they all listened.

"It sounds like a dog barking and I believe it's coming from the stables," the captain grunted.

The captain and Rachael ran to the front door, leaving the house with refreshed feelings of excitement. Rachael knew the Drifter had finally returned and was very concerned about Amy. As they approached the foyer leading from the house to the stables, the barking had grown louder. Rachael was the first to exit the foyer, and when she stopped by the lift, she was able to see Dog standing on the ledge at the opposite side. He was standing by the ladder leading down to the stable floor, and he began barking with excitement when he saw them.

"Okay, boy, we're coming," Rachael yelled, letting her voice carry across the cavern. They stepped onto the lift as it began to rattle on its way down to the bottom of the stables. Before the lift could reach the bottom, the captain jumped out and ran across the stables toward the ladder. He immediately climbed it to the ledge, where Dog was awaiting his arrival. When he reached the top of the ladder, Dog caught a sniff of his scent and began snarling.

"I don't think he likes me," the captain yelled.

Rachael was now standing at the bottom of the ladder when she replied. "Well, grab him anyway; it'll be okay." As the captain moved his hand closer for Dog to smell his scent, he was fortunate to quickly spring his arm back before Dog could take a bite.

"Why don't you give it a shot? Maybe he'll respond to you better than he is reacting toward me," the captain yelled. After Captain Joe climbed down the ladder, Rachael climbed toward the top of the ledge to take his place. She was somewhat apprehensive about putting her hand out for Dog to smell. There was paralyzing fear as she closed her eyes and slowly raised her hand for him to sniff. Dog ignored her gesture and bypassed the hand. He immediately put his nose in her face and sniffed her scent. When he had enough, he backed away, showing no signs of aggression, allowing Rachael to continue her ascent to the ledge. Rachael scoured the area for the stranger, and was now very concerned why the wolf was alone. *How did he get here and where are the Drifter and Amy?* Her questions puzzled her deeply, making her unsure of what to do next.

She glanced down at the ledge close to the ladder and saw the harness attached by a rope. She assumed it was used for lowering the wolf down into the stables. She slowly walked toward the harness and bent down to pick it up. Not sure of Dog's reaction, she moved very carefully toward him with the harness opened. He did not waver or show any signs of resistance, so she slowly placed the harness around his shoulders and under his stomach. She grabbed the rope, which was feeding a pulley attached to the rock wall above the ladder. When she gave it a pull, the wolf lifted into the air and was floating above the stable floors. She gently lowered Dog as she carefully watched him, making sure he did not try to wiggle out of the harness. As soon as Dog's paws touched the floor, he immediately broke free and darted toward the stable door. "I think he wants us to follow him!" Joe remarked. With a blank stare caused by the captain's remark, Rachael's confusion raged. *What's going on here, follow him where?* She climbed down the ladder still upset as to why Dog was here and no one else.

When she reached the bottom she began questioning Dog. "Where's Amy? Where's the Drifter?" She should have not asked the question if she was not ready for the answer, for Dog darted toward her like a flash of light and grabbed her pants leg with his teeth. Stricken by fear, she allowed him to drag her toward the stable door. He did not release his grip until they had reached it. He broke loose and began barking wildly as his paws pounced against the metal.

"I think you're right; he wants us to follow him. We need our coats… why don't you go get them while I stay here with Dog?" Rachael expressed, still confused as to what was happening.

Joe took the elevator back to the ledge and disappeared into the foyer. Rachael remained in place with her eyes on the wolf when she noticed blood oozing from his paw. Carefully she approached until she was standing directly in front of him. She slowly knelt down on one knee as she reached out to check him. Her hands were very close before he lashed out and snapped his teeth. "Okay! I'll leave you alone," she screamed, for she was terrified of being bitten.

Dog must have sensed her fear, so he stopped his growling and moved closer to her. He nudged her hand with his nose, as if asking for forgiveness. Taking one more chance, Rachael again slowly reached out with her hand to check his paw, when he immediately jumped backwards and began barking frantically. Fearing for her hand, she pulled it quickly back and pressed it tight against her chest.

"Are you ready?" the captain said, startling Rachael.

She realized now why Dog might have reacted the way he did, but she remained cautious. Relieved briefly from her fear, she stood up and watched the captain as he came closer. He was carrying their coats and a few extra blankets. "You scared us!" she said, still shaking from Dog's reaction. She was not sure if the wolf trusted her or not, but it was not important, because she did not trust him.

The captain handed Rachael her coat before walking to the switch that opened the stable door. He pushed the button as the sounds of the hydraulic arms pushing on the heavy door rumbled. Barking sounds came from the rear of the stables, causing the captain to turn around. He saw Dog sitting by a workbench.

"What is it, boy?" the captain questioned.

When he got to the table, he unlatched the sliding door and opened it. Dog stuck his head inside, and within seconds returned with a rope clenched in his teeth.

"What's with the rope?" the captain dumbly asked. Standing with a blank expression on his face, he shrugged his shoulders, but obliged Dog by taking the rope from his mouth. Before the captain could get a firm hold on the rope, Dog released it and dashed toward the stable door into the winter storm. The captain placed the rope around his shoulder and followed Dog outside, where he and Rachael waited. They blindly left the warmth of the caverns and closed the door behind them. Dog immediately took the lead as he darted south, following the edge of the mountainside. The wind was blowing with such tremendous force, it felt like tiny needles as it pounded against their faces. They ran as fast as the snow and wind would allow, which wasn't very fast. Dog was forced to stop and wait for them to catch up many times before he would take the lead once again. They traveled south for quite some time before Dog cut left and headed deep into the woods. Without thinking, Rachael and the captain followed him, with no idea where they were going or why.

After thirty minutes of running with all their strength, the captain tripped and fell to the ground. Rachael stopped to help him, but from the sound of his breathing, she feared he was having a heart attack. She yelled at Dog to stop. He stopped and returned to their sides as he patiently waited. While she was checking the captain, he pushed her hands aside, indicating he was fine but needed a short rest. Dog patiently waited as the two of them rested. Soon after, the captain stood up. Dog took that as the okay to go, and with lightning speed, he disappeared into the darkness of the forest. The captain glanced at Rachael, lightly shaking his head as they followed Dog's lead.

(45 minutes later)

When they finally caught up to Dog, he was sitting on the edge of a ledge with a steep forty-degree incline. They examined it carefully as it seemed to stretch deep into the endless darkness. Dog started his barking and kept looking down the slope.

Rachael dropped to her knees as she yelled, "Hello … Is there anybody there?"

No response was heard over the whistling of the strong wind as it shook the snow from branches of nearby trees. Rachael glanced at the captain, waving her hands as if she did not understand.

The captain shrugged his shoulders in the same confusion as he said, "I know. Dog thinks there is something down there, so I guess I should check it out."

He removed the rope from his shoulder and securely tied it to the trunk of a nearby tree. Throwing the rope over the ledge, he slowly and carefully lowered himself down the steep incline. Rachael waited with childlike impatience as the captain disappeared into the darkness. Her rambling thoughts began to plague her as their focus became clearer.

What if it is them and they're both dead. I'll keep my hopes up, but what if they are dead, what then? How are we going to get home? Rachael pushed the raging thoughts from her mind, trying to avoid the dreadful events that might lie ahead.

(The Captain)

The captain slowly descended into the dark shadows until he no longer could see the ledge from which he had dropped. Visibility was low, and the sounds of the wind made it difficult to communicate with Rachael. He had dropped some 100 feet before he saw what looked like a shadow protruding from the whiteness of the snow. As he slowly maneuvered toward the shadow, he was finally able to make out a figure of a man with what looked like a small child on his back.

With excitement, he yelled to Rachael. "It's them. I've got to get a little closer to check to see if they are okay!"

He continued his descent toward the figures until he reached the end of the rope. He was approximately six feet short of being able to check their condition. Discouraged, he pulled himself back up to the ledge where Rachael was waiting. Upon his arrival, she questioned him, hoping for some encouraging words. The captain put his hand on her shoulder for comfort as he explained the situation.

"They are down there, but I ran out of rope and was unable to reach them. I'm not sure if they're alive or not." Rachael sighed heavily as she watched him untie the rope from the large pine and retie it to a smaller tree closer to the ridge.

She questioned his actions and he responded quickly. "I needed a few extra feet, and I'm hoping this will give me that." Again he started his descent, but before he left, he gave Rachael some signals to watch for. He explained since they were unable to talk over the wind that she needed to hold the rope loosely with her hand. If he was to pull on it with three quick jerks, then that meant they were alive, and if he pulled it once, then ... He stopped and said no more.

It seemed like an eternity passed before Rachael felt the three jerks indicating they were alive.

She stood up and began yelling with excitement. "They're alive!"

Dog must have understood what she had said for he started barking and jumping around in the snow.

After determining that the Drifter and Amy were alive, Captain Joe gently shook the Drifter, trying to awaken him. He made several attempts to get a response, but was unable to wake him. He began scouring the area for a safe escape route, when he noticed the bottom of the incline seemed to drop off into a dark hole. Since his rope would not reach the end, he was not able to surmise the outcome if he slipped and fell. Evaluating the Drifter and the surrounding area, he was able to ascertain that they had slid down the incline, stopping only thirty feet from its end. The Drifter's feet were buried in the snow, which seemed to add support for their weight. The way the Drifter was holding on to a large hunting knife indicated that this was the mechanism that stopped their fall.

Very carefully, he drove his foot into the snow, packing it and creating a place to secure his feet. Once secured, he released the rope so he could tie the end of it around the Drifter's shoulders, making a slipknot that would tighten as pressure was applied. This would secure them and prevent the rope from slipping as he pulled them to safety. As soon as he had them secured, he quickly climbed back up the incline, using the rope to prevent his falling over the edge to an unrighteous doom. Rachael's patience had dwindled by the time she saw the captain climbing up the incline. She yelled. "Are they all right?"

The captain softly replied, "I'm not sure. I think they are, but we need to get them to safety soon." By the time Captain Joe had reached the top of the incline, his breathing was hard and heavy. Rachael comforted him until he was able to catch his breath. As soon as he was able, he told Rachael his plans.

"I've tied the rope around them. We need to pull them up, and it's going to take both of us to do this." Rachael nodded as she reached for the rope to help pull the Drifter and Amy to safer ground.

The two of them tightened their grip on the rope and began pulling with all their strength. Rachael's arms began aching as she strained against the weight of their bodies. Every inch gained caused more pain, but her determination forced her to pull even harder. The weight of the Drifter and Amy increased as the snow packed against their upward momentum. Slowly, Rachael and the captain struggled, making headway inch by inch. Rachael's muscles were on the brink of breakdown when someone else came to their aid. She was amazed to see Dog join them in the fight against great odds. With his teeth buried into the rope, he was pulling with all the strength of his body. With uplifted spirits, the three of them continued their slow and agonizing process. Each pull seemed to be harder than the last, but they fought with all their endurance. The captain, Rachael, and Dog worked diligently in unison, until they finally succeeded in pulling the pair to the top of the incline. Captain Joe immediately grabbed both of them and heaved them over the ledge onto safer ground. As he was trying to remove the belt from around Amy, Dog decided to sit by his master and lick his face. The Drifter did not respond, and with every lick, Dog would whine. The captain, not wanting to interrupt, gently moved Dog's head aside so he could finish removing Amy. After he had Amy in his arms, he handed her to Rachael.

"Carry her ... I'll carry him."

At first, Dog offered some resistance, not allowing the captain to pick up the Drifter. After a few minutes, he finally backed away, giving the captain the okay to carry his master home. They all were worried about getting the pair to safety as quickly as possible. Rachael held Amy tightly against her chest, hoping to provide some warmth with her own body heat.

Captain Joe lifted the Drifter over his shoulder as he bellowed, "Home!" Without hesitation, Dog dashed into the thick forest as the two of them followed.

(Back at the mountain home)

The Drifter, lying limp on the captain's shoulder, looked as if all life had left his body. They entered the stables carrying the Drifter and Amy out of the deadly reaches of nature's hand. Amy, in the arms of Rachael, wrapped in the fur coat of the Drifter with her cheeks a deep red, looked like an angel lying on a soft bed of feathers. She was asleep and warm, looking much better than her bearer. Rachael looked as if she had no strength to continue. Worn and beaten from the cold and deadly winds, she stumbled as she entered the stables. Captain Joe noticed her erratic walking and, concerned for her safety, asked if she was all right.

"I'll be fine as soon as I get some rest and something to eat," she replied. He nodded his head, for he understood. He too was exhausted and hungry from the trip. Dog was the last to come through the stable door, as he patiently waited for all others to enter safely, as if he was their sole protector. Without any hesitation, he approached the switch that closed the stable door and pressed it with his nose. The door shook and rumbled as it slowly closed, shutting off the cold winds and snow that steadily blew through the stables. Captain Joe watched in wonder as the stable door closed and again was amazed at the intelligence of this animal.

"Good boy!" he said.

The captain walked to the lift and placed the body of the Drifter inside, supporting him against the railing. He motioned for Rachael to join him. She staggered toward the lift and stepped on board, with Amy still wrapped closely to her chest. Dog was last to follow and was able to find a small spot to sit on the base of the lift. With all present, the captain pressed the green switch, and the lift began to rise. Dog looked up at his friend and whined, but nobody could hear him as the roaring of the lift drowned out his cry. Rachael could see the staring eyes of the captain as he looked at the limp body of the Drifter, and she too had the same worried look in her eyes. Without further hesitation, she turned her head toward the cavern walls, for she did not want to think of their fate if this man should die.

Both stood in silence listening to the roaring sounds of the lift while they ascended toward the upper ledge. The sounds were interrupted when she heard the scratchy voice of the captain: "He never moved or twitched all the way back, and I couldn't wake him on the slope." She turned her glance toward the captain, only to see tears developing and building in his eyes. She turned her head away when she felt a cold sensation sweep through her as the grim possibility made it perfectly clear: They might never get home. The roaring sounds ceased and were replaced with the loud clatter of metal when the lift came to a halt. It shook for a few seconds as the echoes faded against the cavern walls. Dog was the first to exit the lift. He stopped at the entrance of the foyer as he waited for the others to join him. Taking his incentive from the wolf, Captain Joe picked up the Drifter and slung him back over his shoulder. Rachael tightened her grip on Amy, and the two of them left the lift and followed Dog to the house.

Rachael opened the front door and quietly walked into the house as the others followed. The captain softly closed the door and the three of them followed the narrow hallway into the living room. Most of the survivors were sleeping on the living room floor, forcing them to step around or over them. Rachael made a beeline to Jennifer, and gently laid Amy in her arms. She carefully removed the fur coat covering Amy, and tucked the child neatly under the blanket covering with Jennifer. Jennifer awoke when she lifted the covers.

Rachael whispered, "You need to keep her warm. I need to get some rest, and I will be back later to check on her."

As she turned to leave, Jennifer grabbed her wrist and whispered, "She will be fine. You get some rest. If I need you, I will send somebody to get you, okay?"

Rachael nodded as she slowly staggered to one of the bedrooms on the west side of the house. Jennifer pulled Amy very close to her body, wrapping her arms tightly around her with motherly instincts of protecting her young.

Dog was still leading the captain, and they proceeded up the stairs toward the Drifter's room on the east side of the house. After the captain entered the room carrying Dog's master, he very carefully laid him across his bed. Slowly and carefully, he removed the Drifter's clothing while he was checking for frostbite or any other possible wounds. He noticed small patches of frostbite scattered across his upper body, down the arms, and on the back of both hands. Not familiar with first aid treatment for it, he decided it was best to leave it to Rachael. He figured the most important concern was to keep this man warm until Rachael had a chance to examine the wounds. He folded back the covers and carefully maneuvered the Drifter onto the sheets, where he could cover his body. Carefully, he tucked the blankets around the Drifter, trying to keep as much of the frostbite from touching the sheets as possible.

Dog sat there at the foot of the bed, watching every move the captain made. He was curious to see what was going on and what this man was doing to his friend, but he sat there patiently waiting without causing any interference. When the captain had finished and was walking away, Dog moved toward the bedside of his master. He laid his head down across the Drifter's stomach as he let out a short whine.

The captain heard his cry and stopped. He turned around to face the bed as he solemnly whispered, "I'm sorry Dog … that's all I can do for now … It's up to God now."

Dog glanced at the captain and moaned before laying his head back down on the stomach of the Drifter.

Chapter Nine
The Healing

(Early morning hours)

    Rachael woke from her deep slumber as if she had slept for years. She jumped out of bed, only to feel the aches of her tired and sore muscles. She ignored her own discomforts, for she felt the weight of caring for the passengers to be more important. Tired, sore, and hungry, she slowly moved toward the bedroom door to check on the others. Her first stop was with Jennifer and Amy. Amy was still lying in the arms of Jennifer, just as she did last night when she left her. She was awake and looked much better.

    "How are you feeling?" she asked.

    Before anybody could answer, the captain interrupted. "She's fine. Go check on our host upstairs."

    When she glanced at the captain, she noticed his arm was extended and pointing toward the Drifter's room. She ignored the captain's comment and turned her attention to Jennifer. As she reached down to uncover Jennifer's leg, her hands were blocked. Upon a glance, she saw Jennifer shaking her head no, while she also pointed upstairs. Rachael sighed as she took the hint and left for the Drifter's room.

    Her stomach began to growl, reminding her she had not eaten in quite some time. She was very hungry, and that provided an explanation for the weakness in her legs. She pushed the hunger aside, knowing it was crucial to check on the condition of their host lying upstairs. As she climbed the stairs, her fears grew with the realization that the Drifter might not have made it through the night. She felt the pressure from the others to keep this man alive, since she was the most knowledgeable in first aid. At the top of the stairs, she stopped for a moment to give a glance back to the captain.

"Go on... See if he's okay," the captain called up to her impatiently.

She turned toward the door and entered. Once in the room, she saw the man's wolf sitting on the opposite side of the bed, with his head lying on the legs of his master, the Drifter. Dog sensed her presence and lifted his head. He began growling very lightly as she moved closer to the bed. She hesitated with a sense of fear before she moved any closer. Would this animal let her to get close enough to examine this man, or would he attack? She was not sure what to do next.

In a desperate and nervous voice, she said, "Hey, Dog ... I need to look at him and see if I can help ... okay?" Dog stopped his growling as if he understood and left the bedside to sit in the northeastern corner of the room while he waited.

She was amazed at the intelligence of this wolf; it seemed phenomenal. The love and respect she sensed from the animal for the man who lay in the bed was very commendable. She was bound and determined by God that if she could nurse this man back to health, she would. As she uncovered his body for a closer inspection, she began to see the patches of frostbite across the upper parts of his body and down his arms. His breathing was shallow and faint.

She went into the bathroom, on the south side of the room, and filled the washing bowl with hot water from the sink. Grabbing a clean washcloth from the linen closet and some first aid bandages from the medicine cabinet, she returned. Carefully, she washed the wounds on the chest with the hot water and laid bandages across them. She then washed and bandaged his arms and hands. After she had finished, she carefully covered his body with the warm blankets.She glanced at the wolf and smiled, giving reassurance that his master would be fine. Dog walked over to the bed and again placed his head on the body of the Drifter, as Rachael left the room. Back in the living room, she stopped at the foot of the couch. Before she checked Jennifer's wound, she reassured them that the Drifter would be fine. The captain thanked her as she carefully lifted the blanket covering Jennifer. The blood was coagulated and crusty on the large gash running from the ankle to above the knee. She was afraid for Jennifer. Infection had begun to set in, and she had no idea how to take care this type of laceration because of the depth of the cut. She placed the blanket back over the leg and smiled, not wanting anybody to know the critical condition Jennifer might be in. As she was walking away, she was asked an unbearable question, one she tried to avoid. "How's my leg?"

Not wanting to answer, she turned and smiled. She simply changed the subject by asking where Amy had gone. Jennifer pointed to the bathroom on the west side between two of the bedrooms.

Rachael shook her head, understanding Jennifer's gesture, and said, "I'm going to fix me something to eat before I die of hunger. Has Amy had anything to eat? How about you, are you hungry?" Jennifer smiled, knowing Rachael was avoiding her question.

She simply shook her head as she replied. "The captain fixed us something to eat earlier, so go get something for yourself and don't worry about us right now." Rachael left the room to fix herself something to eat. Captain Joe watched her leaving the room, before he took his glance to the fireplace, where the others were gathering around the warmth of the fire. Rachael returned shortly after her departure carrying a bowl of steamy beef stew. She sat down on the fireplace's brick base and began devouring her stew, only glancing at the others briefly, catching expressions of despair. The others patiently awaited the news about the Drifter. She felt helplessness brewing from them, knowing their only hope lay upstairs, possibly dying. Captain Joe sensed the tension that was building. He raised his head as his words pierced the silence. "The weather will let up soon, and we will all be home by Christmas."

The small crowd of survivors ignored his comment by remaining silent. Rachael's guilt took its toll as she leaned back against the fireplace and cried from within, *What am I going to do?* Her burden of helplessness gave her no comfort, which was a righteous punishment for her lack of experience and knowledge. In the meantime, the storm raged on as the night drew to a close with no more discussions about their current affairs. Most of them who were gathered around the fireplace lay back on the carpet and fell asleep. Others sat and listened to the crackling sounds of the burning wood. All were feeling the safety of the Drifter's home, but none was convinced they would ever get home again. Christmas was falling upon them. Their friends and family were worried, with no news to give comfort. The silence of the dwelling was deafening, as the only sounds were the crackling noises of the fire.

(Twenty-four hours later)

As the Drifter opened his eyes, he found himself staring into the beautiful dark blue eyes of what looked like an angel. "Did I die and go to heaven?" he asked the light-haired angel.

Rachael smiled, "No … I'm no angel, but I'm glad you finally woke up. We're all worried about you."

The Drifter stared into her eyes as a sarcastic smile broke the grimness of his face. "You wouldn't have been scared of being stuck here in the event of my death … would you?" Rachael smiled as she bowed her head, feeling somewhat guilty from his question. He placed his hand on top of hers as he mumbled. "I'm very much alive and starving. Is there anything left to eat around here?"

Rachael lifted her head and smiled as she nodded. The Drifter's voice woke Dog from his sleep, and before another word could be spoken, Dog was all over the Drifter's face with his tongue. The licking was tickling his cheeks, causing him to laugh while he was steadily pushing Dog's head away.

"He's glad to see you. If it wasn't for him, you and Amy might very well be dead," Rachael said. The Drifter's confusion was written deep into the wrinkles that formed across his forehead. Rachael smiled as she told him what had happened and how she and the captain with Dog had rescued him and Amy from the treacherous slope.

The Drifter interrupted her story to inquire about Dog's entry. "The area where he was leads into my study, and there is no way in except through the stables. I know Dog didn't climb the ladder, so how did he get in there?" Rachael shrugged her shoulders, for she was also confused on how Dog was able to get in.

"Anyway, Dog took us to the ridge were you and Amy had fallen. The captain tied off a rope to a nearby tree and climbed down the slope. He ended up securing the rope around you and Amy. It took all of us, and that includes Dog, to pull both of you to safety. Once we had you up, we carried you back here."

"Thank you. I owe my life to the two of you and I take that very seriously." The Drifter glanced at Dog, and with a gentle rub, he offered his gratitude. He took his glance back to his rescuer and asked, "How about that food and some coffee?"

Rachael smiled. He watched her as she stood up and left his bedroom. He remembered the warmth of her hand when he had taken it into his. It had been a long time since he had any feelings that caused a tingling sensation in his stomach. The soft glow of the small light shining from his bed stand caused her radiant beauty to glow. He enjoyed the lost feelings she brought back, but feared they would only torment his broken heart. Dreaded thoughts began to cloud his judgment. *She probably already has someone. Besides, I have to go home soon and I'm sure she'll not want to come with me.* He pushed the painful thoughts aside as he removed the bed covers.

Dressing was very painful and the pain increased with every movement. His arms ached the most, but every part of his body made itself known. He was not sure what happened after he slid down the slopped ridge. The last thing he remembered was climbing up the incline, dragging Amy. *Did I pass out? How did Dog get inside? Is Amy all right? Did someone take care of Jennifer's leg? What about George's shoulder?* There were so many unanswered questions causing chaos in his mind, and he still had not had his first cup of coffee. After what seemed an excruciating hour of pain and agony, he finally finished dressing his tired, aching body. As he slowly staggered down the stairs, he began to feel the eyes of everyone watching him. The eerie feeling sent chills down his spine, adding to his current discomfort. Avoiding their eye contact, he continued his slow pace to the bottom of the stairs. After reaching the bottom, he raised his right arm in a friendly gesture as he spoke. "How is everybody?"

The captain answered with a large smile splitting his face. "We are fine. It's good to see you're getting around, and you're looking much better than you did two days ago."

"Two days ago!" he yelled in astonishment. No one answered him, fearing the anger in his words.

He quickly apologized for being somewhat rude with his comment, even though he was still troubled about being unconscious for the last two days. Shaking his feelings aside, he reached out his hand toward the captain. "I owe you a debt of gratitude for saving my life."

The captain shook his hand as he accepted the gesture with a remark of his own. "You saved our lives, and I believe the gratitude is still on us, not on you." He sensed the goodness in the captain's heart, and knew if something should ever happen to him, these people would be well taken care of.From the corner of his eye, he saw Rachael approaching with a steamy cup of coffee. He could smell the brew as she came closer to him. He watched her approach, and graciously took the coffee from her soft hands. "You're a woman after my own heart, thanks."

Rachael smiled. In a soft, sensual voice she said, "If you're hungry, I could fix something for you." He once again felt the warm sensation of the butterfly effect on his stomach. He smiled with slightly parted lips as he answered.

"Breakfast sounds really nice; some bacon and eggs would suit me just fine."

Rachael nodded, turning toward the kitchen without losing eye contact with him, until she was forced to. His eyes remained on her until she disappeared through the kitchen doorway. He slowly walked to the dining room table, where he sat and sipped his coffee. Soon, the aroma of bacon sizzling caused his stomach to growl loudly, as it awaited the arrival of food. Rachael returned with the Drifter's breakfast and sat next to him at the dining table. She refilled his coffee and watched him as he consumed the food. He did not realize how hungry he had been until the taste from the bacon touched his tongue.

"Ummm, you cook a mean breakfast, Rachael," he said as he continued filling his mouth.

"Thank you, but I think you were hungry, because my cooking skills aren't that good," she laughed.

The more time he spent with her, the more attractive she became. He realized how wonderful she was — her wit, humility, desire to help and care for others. These were good qualities in any person, not to mention her beauty and passion. The more he thought, the more he believed it was possible to rekindle his shattered world. The passion that he thought was long forgotten still raged inside.

The thoughts of going home still plagued him deeply. How he was going to settle his affairs, where to start, and finding the best approach. Helping these survivors softened his fears and brought him closer to the realization that it was time to return to his old life. He filled his cup with coffee from the pot sitting on the dining room table, then stood up and walked to the sofa where Amy was sitting. Dog was lying on the floor at her feet, looking very content. He examined Amy with his eyes starting at her head and covering her entire body down to her feet. To him, she was looking very healthy, but something else seemed to be bothering her. He placed his hand on her shoulder and asked how she was feeling. Amy never glanced up, nor did she offer a response. He assumed her disturbance was about her mother's death, so he avoided any further conversation. As he moved his eyes from Amy toward Jennifer, he noticed she was still lying on the sofa exactly where he had previously put her.

When his eyes met hers, he saw that she was staring back at him. Jennifer quietly spoke, answering his question of Amy. "She seems to be okay physically … but I think it's going to take a while for her to get through this. I'll stay with her and try to take good care of her. Your dog has really helped." Dog, overhearing his name, lifted his head off of the floor and stared at the Drifter.

"So, you're going to be a traitor and start hanging out with Amy, HUH?" the Drifter teased. Dog gave a short whine before laying his head on Amy's lap. Amy, hearing the comment, looked up and smiled, before reaching down to give Dog an affectionate scratch between his ears.

From Jennifer's concerned and sympathetic look, he could tell the two of them were getting very close. It gave him a warm sensation knowing that Jennifer was helping keep his promise to Amy's mother. He was somewhat concerned about Jennifer's attitude in general, but knew she would protect Amy at the risk of her own life. Right now, she was perfect for the job, and that satisfied him for the moment.

He knelt down next to Dog, giving his approval as he gently rubbed his neck. He sighed softly before scooting sideways to examine Jennifer's leg. He asked her how she was feeling and only received shrugged shoulders for her response. He knew she was concerned about her condition, but was the type who would not show her weakness. Normally she would speak her mind, bearing no concern for the other's feelings.

He asked again, "How's your leg?" He paused, awaiting a response. "May I look at it?" Jennifer responded by slowly lifting the covers, exposing her bad leg. He thanked her as he slowly examined the cut. It was deep and the blood had dried, crusting over the wound with pus oozing from the cracks. The infection was worse than before, and if something was not done, the result would be the loss of her leg. He slowly covered her leg with the blanket as he was standing up to leave

"Well! What do you think?" Jennifer yelled. "Don't just walk away without saying something!"

When he opened his mouth to respond, his words flowed out as if he lost his control. "You'll be fine! I suppose it'll take more than a bad cut like that to give you any character." When it was all said, he felt the eyes of everyone on him. Slightly embarrassed for the sarcastic remark, he turned his back to them as he walked toward the kitchen.

Deep inside, he was sympathetic toward Jennifer, but sometimes being in her presence provoked his responses. A smile cracked his lips, for he could not help feeling good about his triumph over her. As he was pouring another cup of coffee, he tried to justify the good feeling. *I really want to help her, but she is so cruel to me. I'm not sure why she hates me so much, but it doesn't matter; she doesn't deserve to lose her leg. That would destroy her career and her life. If I'm going to help her it has to be now; waiting could be disastrous.*

His thoughts were broken when Alice entered the kitchen. She was disturbed by his actions toward Jennifer, but more by his lack of response for her husband. "George's shoulder is causing him great pain. He hasn't slept and I can't seem to make him comfortable. Can you help him … please?"

The Drifter remembered his promise to take care of the shoulder once they were safe in his home. "Okay, first I need to get something from the outside closet. Something that will ease the pain and make it easier on George." He passed her as he exited the kitchen and headed for the closet outside of the house. Alice shook her head in disappointment as he passed. She took her frustrations and left the kitchen to go comfort her husband, George.

The Drifter walked from the house into the small corridor leading toward the wind generator. His freezer was in the food pantry, which was built inside the cavern wall that opened up to a smaller cavern. It sat on the northwest side, only a few feet from the corridor leading into the generator room. This is where he hid the good stuff. As he opened the pantry door, he reached up to the top shelf and removed his last fifth of Crown Royal.

"Oh, Crown Royal, how I missed you," he said in a low voice, as if he feared someone would hear him. He removed the cap and placed the bottle against his lips, when all the memories of the drunk and lonely nights returned. His addiction had almost destroyed his life. He thought again before he took the drink, stopped, shook his head, and said loudly, "No! George and Jennifer will need this much more than I will." He placed the cap back on the bottle and closed the pantry door.

As he headed back into the house to get some glasses for them to drink from, he thought how ice would help the swelling in George's shoulder. If the swelling was lessened and the muscles were more relaxed, the shoulder would be easier to reset. When he entered the front door, he did not break stride, as he headed for the kitchen. From the freezer, he took out an ice tray and dumped the ice into a plastic bag, then grabbed two glasses from the cupboard. He left the kitchen in a hurry, with the essentials currently needed, and headed straight for George. He handed the bag of ice to Alice and instructed her to hold it against George's shoulder. He once again removed the cap from the Crown Royal and poured it into one of the glasses, until it was full.

"Here, drink this. I'll keep it coming until I see the effect I'm looking for," the Drifter explained as he handed the glass to George. George slowly sipped on the glass of whiskey and was shocked when he heard, "NO! Drink it fast, I don't have enough for you to just sip on it." George lifted the glass and guzzled it down. Before he could drink the whole glass, he began coughing and gagging from the effect of the liquor, as it took his breath away. In the background, Jennifer began giggling about poor George's demise. Some of the other survivors joined in with Jennifer, laughing with her, also thinking his reactions were funny. The Drifter gave them all a cold, calculated, scornful look that caused them to promptly quit their laughter.

"That's much better, George," he said while he refilled the glass. George downed the second glass and again gagged as it took his breath away. The Drifter smiled as he poured some of the whiskey into the other glass and walked toward Jennifer. He handed her the glass. "It's your turn and I expect you to drink it fast also."

Jennifer looked at him, and with sarcasm in her voice responded, "No thanks, I'm not thirsty." Again she was displaying her nasty attitude with the Drifter, and he wondered how he ever could have felt sorry for her. If a man needed a drink, this was the time.

As calmly and coolly as he could at this point, he again handed her the glass. "You will need this very shortly, or if you prefer, I can sew up your leg while you're sober."

"Sew up my leg!" she screamed. "You're not a doctor and I'll be damned if I let you touch me!" He thought for a moment and decided not to fight Jennifer, for to do so would be a losing battle. He left Jennifer to wallow in her hatred of men, and turned his attention back to George, who by now was beginning to feel the effects of the Crown Royal. Alice, with a concerned look in her eyes, questioned the Drifter. "Why is Jennifer acting this way? Why didn't you force her to take the drink?"

The Drifter smiled, and in a very boisterous voice, being sure Jennifer could hear him, said, "I really don't care whether or not she lets me help her. It's a real shame she may lose that leg though … and it's such a pretty leg at that."

He heard Jennifer's scream from behind. "What do you mean I could lose my leg?" He steadily ignored her comment and continued his conversation with Alice.

"By the time we get her to a real doctor, well… infection will have set in and taken over. If it turns to gangrene, it's off with the leg." Alice was disturbed by his comment, and he saw the misunderstanding building upon her face, so he lifted one eyebrow as he shrugged his shoulders, hoping she would get the hint. Noticing George had finished his last glass of whiskey, the Drifter picked up the bottle and refilled his glass. George's arm was shaking. In a drunken but concerned voice, he asked, "Don't you oughta save some for Jennifer?"

The Drifter smiled again. "Nope, don't believe in wasting good brew." He could hear Amy from behind talking to Jennifer. "I don't want you to lose your leg."

Jennifer let out a short "Humph!" in response, making sure she was loud enough for the Drifter to hear. "I'm not going to lose my leg, Amy. That bastard doesn't know what he's talking about. He's not a doctor, so you don't have to listen to him, okay?" Alice grabbed the glass off the end table and forcefully took the bottle of Crown out of the Drifter's hands. She took the glass to Jennifer and demanded she take it. The Drifter cocked his head around to get a better view of how Jennifer was reacting to Alice's demands. Without a word of protest, Jennifer took the glass from Alice and guzzled it down without even gasping for air or choking. He stood impressed on how well Alice handled the situation and how well Jennifer could hold her liquor.

"She needs a refill!" Alice said as she gave him a scornful look. He now knew Alice was a very strong-willed woman and was a force to be reckoned with. He smiled and nodded for her to pour Jennifer another glass. Alice took the glass from Jennifer and refilled it, taking it to the rim. Jennifer drank it as if it was water, but he knew she would soon feel the effects. *I wonder if she will be a good drunk or worse than she already is?* He shrugged at the thought before moving closer to Alice. With his hand on Alice's shoulder, he leaned close to her ear and whispered, "Take Rachael and the two of you start preparing some hot water. Oh, by the way, thanks for the help; I couldn't have done it without you." Alice grabbed Rachael's arm and strutted off toward the kitchen as the Drifter poured Jennifer another glass.

Amy tugged on his shirt, so he knelt down beside her. She looked into his eyes and he could feel the concern in her words. "Will she be okay?"

He smiled and nodded. "Yes, she will be okay. I won't be able to make her better, but her leg will be just fine." Amy cocked her head, confused by his comment. He gently laughed, trying to feel better for his sarcastic remark. He knew this little lady had become very attached to Jennifer, and he really needed to be more careful about what he said the future. He reassured Amy that Jennifer would be fine. In the background, he could hear Jennifer mumbling, but could not make out what she was saying, and felt better about not knowing. The Drifter motioned for George to sit on the loveseat, which was parallel to the sofa. George acknowledged him and staggered as he approached it. He was holding out his glass for a refill. It seemed that George was handling his liquor much better than he did the first two glasses. By the time he had plopped down on the loveseat, the Drifter was standing by his side, refilling his glass. The Drifter was laughing a bit, not at George, but with him as he asked how he was feeling. George responded in a very slurry and slack voice, *"Nooooo, I don't feeeeel any…thing."* The other survivors began laughing out loud after hearing George having trouble talking. George was also laughing at himself. He was a big man, and seeing him this way was pretty funny. The Drifter poured the last remaining whiskey into Jennifer's glass. He was hoping she would feel the effects better than George; her pain would last quite a bit longer than his would.

Alice had come back from the kitchen with Rachael and was patiently awaiting further instructions. "The water will be boiling very soon; what else can we do for you?" she asked. The Drifter pointed down the hallway toward the large bathroom on the south wall and asked her to get a handful of towels. She nodded and scurried away toward the bathroom. Rachael slowly moved to the Drifter's side and wrapped her arm around his.

She whispered in his ear, "You're a good man. Thanks for your help; I don't believe we will ever be able to repay you. How are you feeling?"

The Drifter thought about her question. *I'm not feeling that good, my body is aching all over and I didn't even notice it until she asked.* He smiled and told her he was doing fine. Rachael was a good woman, and thanks to her, he was beginning to regain his confidence and self-respect. The Drifter could not afford the time to enjoy Rachael's company, so he gently removed her arm and stepped away. She seemed to take the hint and was more than willing to let him go. She moved away from him, allowing him the freedom to do his work. The Drifter called for the captain to come help with George. When the captain was close, he instructed him to select a few of the stronger men. They were needed to hold George perfectly still. He went on to explain how they were going to reset George's shoulder, a procedure that would be very painful. The captain nodded, as he walked off to gather three men from the group of survivors.

The Drifter turned his attention back to Jennifer. He needed to clean her leg before the stitching operation could be accomplished. The poison and infection present had to be cleaned from out of the wound. He gently reached for Rachael's hand as he pulled her toward the kitchen. As they passed the dining room table, he removed three of the towels left by Alice. When they reached the kitchen, the water in the large pot was already boiling. He pulled a smaller pan from the cupboard and set it on the stove, next to the large pot of boiling water. He picked up one of the towels, slowly unfolded it, and dipped it into the boiling water, until it was fully submerged. He continued with the other two towels until all three were inside of the pot.

Rachael gently put her hand on his arm as she apologized for Jennifer's behavior. "Jennifer was raped two years ago and she hasn't been the same since. I've never seen her act this way toward any man. I don't know what happened between the two of you, but she seems to be holding it against you."

The Drifter thought about the large hunter and what he asked her to do as he mumbled under his breath, "I think I know."

Rachael did not understand his comment and asked, "What is it you said?"

The Drifter shook his head and remained silent, as he took a long barbeque fork hanging on the wall and reached into the pot of boiling water and removed one of the towels. He wrung out the loose water from the towel with his bare hands and placed it into the smaller pan.

Rachael realized he was not going to tell her what happened, so she dropped the subject. She watched as he continued wringing out the towels with his bare hands. When he had finished the last towel, he motioned for her to follow him back into the living room.

As they passed the dining room table, he asked her to get the rest of the towels. She stopped by the dining room table as she watched his every move. He had dropped to his knees beside Jennifer and had carefully lifted the blanket away from her leg. Amy had come over and knelt beside him, watching in silence.

He gave Amy a quick glance and asked if she knew how Jennifer was feeling.

Before Amy could reply, a God-awful noise came out of Jennifer's mouth, "Why don't you ask me how I feel?"

The temptation was overwhelming, causing him to lose control of his emotions; he took advantage of the outburst. "I would much rather talk to Amy than you. She has a much nicer disposition than some drunk female that I happen to have this un-delightful pleasure to be here with."

"Druuuunk? You insisted I get drunk, sooo don't blame me!" She sputtered and stuttered as she spoke. He knew from her speech that she was where he needed her to be. Rachael finally picked up the towels and went to the Drifter's side, opposite Amy. She knelt beside him, trying to calm Jennifer. The Drifter glanced at the captain standing next to George and motioned for him to join them. He asked the captain to lift Jennifer's leg off of the sofa. Once her leg was in the air, he took one of the steamy hot towels, folded it in half, and wrapped it around Jennifer's leg.

Jennifer jerked her leg and yelled, "You bastard … that's hot!"

The Drifter sighed as he looked toward the captain. "Hold her tight." The captain put a firm grip on her leg while the Drifter continued wrapping it below the knee.

The foul words continued spewing from Jennifer's mouth, as he wrapped the other two towels around the leg, making sure the laceration was completely covered. When he was finished with the last hot towel, he began wrapping the dry towels around the steamy hot towels to help hold the heat. After he had Jennifer's leg wrapped securely, he motioned for the captain to lower it to the sofa. With a short sigh, he gave Rachael instructions on what to do next, so he would not have to endure Jennifer's anger.

"Let that work for a little while. Then I need for you to unwrap the towels, reheat them, and do it again." Rachael agreed as he stood up to talk to the captain. After a few words, they both left Jennifer and turned their attention back to George, who seemed to be in a very happy mood. The Drifter thought about George and how he was a much better drunk than Jennifer. He knew that handling George's shoulder was not going to be easy. He had no way of determining if any bones were fractured or how much tissue damage there was. By resetting the shoulder, there was a possibility it could cause more damage to the surrounding tissues or even break some bones. He could only hope no other damage would be caused from the procedure. The Drifter sat down next to George as he said a few words. When George spoke, he laughed a little and smiled a lot. This made the Drifter feel more comfortable about the pain he was about to put George through. He removed the ice pack from George's shoulder and very carefully pushed on the tissue as he examined the bone around the injury. He could not find any obvious breaks, but the extent of the damage was still unknown. The swelling had subsided some, and the ice helped numb the injured area. He felt that George was as ready as he would ever be, even though the procedure was going to cause severe pain.

Remembering that George had recognized him, he still wondered how and where they might have met. He respected George for not revealing his identity to any of the passengers. In his short time of knowing George, he had grown to admire his strength and trust. George seemed to be a good man with a loving heart. Hurting George was going to cause him great discomfort.

The captain shortly returned with three men, and they stood in front of the Drifter, awaiting his approval. The Drifter began wishing he had saved some of the whiskey for himself, for right now he felt he could use a shot or two. He glanced at the three gentlemen the captain had selected, noticing that one was a tall, slender-built man in his mid-thirties. He introduced himself with enthusiasm as Paul, with his hand extended openly toward the Drifter. He took Paul's hand and shook it with as much enthusiasm as he could muster. The other two gentlemen were less responsive. Both had the look of wanting to be somewhere else. He felt the same as they did, so he had no right to hold that against them. The Drifter stood up and explained the procedure to each of them and gave them their specific jobs.

Gently the Drifter placed his right hand under George's left shoulder, and with a slight lifting motion, helped him to his feet. Earlier, he had cleared a small spot in the living room, which was empty of furniture. Slowly he directed George to the spot he had chosen. He instructed George to lie down on his stomach, flat against the floor. He supported George while he slowly bent his knees, lowering his body to the floor until he was lying flat on his stomach.

Once George was in position, the Drifter was ready. He motioned for the others to come join him and do as he had instructed them to do. The Drifter began bellowing out his orders as they prepared to reset George's shoulder.

"You two gentlemen hold his legs; Paul, hold his head and left shoulder. Captain, take his wrist, and when I say, pull his arm toward you very hard and very quickly." He then placed his hands on George's right shoulder, ready to apply pressure to help push the joint back into its socket.

"George, I want you to take a deep breath and breathe out slowly." He glanced at the others, who were waiting for the word. "Get ready, gentlemen." After George had taken a deep breath and was starting to exhale, the Drifter gave the word, "Now!" He pushed the shoulder down and upward toward George's head while the captain pulled the arm with a short snap. George screamed the most awful scream that any of them had ever heard. The Drifter felt a pop as the shoulder dropped back into its socket. He took in a deep breath of relief and fell backward onto the carpet, releasing a big sigh.

The worst was over for George, and before the Drifter had the opportunity to sit up, Alice had run to her husband's side and was knelt down next him. She looked inquisitively at the Drifter with an angry expression on her face. Understanding Alice's stare, he began his inspection of George's shoulder. Much to his surprise, there was no visible damage and the muscles had relaxed. He assured Alice that George would be sore for a while, but the procedure looked successful. He motioned for the other gentlemen to help get George off of the floor and back to the loveseat.

The Drifter left the living room for a short while, returning with a spool of gauze bandage. He bound George's shoulder by wrapping the gauze around his chest and over his shoulder. By the time the Drifter was finished, George's upper chest and halfway down his right arm looked as if they had been mummified. Before he had a chance to leave, he felt the soft touch of Alice's hand on his arm. When he glanced at her, she was smiling. She thanked him for helping George and then sat next to her husband.

He smiled, feeling good about the operation, and returned his unwanted attention to Jennifer. When he stopped at the foot of the couch where Jennifer lay, he took a long look at his next adventure and slowly shook his head. Jennifer had the fear of God written into her eyes after seeing his last performance. He wanted to comfort her, but decided it was not worth the effort. He knew the pain she was going to endure was going to be much worse than George's. Catching his stare, Jennifer hardened her face as she stared back at him. A smile uncontrollably worked its way across his face as he stooped over to retrieve the small pan sitting on the floor next to her.

"What are you smiling about ... you bastard?" Jennifer said hatefully. He ignored the question and left to get some fresh hot water and a clean washcloth.

Upon his return, a few minutes after his departure, he handed the clean washcloth to Rachael. He placed the hot water on the floor next to the couch and instructed Rachael on the next steps. "I need all the dried blood removed. The wound has to be as clean as you can possibly get it. I will be back shortly." While Rachael was cleaning the wound, he left the house.

"Where in the hell is he going?" Jennifer yelled. He heard the comment from outside of the door, but chose to ignore it as he headed toward the stables. He thought about the surgery, and what he needed in the way of supplies. As he thought about the pain the stitching would inflict on

Jennifer, he began to see the pleasure he would gain from the operation. It was a way of getting even for all her sadistic remarks without having the feeling of guilt. An evil smile lifted the corner of his lips as he gathered some stitching implements from the stables.

The only stitching needle available that could perform the operation was the needle he used to sew up the holes in his fishing net. It was the largest needle he had that would hold very fine fishing line. It was semi-circular in shape, which made it a perfect instrument for stitching. Along with the needle, he needed something that could hold the skin until it healed. He saw a small roll of fishing line lying on the shelf above the cabinet and realized it would work perfectly. He grabbed the fishing line and the needle, and headed back to the lift.

When he reached the house, he headed straight for the kitchen. Once inside the kitchen, he wedged the needle into the fishing line and dropped both into the boiling water. While the line and needle were being sterilized, he left to get the alcohol and bandages from the medicine cabinet in his room. When he returned to the kitchen with the alcohol and bandages, he fished out the needle and thread from the pot of boiling water and walked into the living room, where Jennifer waited patiently. He was now ready, but the question at hand remained, was Jennifer ready for the terrible pain she was going to be forced to endure?

He knelt down beside Jennifer to prepare himself for the worst brutal tongue-lashing she could deliver. "I'm ready to start, Jennifer…and this is going to hurt. I am truly sorry, but it has to be done," he said with as much regret as he could.

"You go ahead, you bastard. I'm sure you are going to enjoy this!" she yelled in her cold-hearted voice. A smile crept into his lips once more as he motioned for the captain to hold her leg. The captain could see the expression on his face and began to wonder if the Drifter was enjoying this operation. He stopped at the end of the sofa and firmly held Jennifer's right ankle. The Drifter glanced at Rachael with raised eyebrows, as if he was waiting for her approval. She smiled with a word of confirmation.

He examined the wounded area to make sure it was clean of infection and dried blood. Satisfied with the results, he picked up some gauze and poured the alcohol over it, soaking it thoroughly. Very carefully, he rubbed the lower leg with the gauze to clean the wound even more. Jennifer's words begin to fly as the alcohol burned inside the wound. He gritted his teeth and continued cleaning the wound.

After cleaning the wound with the alcohol, he unrolled the fishing line and cut several small pieces of line. Carefully he threaded the needle, preparing for his first stitch. To his surprise, it was as painful to him as it was to Jennifer, but he continued without hesitation. The horrible words continued for quite some time as he stitched Jennifer's leg. He was not quite sure when Jennifer lost consciousness during the operation, but it was good that she did, because he no longer felt her pain. The Drifter sewed up Jennifer's leg with accuracy and competence. All were amazed at his skills, and thankful for the assistance he had given them. Amy went back and lay in the arms of Jennifer after the Drifter was finished. All was getting back to normal and the injured were taken care of. This had been a long, dreadful day, but night was closing in. They all decided to get some needed rest.

Chapter Ten
The Mutiny

(The Drifter's Home)

    Morning came with no changes in the weather. The storm was still raging with little hope of clearing in the days to come. The Drifter stood by his bedroom window as he stared gloomily into the darkness of the night. Watching the snow dance across his window and hearing the sounds of the howling wind cut its way through the valley caused his sadness to grow even more. The weather today was not going to be any different than the day before. In time, he feared the survivors' hopes would turn to impatience as they began to get more restless.

    The sweet smell of freshly brewing coffee melted away his sadness. He brushed the bad thoughts of the weather from out of his mind as he took his eyes away from the window. He hoped the coffee would help give him a better perspective, giving him strength to face another day.

    As he walked down the stairs, he began to perceive the stale stench of strife in the air, which clenched at his throat, choking the air from his lungs. He was surrounded by the angry cries from those who felt they were unjustly condemned to an undeserved fate. He forced a *good morning* from his lips with as much enthusiasm as he could, knowing this was not what they were hoping to hear. There was no good news to report and he was not going to make this day harder by telling them the truth.

    The captain and Rachael responded to his *good morning* comment with roughly the same sentiment he had projected. He so desperately wanted to tell them that today is the day to leave, that it was time to get prepared and after breakfast, he would take them home. They did not even realize how much he wished he had minded his own business and left them at the crash site to their own fate. It was too late to go back to that day, and he was forced to accept his decision.

Before he was allowed to reach the kitchen for the coffee he so desperately needed, he was confronted by one of the passengers. Stopping short of the table, he turned his gaze upon the spoken words of a young man in his mid- to late twenties. "How are you this morning? ... I hate to inquire, but do you have any idea when we will be leaving?"

The Drifter, trying to be polite, responded, "What's your name, son?"

"Anthony ... Anthony Stevens," replied the young man. He could feel the cold stares from the eyes of everyone as they patiently awaited his answer to Anthony's question. He knew this day was going to be the worst day of his life as these survivors transitioned their hopes to anger. With a grim look and a quick smile, he turned his eyes away from Anthony and up toward his room, allowing the vision of the storm to return. Without answering the question, he left the company of Anthony and walked into the kitchen for a cup of the freshly brewed coffee. As he entered the kitchen, he saw Rachael standing there with her arm extended, presenting him a cup of the steamy brew. He was not sure how she slipped past him and was able to get to the kitchen first, but he graciously accepted the cup, with a friendly smile.

He left the kitchen to find a friendly chair at the dining room table to sit, while Rachael followed. She sat next to him and they both sipped their coffee in silence. He felt the concern displayed in her eyes. He understood the restlessness of the passengers, but there was nothing he could do about the weather. Before she had a chance to speak, he said, "It will be at least a minimum of three days before we can leave, that is if the weather clears right now."

Rachael sighed and bowed her head as if she was in deep thought.

No more words were shared between them as he finished drinking his first cup of coffee. Before he could stop Rachael, she had grabbed his cup and was headed toward the kitchen to refill it. When she returned shortly afterward, she once again sat beside him with a questionable look, as if wanting to speak. He quickly ignored the glance as he moved his eyes toward the living room, where most of the survivors rested.

Rachael did not allow him to ignore the situation, and in a low, whispery voice, she said, "They're not going to like your answer. I have heard some of them talking about leaving without your help and finding their own way home."

He slowly lifted his right eyebrow with a half-crooked smile, for he already expected that there was going to be unrest this day. Rachael waited for some sort of acknowledgement to her statement, but the Drifter kept silent. His mind was rambling in deep thought as he tried to digest Rachael's words. He hoped he could find a solution to rekindle their hopes, but no answer came to mind. He could only hope they would be patient and wait it out, for leaving now would mean certain death to those who attempted it. His thoughts began to dwindle, as he focused on the chores that had been neglected for the last few days. After finishing his second cup of coffee, he stood up and returned to the kitchen, leaving Rachael sitting alone at the dining room table. While he refilled his cup, he decided it was time to check on his favorite patient before starting his chores.

As he sat beside Jennifer on the sofa, he casually and in a quaint voice asked how she was feeling. Her response was not quite what was expected, for he still felt uncomfortable in her presence.

In a soft gentle voice, she said, "I'm doing very well. I don't know what you put on my leg, but it doesn't seem to hurt anymore. It stunk really bad and it took me a while to get over the smell, but I really believe it's helping." Jennifer smiled when she noticed the surprised expression on his face caused by her comment. As he explained about the ointment of specially mixed herbs and roots an old Eskimo had taught him, he began to feel more comfortable in her presence.

As she listened intently to every word, she too began to feel more comfortable around the Drifter. The warmth of his heart spilled from his soft-spoken words, revealing the sensitive man she once perceived to be unworthy of her respect and trust. When the Drifter had finished telling her the story, she thanked him. With a simple smile, she went on to apologize for her behavior since they had met. "I've come to realize that you seem to be a good man, one who was only trying to help us and didn't deserve the harsh treatment that I've given you." The shock of hearing these sweet words come out of her mouth almost caused him to fall backward off the sofa.

After getting over his initial shock and slowly regaining some mental stability, he was still left speechless. Since the two of them had met, there seemed to have been an unspoken rule that caused them to take on the roles of mortal enemies. Not sure how to respond to Jennifer's apology, he remained silent. She could sense his discomfort so she did not pursue the conversation any further.

After the Drifter had examined her leg, he questioned Jennifer about Amy. He needed to know how she was feeling and how well she was coping with her mother's absence. The motherly side of Jennifer took over as she explained the relationship that was building up between her and Amy. The friendship that had developed a trusted bond, like that of mother and daughter. How Amy would sleep in her arms at night as if needing her comfort from the pain she suffered. The Drifter nodded with a loving smile as he took his eyes away from hers to scour the house.

Not seeing Amy, he silently whispered, "We need to talk soon about Amy's future, but now is not the time." Jennifer gave him a startled look as she pondered his words. After careful consideration, and with a little bit of caution, she agreed to talk later, even though she was somewhat apprehensive about his intentions. The Drifter smiled as he left Jennifer to go check on George's shoulder. "How are you doing today, George?" he asked. George answered his question with a painful look. The Drifter knew the shoulder would give George a constant reminder for the next few days, even though it was set correctly.

George swayed around the answer, trying to show his manly strength by saying, "The pain isn't as bad, it's doable right now. I just hope it settles soon."

The Drifter nodded as he placed his hand on George's good shoulder. Knowing how much pain a dislocated shoulder could bring, he tried to give George some comforting words.

"I know it hurts right now. It will get better and soon the pain will subside; until then, there is nothing else I can do." George understood, and with his best effort, cracked a smile from his lips.

Alice followed him as he left their company and headed toward the front door. Before he could exit the house, she stopped him. She warned him about some of the passengers, especially the one named Anthony.

"I'm afraid someone is going to do something stupid," she said.

He assured her that between Dog and himself, they could handle Mr. Stevens. Dog would die before allowing anything to happen that would cause him any bodily harm. Feeling satisfied from his comment, she returned to her husband to give him comfort. The Drifter smiled, shaking his head as she walked away. He sighed, not looking forward to the hard work ahead as he turned his attentions back to his chores, which had been severely neglected.

(Hours later, inside the stables)

The Drifter was feeding Horse when the sounds of the lift echoed through the stables. From the position he was standing, he could not see the lift, so he ignored the sound and returned to feeding Horse. Shortly after, he caught a glimpse of George approaching. With a quick glance, he could see George walking very carefully in order to protect his injured shoulder. He smiled, knowing that George's discomfort would soon fade away.

The Drifter grabbed a horse brush hanging on the stall wall behind him and began brushing Horse's coat. He continued to ignore George's presence until he stopped in front of the door leading into the stall. The Drifter gave George a quick greeting before returning to brushing down his horse. George returned the greeting and patiently waited for the Drifter's complete attention. After a period of waiting, he realized the Drifter was too busy to pay him any mind, so he decided to leave and return to the house. As he was walking away, the Drifter put down the brush and asked George a question in a low, self-controlled voice.

"You said you know me. Where do you know me from?"

For the first time since the crash, George felt triumph over the Drifter. He smiled briefly before he broke out into laughter. The Drifter was puzzled by his outbreak. He shook his head and smiled a discouraged smile before sitting down on a small stool inside the stall. George turned to face the Drifter, but was still having a problem controlling his laughter.

The Drifter offered George the other stool that was next to the stall door. George forced control over his laughter and placed the stool in front of the stall door so he could have good eye contact with his host. With a smile on his face and a quaint laugh he said, "It's a long story."

The Drifter shook his head and smiled. "Go ahead, we have all the time in the world. The storm is starting to let up, but you have time to explain yourself."

George nodded as his expression became stern. "You and I are much alike. I know I'm older than you, but our lives have so much in common that it's truly remarkable. I lived in Richmond, Virginia, not too far from where you lived. When I first started in the architect business, I too was ambitious. I became a workaholic, much like you. It took me almost ten years to build my business. I had all the city and county contracts. I was even getting them from neighboring counties. I was the number one architect in Richmond; that is, until you came along and took all that business away from me."

The Drifter began to interrupt when George raised his good hand and stopped him. "I'm not blaming you for stealing my business," George replied. "Please let me continue.

"One day, I realized I was losing my wife and son because of my work. I came home late one night and found a note on our bed. My wife Priscilla had taken my son Jeffery, and the two of them went to stay with her mother in Tampa, Florida. As you might think, this brought some reality into my life. I knew then that if I wanted them back, I was going to have to slow down at work and spend more time with my family. I spent many long, lonely nights with Priscilla on the phone telling me how I neglected them and how she couldn't take it anymore. A couple of months had passed before I was able to convince her that I was going to hire a vice president and let him run the business so I could spend more time with them.

"She finally agreed to come home and try once more. I was so excited that I couldn't sleep that night. I knew it would take a couple of days for her to drive back, but my mind was so engrossed in seeing them again that it was driving me mad. It was late the next morning when I received a phone call. They were driving through Atlanta, Georgia late the night before and a drunk driver crashed into their car head-on. They were killed instantly. My life was shattered from that point on.

"I had built my business around them, and now it didn't seem important anymore. I had heard about you and how you were building relationships with the city council. You had already managed to get some of my contracts, but it didn't seem to bother me anymore since I lost Priscilla and Jeffery. Before long, you managed to steal all my business, and I ended up closing shop. I took on some smaller jobs to make ends meet, but lost my house and everything else I owned.

"It was about eight years ago when I met Alice, and she captivated me from the start. Soon after we met, we were married, and I was starting a brand-new life. I'm a very happy man today and have no regrets losing my business to you. Alice and I moved to Seattle, where her parents lived. I started another architect business there and have been doing quite well for myself. Your brother John is a remarkable man. I knew him much better than I knew you. I was there the night you had your fight with your wife Janelle.

"I spoke to your brother about it, and he explained what was going on. I was heartbroken when I read in the papers the next morning that your wife and daughter were killed in an automobile accident. I came to the funeral, but I guess you don't remember. I'm sorry you lost your loved ones at the height of your life. I can relate to that, even though it doesn't ease the pains of their loss. I have noticed you and Rachael. Amy seems to be taking a liking to you also. I believe your daughter's name was also Amy?

"Anyway, what I'm trying to tell you is that you have an opportunity to turn your life around, just like I had. Whatever you do, don't let this opportunity get away from you without a fight. Believe me when I say, you'll regret it the rest of your life if you do. I promise not to tell anyone about you. When you're ready to tell them, you'll have to do it for yourself."

When George had finished telling the Drifter his story, he patiently waited for a response from his host. The Drifter sat as he recalled the past, trying to place George, but was not able to remember too much about him, except for his name. He was now angry with himself for not taking the time to get to know George earlier in his career. He stood up and shook George's good hand, thanking him for not revealing his identity to the others.

George nodded as he asked, "Why do you want to keep your name a secret?"

"Maybe someday I'll tell you; for now, let's keep it the way it is."

George agreed as he stood up and returned to the lift. The Drifter watched his departure as he thought about George and his words of advice.

He returned to his chores, and after hours of cleaning the stables, feeding and brushing Horse, he decided to go to his thinking room instead of the house. He was not ready to face his guests and listen to their elevated complaining.

While he sat in his easy chair, looking out of the window and observing the storm in his thinking room, he realized Dog was not with him. It seemed the last few days, Dog had taken a liking to Amy and always remained by her side. He wanted Amy and Dog to get close, hoping this would help her, but now he was beginning to miss his old friend. Shaking off the feeling of loneliness, he took his gaze to the window. His eyes slowly closed as the whistling winds mesmerized him into a deep sleep.

(Back at the house)

Anthony and a handful of others were sitting around the fireplace in the den, discussing their current situation. He was telling all those who would listen how he could force the stranger into giving him directions to

Cyprus Springs. All they had to do was trust in him, for he could be relied upon to get them to safety. The other passengers sitting around the fireplace would glance at one another and then at Anthony, listening and believing his every word. They were anxious to get home before Christmas and were willing to believe and accept anybody's idea that would offer them this opportunity. When Anthony finished his speech, he stopped and looked at the others, waiting for an indication from them. After not seeing or hearing anything, he asked, "Are you with me or not?" The others began murmuring among themselves for a brief moment before they all agreed. Anthony nodded his head in defiance before leaving the others to sneak into the Drifter's room. As he explored the room, he found the Drifter's handgun hanging on the wall next to his bed. He carefully looked about the room, making sure he was alone before removing the gun from the holster. He placed it in the back of his pants, covering its appearance with his shirttails. He then removed the holster from its resting place and hid it under the bed before leaving the Drifter's room. When he returned to the den, where the others awaited his arrival, he proudly waved the handgun for them to see.

"I have his gun … now we just wait for the opportune moment to strike." Guilty silence fell upon the small group as they sat by the fireplace, trying to justify their intent.

(The Drifter)

The silence fell upon the small thinking room, awakening the Drifter from his deep slumber. As his eyes opened, he realized the small room was very quiet and still. The howling of the wind could no longer be heard and the snowflakes had stopped falling in front of the window. He slowly arose from his comfortable chair and walked to the window for a closer look. His eyes filled with a childlike excitement when he searched across the valley and saw that the storm had lifted. The timing was just right, for now he could prepare for his journey to Cyprus Springs.

He left his little study, moving quicker than usual, wanting to get to the house with the good news. As he climbed down the ladder into the stables, a horrible thought entered his mind: *What if the storm has just let up for a while and will start again?* Thinking this was a possibility, he decided not to give anybody the news until he was absolutely sure the storm was over.

As he crossed the stables to the lift on the opposite side, he was still highly excited about the clear weather. He rode the lift up the rocky wall to the small cliff leading into the cavern hallway. When he entered the front doors, he was almost knocked off his feet when Dog put his paws up against his chest. He gave Dog a brisk rub across his neck as he whispered, "The storm is over and we can take them home soon."

Dog barked with excitement as he dropped to all fours and the two of them entered the living room together. Immediately he began observing his guests. Some of them were napping on the floor next to the living room fireplace, while others were pacing the floors. He glanced toward Amy sitting on the couch with Jennifer, and noticed she was watching him. He smiled as he motioned for Dog to join her. He left the living room and climbed the stairway to his bedroom.

When the Drifter entered his room, he was still excited. He made a beeline toward his closet to prepare for the upcoming journey, and never noticed his pistol was no longer hanging on the wall next to his bed. As he opened the closet door, Amy's Winnie the Pooh bear fell to the floor next to his feet. He passionately reached down and picked up the bear. Slowly he backed up and sat down on the bed, gently holding the bear tenderly in his hands. Tears slowly filled his eyes as some of his daughter's memories returned. The hardest memory to forget was the night of the fateful tragedy that might have been prevented, if he had not broken his promise. It seemed there were many broken promises, and he wished for the opportunity to set it right.

His guilty heart and thoughts of self-pity were disrupted when he heard a small, soft-spoken voice from behind. "That's my Winnie the Pooh, where did you find it?" As he turned to the voice, he saw Amy and Dog approaching him. He watched Amy's every move until she stood directly in front of him. He then lowered his eyes to glance at the bear in his hands, when he was completely taken by surprise. Amy had reached down into his hands and snatched the bear from his tender grip. Dog began barking and snarling, for he knew the bear belonged to his master. The Drifter gave him a stern stare before he motioned for him to sit down and stop his barking.

Unable to speak and stumped for words, he remained silent. As he reached to wipe the tears from his eyes, Amy asked an unbearable question. "Why are you crying?" He had hoped she had not seen his tears or his attempt to conceal them. Not sure of how he was going to answer her question, and unable to hold back his feelings of guilt, he tried to change the subject. His futile attempt failed when Amy asked, "Where did you find my Winnie ... and why did you keep it?"

Forced into submission, he admitted his guilt. "When I found this bear next to the broken-up airplane, it brought back memories of my little girl. I never thought it was yours, or I would have given it to you when I found it. You see … a long time ago, I gave my daughter a Winnie the Pooh bear just like this one when she was six years old. I'm sorry I kept it, but I really had no idea it was yours."

The two of them sat in silence for a few minutes while Amy hugged the bear tightly against her chest. She looked into the Drifter's eyes and asked the question he was hoping not to hear. "Where is your daughter now?"

Tears uncontrollably rolled from his eyes as he explained the fateful accident to Amy. "My wife and daughter Amy … died in a car accident on the night of October 17, 1995." A strange and spirited feeling shook his soul, when Amy told him that was the night she was born. He turned his head toward her to make eye contact, and for a brief moment, he could see the reflection of his own daughter. A smile lifted the corner of his lips as he realized how much this child resembled his daughter in so many ways. For the first time since they met, he now understood why his heart was overwhelmed in her presence.

From the look in his eyes, Amy could sense a strong, glowing emotion emanating from the Drifter. She stared into his eyes, even though it caused her to feel uneasy. Finally she broke eye contact as she politely asked, "Sir, are you okay?"

The Drifter solemnly lowered his head before he replied with a soft and tender voice, "I'm okay, Amy. How about you and Dog helping me gather some fresh vegetables from the garden?" Amy perked up with excitement after hearing that he had a garden. Dog barked once while Amy kept smiling from ear to ear. The Drifter sensed the warmth of her smile, and it reminded him of his daughter.

He smiled and asked, "I take that as a yes?"

Amy nodded, giving her approval. Dog laid his head on his lap, and with a simple whine, gave his approval.

He rubbed Dog's neck with one hand, and with the other, he gave Amy a gentle hug. "Good. Dog, you and Amy wait for me downstairs. I'll be there as soon as I can get ready." Dog lifted his head and headed toward the door. Amy smiled once more before she left carrying her Winnie the Pooh bear tucked against her chest.

He sat down on the bed, feeling a bond for Amy rooting itself deep within his heart and growing rapidly. He had to sacrifice his most valuable possession, but felt it was needed to help Amy overcome the tragedy she would soon be faced with. His guilt of not telling her about the death of her mother haunted his dreams every night. *The time isn't right and to tell her now ... could destroy her. The burden of the bad news will have to come someday, but today is not that day.*

He sat on his bed, reminiscing of times gone by. It was as if Amy gave him a gift by purposely reaching inside his mind and reviving the long-forgotten memories. His eyes filled with tears as the broken promises to his daughter flashed before him. *I know I failed you, Amy, but I will not fail again.* Unable to bear the past any longer, he broke away from the memories and left his room to join Amy and Dog.

Chapter Eleven
Going Home

(Day 2 after the passing storm)

    The Drifter stood by his bedroom window with the view of the entire valley. No snow fell again today. All was quiet and still. He felt assured at last the storm was over, and now his patience would be taxed over the next few days while the snow packed. His desire of getting these people home before Christmas was as strong as relieving his burden of having to take care of them. It had been almost twenty-four hours since the snowstorm had passed, and he had kept it a secret. As he stood there looking over the valley, he contemplated whether or not he should give them the news now or wait until it was time to leave. After much deliberation, his decision was to tell them, hoping this would reinforce their hopes and help suppress their fears of not getting home before Christmas. He turned from the window and left his bedroom, ready to face his guests. As he walked down the stairs toward the living room, he noticed Anthony standing at the bottom of the stairs. Their eyes met when he reached the bottom of the stairs, where he quietly stood in silence. Anthony seemed nervous, with little twitches in his movement, which began to alarm him. He was not surprised when Anthony pulled a pistol from behind his back and stood there with it pointed toward his face. The Drifter remained motionless but stood strong as he waited for an explanation. The longer they stood face to face in silence, the more Anthony's twitching steadily increased. The Drifter noticed the gun Anthony was holding happened to be his, and wandered how Anthony was able to take it without his knowledge.

    Dog, who had seen the events against his master, began growling, sounding more fierce with every passing second. The wolf moved slowly toward Anthony, now flashing his teeth as if he was ready to attack. The Drifter motioned with his right hand for Dog to silence his growling and wait. Dog howled a gruesome sound before he sat where he last stood and patiently waited for the sign.

The Drifter's patience had come to its end when he heard the shaky voice of Anthony say, "Please keep your dog away from me … I don't want to hurt anybody, but I will if I have to. I don't want any problems from you, Mr. Drifter, or anybody else. A small group of us have decided we are ready to leave your hospitality. We are tired of waiting here and we want to get home before Christmas. All I need from you is a compass and directions to that town you were talking about."

The Drifter sensed Anthony's nervous condition, as if he was not sure about his decision to leave. Using this to his advantage, he decided not allow Dog to attack until he had a chance to end the confrontation peacefully.

With as much strength of character as he could force through his squinted eyes, the Drifter used Anthony's fear of the wolf to scare him into releasing the pistol.

"He'll rip you into shreds if you don't put that gun down."

Anthony's fear increased even more as he continued glancing between the Drifter and his wolf. He still held fast to his decision by holding the gun firmly pointed at the Drifter's face. "I told you … all I want from you are directions out of this place. We've discussed this, and if you give me directions, we'll go in peace and no one will get hurt." By this time, Anthony's voice was scratchy and full of skepticism. The Drifter decided not to move from his position or volunteer any information. The two stood in silence while he reframed from releasing Dog's fury on his assailant.

He stood alone against Anthony, and there seemed to be no actions from anyone to help him. The tensions were building in the air, and he began to realize Anthony was not going to give. His greatest fear was, he stood alone and all of them were behind Anthony in the making of this mutiny. Minutes passed as they stood face to face before the Drifter decided to take a different approach and deliver the news about the passing storm.

"The storm cleared from the valley yesterday. It will take another day for the snow to pack, and I will be more than delighted to take you to Cypress Springs. Now give me back my pistol and let me have a cup of coffee." Anthony did not waver from his position of power, as if he did not believe about the passing storm. The Drifter lowered his head slightly, trying to shake the feeling that the only way to end this nightmare was to let Dog attack. He was about to give the signal when he saw the captain circling around to come up behind Anthony.

As the captain approached their assailant from the rear, with an undetected sneak attack, he found his attempt was futile, for Anthony sensed his presence. With a quick movement, Anthony turned around and pointed the gun at Captain Joe, still keeping a quick eye on the Drifter.

"Nice try, Captain. Now just back off. I said that I didn't want to hurt anybody, but I will if necessary!" Anthony politely said. Captain Joe used his powers of persuasion, trying to convince Anthony to put the gun down and return to the others. After several minutes of listening to the two talk, the Drifter decided to use his last approach. He interrupted their conversation by saying, "I know you didn't believe me about the storm clearing, but the storm is over. Now this is your last chance to give me the pistol without any further action, and we will ignore this incident, putting it behind us. If not, I'm going to allow my wolf to attack, and I will not be responsible for your life. You have until the count of three." Anthony listened intuitively while the Drifter spoke, still holding the gun toward the captain.

Before the Drifter could reach the count of two, Anthony had already decided to lower the pistol. As Anthony bowed his head in shame for his aggression, he slowly lifted the pistol, trying to surrender it to the Drifter.

"I'm sorry! We just want to go home." The Drifter could empathize with Anthony and the rest of the passengers, but was still angered by the attack.

The captain yelled, "What did you mean the weather cleared yesterday, and why didn't you tell us then?"

The Drifter grinned with a slight look of repentance as he responded to the captain's question.

"I didn't want to tell you in case I was wrong. It stopped snowing but I could not be sure it was over. I was on my way downstairs this morning to tell all of you that we would be leaving tomorrow … until this happened." The murmurs could be heard all over the house, like soft, shadowy whispers of a dream. He felt as if he had done no wrong by not telling them, so he ignored the whispers and left the stairs toward the kitchen for his cup of coffee.

Silence fell upon the small group of passengers when the Drifter re-entered the dining room carrying his coffee. They watched as he climbed the stairs to return to his room. Dog followed his master upstairs, leaving Amy sitting by Jennifer on the sofa.

After the Drifter disappeared into his room, Amy leaned forward and whispered into Jennifer's ear, "This isn't my Winnie the Pooh." Jennifer, with the look of puzzlement, softly asked her to explain why she did not believe it was her bear. Amy looked at her and sniffled before she answered, "My father was mad at me when he found out we were leaving, so he burned my bear, here in the back, with his cigarette." She pointed to a spot on the lower back of the bear, close to the butt. "This one doesn't have a burn on it."

Jennifer shook her head, still confused. "If it's not yours, whose bear is it?"

There was a hesitation before Amy took a deep breath to answer her question. "I think it belonged to his daughter."

Jennifer, still unable to grasp the concept of her meaning, asked Amy once again to explain in more detail, telling her about the Drifter and his daughter. Amy nodded as she continued. "His daughter died in an accident the night I was born. He told me that he gave her a bear just like this one when she was six. … Why would he give me her bear and lie to me about finding this one next to the plane?"

Jennifer was flabbergasted by Amy's question, and was unsure how to answer. With a silent hesitation, she tried to find the words to solve the equation. She motioned for Amy to come closer, and when she was next to her, she placed her arms around Amy's shoulders, giving her a motherly squeeze. This gave her the time she needed to find the words. While she held Amy tight against her chest, she softly answered the question.

"From watching and listening to him, I know he is a very good man. He probably didn't know how to tell you that this bear belonged to his daughter, but by his giving this bear to you … he must love you very much. This bear is probably the only thing he has left that once belonged to his daughter, who he loved very dearly. I know he loved his daughter very much, because he wouldn't have carried the bear with him and still have it here in the middle of this godforsaken place. To give up his most valuable possession to you means he truly, truly loves you."

Amy remained silent while her tear ducts filled, causing her eyes to glaze. Jennifer's motherly comfort came to a surprising halt when she heard Amy's whining voice ask, "If he loves me so much, why hasn't he found my mommy?"

Jennifer felt ambushed by the question, with the feeling of guilt for having deceived Amy by not telling her about her mom. Unable to muster the courage to tell Amy herself, she lay there, forcing her tears of sorrow from filling her eyes. As much as her heart was breaking by not telling her, she still was not ready to face the emotional trauma. After a moment of trying to clear her conscience of the formidable deed, Jennifer decided to put the burden with the Drifter and told Amy she would ask him to explain. Relieved from the current pressure, Jennifer laid back on to the sofa as she contemplated her next move.

(Three hours later)

The day seemed to be running smoothly without any further incidents from the survivors of Flight 493. Their hopes were strong with all the excitement of going home as they scuttled about the house, gathering what was left of their belongings in preparation for their departure. All seemed to have forgotten the incident that had transpired that morning with the mutiny, all except for one.

Anthony sat alone in the den, ashamed of his part in creating the mutiny, but felt he carried the burden for all who had participated. He stood against the Drifter without any support from the others, and when it was over, he felt like an outcast.

As the Drifter was on his way out the front door to prepare Horse for the journey, Rachael stopped him. After a few brief words, he nodded and headed straight toward the den. As he and Dog entered the small room, there was no hesitation in their step as they approached Anthony, stopping short of standing over him. Patiently, the Drifter waited to be acknowledged, but it seemed Anthony was sulking in such deep self-pity that he never paid them any attention. The Drifter cleared his throat, which forced Anthony to raise his pitiful head to make eye contact with the man who towered over his presence.

Anthony's smile was solemn as he tried to apologize once more for his stupid participation in the mutiny. The Drifter silently stood, not giving Anthony the self-satisfaction for his apology. Minutes passed before the Drifter released Anthony's tension when he casually asked if he was married. Anthony's lazy nod sent the feeling of remission through the Drifter.

"Do you have any children?" the Drifter asked.

"I have a six-year-old daughter. I travel a lot, and she was very upset that I was leaving before Christmas. I'm usually gone for long periods of time and I promised her I would be home before Christmas," Anthony said in a pitiful voice.

The Drifter now understood the meaning behind his actions, even though they were not right. Without changing his expression, he placed his hand on Anthony's shoulder.

"I understand why you did it, but you and the others could have died out there in the middle of that storm, then your daughter would no longer have a father. I want you to believe me when I tell you that I'm not holding this against you. You seem to have some leadership abilities, and if you don't mind, I would like to call upon you to help me get these people home safely. I will do my best to make sure you keep that promise you made to your daughter."

Anthony's eyes lit up with excitement as his pride sparkled in his expression. Color rushed back into his face just before a smile parted his lips from cheek to cheek. He stood up and shook the Drifter's hand, assuring him that it would be his pleasure to help in any way he possibly could. The Drifter, feeling satisfied with the conversation, accepted the handshake before departing with Dog.

(The Evening before Leaving)

The Drifter was checking Jennifer's leg when she motioned for him to lean closer, indicating she had something to say and it was for his ears only. As he leaned and placed his ear next to her mouth, she whispered, "Amy asked me this morning why you haven't found her mother." Shocked by the comment, the Drifter leaned back as the two of them shared eye contact with horror for quite some time. Jennifer, seeing the pain in his eyes, remembered that she too felt the burden of shame. Thoughts of how he was going to explain the truth to Amy about her mother flashed erratically through his mind. Eye contact was broken when he turned his head away in search of Amy.

Jennifer watched the ever-changing expressions on his face, before realizing he was looking for Amy. She softly touched his hand. "She is sitting in front of the fireplace in the den, with Dog."

The Drifter acknowledged her and asked if she would care to join him when the truth was revealed. Jennifer agreed. He stood up, leaned over, and gently lifted her off of the sofa, carefully carrying her into the den, and laid her on the carpet next to the fireplace. With great ease and passion, he placed one of the throw pillows under Jennifer's leg for support. Both of them stared into the fireplace, listening to the cracking of burning wood. The Drifter was hesitating bringing the moment of truth to a close as he glanced into the face of Amy and then back to Jennifer. Jennifer had been indicating with slight gestures from her eyes and hands that it was imperative to tell Amy about her mother and not delay any longer. His eyes finally settled on Amy's face. Her head was bowed, so the Drifter gently lifted her chin so he could face the young child. When Amy's eyes made contact with his, he asked, "Amy ... do you remember back at the campfire when I told you that I made a promise to someone? That someone asked me to take care of you and protect you from the hunters."

Amy's thoughts swirled for a while before she remembered the night at the campsite. When the horrors of that night returned, she nodded her head and looked as if she was about to cry. Seeing Amy's pain caused him to hesitate slightly, being more apprehensive in telling her the truth. "Amy, that person I made a promise to was your mother, Jessica."

Amy stood up and painfully shouted, "If you know my mother, why haven't you found her?" Some of the passengers sleeping in the den were awakened by Amy's loud words. The Drifter shook his head toward them, giving the indication for them to lie back down and return to their sleep.

He motioned for Amy to sit down and listen. She sat next to Jennifer and leaned back into her arms for comfort. He slowly began again by asking Amy if she remembered the hunter Tom. Amy acknowledged slowly as if she was now afraid of what this man was about to tell her. The Drifter returned the nod, took in a deep breath, and decided now was the time to reveal all.

"When Tom decided to use your mother for his sick little game and sent her into the woods ... well, he caught up with her. What he did to your mother was not very pretty, but he left her for dead. When I arrived, she was barely alive. She asked me to care for you and protect you ... and I gave her my word I would. A few minutes later, she passed away. I carried her body into camp before we came here, and she is buried with the rest of the passengers. Your mom is in heaven right now, watching over you, making sure you're going to be okay."

The Drifter wiped the tears from his eyes as he bowed his head in silence. Amy did not respond or move for quite some time. The look on Amy's face was ever-changing, from anger to fear and loneliness to hate. He was more worried than ever before about her disposition, and was anticipating the worst, when without warning, Amy threw her head into Jennifer's chest before bursting into tears. He reached over to gently touch Amy on the shoulder, wanting to give comfort, only to have his hand brushed away by Amy, when she pulled her shoulder away from his touch.

Jennifer shook her head, wanting him to leave while she comforted the hurt child. Saddened by rejection, he stood up and left the den with tears building from deep inside of his broken heart. He understood the time was not right, but he still wanted so much to help and comfort Amy. He and Dog left the den, listening to Amy's soft cries echoing though the small room.

(The Cabin)

Tom was preparing to leave when the front door opened and an older gentleman stepped in. Tom gave the man, who had entered unannounced, a sly, hateful look. The older gentleman noticed Tom's stare and boldly spoke. "Hello, nephew. I come to check on you and the other boys. I was afraid that you all might have got caught up in that storm."

Tom shook his head as he answered the older gentleman. "No, Uncle John, we made it back to the cabin before it hit." Uncle John nodded as he walked toward the small card table in the middle of the cabin. He inquired about Jack and Pete but got very little response from his nephew. As Uncle John sat in silence, watching Tom prepare his pack, he became inquisitive, wondering what Tom was doing.

Very shortly after his uncle's arrival, Tom bid him farewell and left the cabin. Uncle John helped himself to a cup of coffee sitting on the wood-burning stove and returned to the card table to sip it in silence. He looked around the cabin and noticed all the weapons were missing from the gun rack. Something about them being missing along with Jack and Pete began to spark his curiosity. As he sat there, he remembered watching Tom load his .30-06, which was not his favorite rifle. His interest spiked even greater when he saw the hateful look from his nephew's eyes as he was leaving. Not sure of what was going on, he grabbed his rifle and decided to follow his nephew.

(The Drifter's home)

The Drifter peeked around the wall to catch a glimpse of Jennifer and Amy, trying to check on their progress. The night was getting late, and they had remained sitting in front of the fireplace for several hours, leading into the early hours of morning. Every once in a while, Jennifer would notice him peering around the wall, and shook her head, indicating it was not the right time. This went on for quite some time until the Drifter decided it was time to end their silent treatment. Time was passing and he knew they needed their rest before the long trip to Cyprus Springs.

He entered the den with Dog following and ignored Jennifer's attempts to make him leave. As he gently picked Jennifer up from the floor, he whispered, "It's time to get some rest, so don't argue with me." He carried her up the stairs and into his bedroom, with Dog and Amy following. He laid Jennifer on his bed and invited Amy to lie with her. Amy, being tired and sleepy, lazily crawled into the Drifter's bed. She pulled her body up next to Jennifer's and snuggled in for the night. He covered them both, wished them a good night, and left to sleep on the sofa, where Jennifer had lain since her arrival.

(Tom)

Tom scurried back to the crash site, leaving his uncle sitting alone in the cabin. He left in a hurry, for he was not prepared to explain the whereabouts of Jack and Pete. His uncle was a kind old man, and had allowed him the use of the cabin every year without ever questioning his motive. Tom knew from the stories his mom used to tell that he was an honest, hard-working man. He was a policeman, and one night an innocent child was killed by one of his stray bullets during a police raid. He never forgave himself for that night, and it seemed to affect his life. One day, he disappeared from civilization and was not heard from for years. Later, he had found out that his uncle moved to Alaska and was living in the wilderness for the solitude it gave him.

For Tom to tell his uncle of his deadly deeds with the survivors from the plane crash would probably drive him over the edge. He picked up his pace as he hurried to hide his sadistic activities. Several hours passed before Tom arrived at the crash site. His first order of business was to locate Jack and Pete's bodies. He had to remove any identification and bury their bodies from the authorities. As he strolled through the campsite, he found Pete still lying by the old campfire, almost completely covered with snow. He brushed away the snow until Pete was uncovered from his cold, white grave.

He began his search through Pete's pockets, trying to locate his wallet. After a few seconds, he found it in the back pocket of his frozen camouflage pants. With a great prying effort, he managed to release the wallet from its frozen grave. When he opened the wallet, checking for Pete's identification, he found it still intact. Relieved that their identities were safe for the moment, he sighed a deep breath of relief. Tom stuffed the wallet into his jeans and dragged the frozen body across the plateau, deep into the woods. Approximately two hundred yards from the plateau, he left Pete's body lying in the snow next to a large cedar tree, as he began his search for Jack. Several hours passed as he searched throughout the forest, not knowing that he was being watched from afar. Coming up empty-handed, he decided to temporarily suspend the hunt for Jack, and bury Pete. As soon as he was able to locate Pete's body, he continued to drag him further away from the crash site and deeper into the woods. Along the way, he would stop for a short rest and search the area once again, hoping to find Jack's body.

Hours passed as he dragged Pete further south toward the mountains' edge. Along the way, he tried very hard to remember the direction Jack had traveled when he was hunting the stewardess. Over and over, he stepped through his mind that God-awful day, retracing all the events that had occurred. He thought he had covered the area thoroughly where he suspected Jack had gone, but being unable to find him only confused and frustrated him more. By the time he found a place where he could bury Pete's body, his arms were aching and he was totally exhausted. The frustration of not finding Jack only angered him more as he rested his weary body, before attempting to dig Pete's final resting place.

(The next morning)

Morning came quickly to the Drifter when the passengers of Flight 493 began scurrying about the house in excitement. The noise continued to wake him, even though he tried desperately to return back to sleep. Rachael presented him with a cup of coffee as she awakened him on the sofa. He slowly opened his eyes as the aroma of the coffee tickled the senses of his nose. He gratefully accepted the coffee from Rachael as he asked about the commotion. She smiled as she explained the excitement the passengers were all feeling about their trip home. Their spirits were high because they knew they would soon be leaving. The Drifter sheepishly nodded as he sat up on the sofa to sip his morning brew. Rachael sat beside him, wanting an answer to a question that was haunting her. She hesitated no longer to ask the Drifter about his feelings toward Jennifer and Amy. She had been awakened by Amy's outburst last night, and had listened to their conversation. She was concerned about Amy's emotional state of mind after he had explained the death of her mother.

The Drifter had bowed his head while Rachael was talking and now he shrugged his shoulders, for he had no answer to her question. "I'm not sure how she is doing. Jennifer asked me to leave, so I left, even though Amy's crying burned deep inside me."

Rachael nodded before asking the whereabouts of Jennifer and Amy. She did not see them with the rest of the group, and wondered why he had slept on the sofa. He explained to Rachael about letting Jennifer and Amy sleep in his bed so they could get a good night's rest before the trip. Rachael smiled as she put her arms around his neck, gave him a gentle kiss, and whispered, "I love you so much."

(Preparing for the trip)

Before they began their preparation for the trip, the Drifter explained the treacherous conditions they would face together. How they would be forced to keep quiet and stay close together when they traveled through the mountain pass to Cyprus Springs. He also tried to relay the difficulties of the trip, and how all of them would have their own tasks with finial responsibilities to each other. The passengers listened attentively, nodding as the Drifter spoke. Seeing them understand the conditions of the journey, he began barking orders. Captain Joe and Anthony were listening to the orders as they were given, and began organizing the survivors into groups. As the passengers were grouping together to carry out their chores, the Drifter decided to prepare Horse.

Down in the stables, he had dragged the travois from off the stable wall where it hung, and already had it attached to Horse. Jennifer was still unable to walk sufficiently, and she would have to ride on the travois. After he had it secured, he crossed the stables to his workbench and retrieved some large canvas covers. These covers would lie across the snow, protecting them from the cold like a beach blanket across the hot sand. After securing the canvas covers across the back of Horse, he left the stables to get Jennifer.

When he arrived and entered the house, everyone was there to greet him. Confused and somewhat apprehensive, he slowly walked among them, shaking their hands and being thanked for their salvation. He nodded his head in acknowledgement so many times returning a response that he began to feel a headache approaching. Rachael had already prepared Jennifer for the journey, and the captain had carried her down the stairs. While he checked Jennifer's leg, he noticed her spirits were just as high as the others'. He wondered what she was thinking about the night before, but considered the knowledge may be too painful to hear. Amy sat next to her, petting Dog, with her eyes pointed toward the floor. Several times, he tried to get her attention, but it seemed she wanted to avoid his glances. He began to feel that Amy was holding him to blame for what happened to her mother. The Drifter with Rachael's help carried Jennifer out of the house and to the stable lift. The captain gathered the rest of the passengers and formed a single line behind them. The Drifter was the first to be lowered into the stables, along with Rachael and Jennifer. Rachael remained at the bottom to help the others, while the Drifter carried Jennifer to Horse and prepared her for the long journey. Amy and Dog, along with Anthony, were the next to be lowered. He watched them as they reached the bottom, hoping that Amy would at least give him a glance. There was no response from her, so he gently laid Jennifer onto the travois and secured her to it.

One by one, they gathered around Horse, patiently waiting for the rest to arrive. Dog remained by Amy's side, following her every footstep, as his master had ordered. He glanced back at the crowd as they gathered, and noticed Amy was carrying the Winnie the Pooh bear. She had it secured against her chest with her arm wrapped around the bear. His heart was breaking with the sense of helplessness. Finally, the last of the survivors, followed by the captain, gathered with the crowd standing by the Drifter's horse. The captain informed him that all were present and ready to leave. The Drifter nodded and proceeded toward the stable doors, leading Horse. When he was by the door, he pressed the switch and the rumbling sounds began, as the door echoed its musical notes throughout the caverns. As the door opened, the Drifter heard a loud cheer coming from the passengers behind him. A smile cracked his lips, knowing they were all excited about getting home before Christmas. He enjoyed the moment of their happiness, but he knew the journey would be long and hard. Their excitement would soon turn to mumblings of misery.

The Drifter led Horse outside while the others followed. Rachael escorted Amy at the rear of the small caravan, and was last to exit the corridor. The Drifter waited for the last to leave before he reached inside the small crack of the rocky wall and pressed the switch. The huge stable door slowly creaked and cracked as it closed against the rock once again, concealing the Drifter's home. He turned away from the door and whistled for Dog as he knelt in the snow to wait. Dog came running to his side, and a slight gesture of his hand and the words "Cyprus Springs," was all it took for Dog to understand. Off he ran toward the front of the caravan, barking as the Drifter stood up. In a few minutes, Dog had the reins of Horse clenched in his mouth and was leading the horse east across the valley. The Drifter remained close to the rear so he could keep an eye on Amy, for he did not want to lose her again. Their journey would take them straight across the valley toward the east, south of the frozen lake and slightly north of the wolf den he had accidentally stumbled on while searching for Amy. He could only hope that the winds would continue to blow from the south, carrying their scents away from the wolf den. Slowly the caravan moved across the valley toward the frozen lake. He felt that if they could make it there before deciding to camp for the evening, they would have made good progress. The snow was thick and deep, not having enough time to pack before leaving, but due to the stress levels back at the house, this still gave them the hope they so desperately needed. As the day dwindled by, the rest stops seem to get closer and closer together, making the Drifter wonder if they would make it the lake before retiring for the night.

(Tom)

Tom was persistent at burying Pete's body deep under the snow and into the hard frozen ground beneath. He struggled for hours with a worn shovel and dull pick to dig a pit deep enough to conceal Pete's body. Throughout the entire time he was digging, all he could think about was his uncle John finding out what he and the others had done. He kept hoping his uncle had left the small cabin before his return and disappeared into the mountains as he always did in the past. He was still confused at why his uncle showed up on this particular day, when he never came around in the past. *Did he know something or was he truly worried about us?* Tom thought, as these and other thoughts continued to plague his mind throughout the painful task of digging a hole.

After several hours of sweaty, hard work, Tom finally finished Pete's eternal tomb of rest. He hoped his friend would enjoy this place of serenity in the northern Alaskan mountains. This was the perfect place for his dear, rich friend to spend eternity. Tom climbed out of the rocky grave, and with his foot, pushed Pete's body over the edge and into the pit. A loud thump with breaking sounds of cracking bones echoed through the silent forest. Tom stood above the grave as he mumbled a farewell to Pete. "I'm going to miss you, Petey, especially your money. Rest in piece, my old friend." Tom slowly covered the grave with the rocks and dirt that came from the ground. After he was finished with the loose dirt, he finished covering it with the snow, leaving the area looking as if it had never been touched. He smiled, with a satisfaction of success at burying his deeds, as he returned to the crash site in search of Jack.

(The caravan)

Hours barely passed before the mumbling began. The Drifter knew they were already getting weary of travel, with the thick snow making the trip more tiresome and difficult. Their muscles ached from walking, being forced to step high with each step. He realized that the journey would take longer than the two days he had hoped for. At their current pace, it could take more than the three days he had originally predicted. The captain had approached him earlier, trying to get him to stop and make camp, but he refused to give in so easily. However, with the current mumblings, he decided it was time to stop for the evening, after only six hours and four miles of travel. When he yelled for them to stop and make camp, the passengers dropped to the ground to rest. While they were resting, he began his search for a suitable clearing, large enough to build four ice huts around a large campfire. After a short time, the Drifter found an area large enough to support the ice huts and fire. He returned to the resting passengers and motioned for them to follow him to their new resting place for the evening. Once there, the Drifter approached the captain, giving him instructions on how to prepare the ice huts. He explained to the captain that all of the able-bodied men needed to dig four large holes in the snow. The holes needed to be at least eight feet square with an opening pointing toward the center of camp. He continued to explain: After the holes are dug, they needed to pack three feet of snow around the sides, making a solid wall of ice. The opening that led to the center of the camp needs to be left open, allowing the heat of the campfire to warm the huts. The captain agreed and left to gather some men to begin their task. After two hours of hard work, they had dug the four holes. An hour later, they had the ice walls stacked about three feet high around the holes.

The Drifter, satisfied with the making of the ice huts, motioned for the captain. When the captain arrived, he told him to gather some men and bring back some firewood for the campfire. The captain nodded and left with his forces to gather the wood for the fire. While the captain was out gathering wood, the Drifter removed the canvas covers from Horse and placed one cover at the bottom of the hole and laid a second cover across the top. With some large metal stakes and rope, he secured the canvas tops against the packed snow, making a small, cozy ice hut to sleep in. While he was busy preparing their sleeping quarters, he never noticed Amy's eyes had been watching him the whole time. Dog had left camp earlier, scouring the area making sure it was safe, but now he had returned, and he too was watching the Drifter's every move. When he finished the ice huts, he moved to the center of the campsite to build a campfire. The campfire would feed warmth into the huts, with their openings strategically positioned in the middle of the campsite. After several minutes of a blazing fire, the heat had begun to warm the huts. A small group of passengers had pulled up some of the larger logs the captain's crew had dragged in earlier, and used them as seats. Slowly they all gathered by the fire to enjoy its warmth. They sat in silence as some of them slowly chewed some jerky. Rachael had set up a metal tripod over the fire and used it to warm the stew. After several minutes, the stew was steaming and ready to eat. The crowd gathered around as Rachael dished each a small portion of the warm meal.

Shortly after the passengers had consumed the riches of the stew, they began to turn in for the evening. It was not long after dinner that the campfire was empty, except for the Drifter and his wolf. He had stayed to feed the fire, allowing the huts to retain their heat and help the others rest more comfortably. The air was very heavy with cold, but still with the absence of wind. The Drifter was not alone at the fire very long, before he was blessed with the presence of George Stickler. George sat on a small stump across from the Drifter, so he could share eye contact with the man who had saved his life.

The two of them shared no words; each sat in reverence of the other. The Drifter had been noticing George twiddle his fingers, showing signs of being nervous. After watching George for a while with no indication that he was going to say anything, the Drifter decided to break the silence by asking him to speak his mind. "Say whatever you have to say and get it off your chest."

George casually and calmly glanced into the eyes of the Drifter when he asked, "What do we tell the authorities when we get home? ... You know they'll ask."

The Drifter lowered his head, breaking eye contact with George. Several minutes passed before he answered the question. "Tell them what you will. Just keep my name out of it." George elegantly savored the Drifter's words while he thought of an appropriate response.

"You've earned the right to use your name. For all the lives you have saved this day, no one here will disagree with me that you have earned our love and respect. The authorities will want to know who you are." The Drifter nodded, thought about George's words, and repeated his answer.

George stood up, shaking his head, not believing this man would not give in to that which he deserved. As he passed by the Drifter, he laid his hand gently on his shoulder. "God bless you, Jeee ... Sorry. Good night, Mr. Drifter." The Drifter lifted his head and wished George a good evening, as he continued to feed the fire with more logs.

When George entered the ice hut, Jennifer questioned him. "Is he okay?" George gave her a quick look, nodded, and lay down on a blanket next to his wife. Jennifer sat up, checked to see if Amy was still asleep, and began telling George about the night before. She explained that the Drifter told Amy about her mother, and since then, he seemed very distant, not speaking much. George felt her concern, so he slowly tried to explain the life tragedy of the Drifter. "Many years ago, he ... I'm sure he has a lot on his mind. He has taken on the responsibility of our lives, and that would make any man worry." Before George could lie down and retire for the night, Jennifer quickly asked him what he meant by "many years ago." George brushed the question aside by telling her he was tired and not thinking clearly. Someone else he knew popped into his mind just before he realized it had nothing to do with the man outside. Jennifer, taunted by his lack of response, decided not to question him any further.

(Tom)

Tom had searched for many hours without any success in locating Jack's body. As his search continued to come up blank, his anger turned to fear. Questions filled his mind as the fear grew stronger inside. *Was Jack dragged off by wolves? Did they bury him? Did they keep his wallet with his identification? Is his body completely covered by snow and that's why I can't find him?* All these questions with no answers started to feed his fury. The more thoughts that popped in and out of his mind, the more furious he became. After hours of analysis, he finally decided the Drifter had to be responsible for the disappearance of Jack's body. Tom decided to return to the cabin and prepare for several days in the wilderness. His fury had turned to revenge, and now he would track this man with every intention on destroying his life.

On the journey back to his uncle's cabin, he prayed that his uncle John would not be there. *What if he is there? What am I going to tell him about Jack and Pete? God, I hope he's gone when I get there.* These and other thoughts provoked his anger, driving his passion to destroy the Drifter. He blamed the man for spoiling his fun and putting him in the predicament he was now facing. Tom continued to think of a convincing story he could tell his uncle, just in case he was still at the cabin. The more he came up blank about a good story, the angrier he became. By the time he reached his destination, he still had no story to tell, so he decided to stalk the cabin, making sure it was empty. He peered through the windows of the small cabin from the outlying trees. At first glance, the cabin looked empty, so he moved closer, keeping clear of the window. With his back planted against the outside wall, he slid closer to the window. Slowly and quietly, he moved until he was next to the small kitchen window. He scoured the small cabin through the window, trying not to be detected. After careful investigation, he discovered the cabin was empty. With a sigh of relief, he walked to the front door and entered the cabin to prepare for his grand finale, the greatest hunt of his lifetime. The thought of getting his revenge gave him satisfaction, bringing a crooked smile to his lips. The Drifter took his best friend Jack and destroyed his adventurous days with Pete's money. He was going to get even, and this time he would not fail.

Chapter Twelve
A Broken Promise

(Campsite)

It was late in the morning before the Drifter decided to retire for the night. He stacked fresh wood onto the campfire to keep it blazing for hours to come. When he entered the small ice hut where Amy slept, the only spot open was between Rachael and Jennifer. Amy was on the opposite side of Jennifer, cuddled up in her arms and fast asleep. The Drifter carefully crawled between the two ladies while Dog lay next to his feet. Rachael had awakened when he entered the ice hut, and watched his every move. When the Drifter was comfortable, lying on his side, Rachael turned toward him and put her arm across his chest. He felt slightly uncomfortable from her affection, but did nothing to stop her.

His mind wandered, as he thought of Amy and how close they were getting. Now, because of his delay in telling her the truth, she had drifted far away. The guilty feeling in his heart was heavy for not telling her earlier about her mother. He regretted it now, but it was too late to start over, leaving him with only a slim hope of winning her heart back. As he began to fall into a deep slumber, thoughts of his daughter flashed before his mind. His feelings of guilt consumed his thoughts, preventing him from sleeping. He turned toward Rachael, trying to clear his mind, only to see her eyes open and focused on him.

"Are you all right?" she asked. He sensed her concern, but was unwilling to explain the depression that once again held him firmly against his will. Instead, he nodded and closed his eyes in an attempt to sleep. Several hours passed and sleep did not come. He finally sneaked out of the ice hut with Dog, and they both returned to the campfire for the rest of the morning.

(Breakfast – Day 2)

The next morning, the Drifter had a fresh brew of coffee waiting for the others to awaken. It was not long after the captain first appeared from the east ice hut, that the rest of the survivors slowly gathered around the campfire. The Drifter was sipping his coffee when he caught a glimpse of Rachael approaching. He immediately grabbed a cup and poured her some.

"What happened to you last night?" she asked as she took the coffee.

"I couldn't sleep, so Dog and I came here to keep the fire going." He knew she did not completely believe him, but he was not prepared to share his feelings with her.

They sat around the campfire, eating a light breakfast of eggs and oatmeal prepared by Rachael and Alice. The used paper plates and bowls were flung into the fire to burn for proper disposal. The pans were scrubbed in the snow until they were clean and ready for their next meal. After their breakfast, the campsite was broken down and all the supplies were gathered and secured for the second day of the journey. After they had finished packing the supplies, and before they left the campsite, the Drifter asked everyone to police the area for any remaining trash. When the area was clean, they left camp, heading east toward Cyprus Springs.

The second day of their journey began routinely. The snow had packed during the night, making the ground more solid for walking. The snow offered more resistance to weight, not inhibiting them as it did the prior day. Hopes were high and anticipation of getting home was the greatest force that drove this small caravan. The Drifter had Dog set a fast pace to make up lost time from the day before. Without their mumblings of protest, he figured today would prove to be the best. This would allow them to cover most of the remaining distance, leaving only a few miles for the last day.

Four hours and one break later, the Drifter began to feel an uncomfortable sensation running up his spine. Again, he had an eerie sense of being watched, and could not shake it. As he scoured the area for a presence, he decided to slowly drop further behind the caravan. His search took him in a wide "S"-shaped pattern. As he walked, he examined the snow for tracks or any other signs of presence. After forty-five minutes of not finding anything, he gave up his search and felt it was safe enough to return. The caravan was out of sight by this time. So he continued his search pattern until he could see the small group resting leisurely on another break. He still had a hard time shaking the feeling, even though there were times when the feeling was very strong.

(Tom)

Tom carefully walked toward the resting passengers, keeping with the trees to hide his approach. When he was close enough to the small group, he dropped to his belly and shimmied toward a large tree on the outskirts of the resting area. He had to remain far enough away so the animal could not smell his scent and give away his presence. He lay there in the snow behind the large cedar and listened intently to the conversations. He could hear Anthony talking to a young lady about his wife and daughter back home; how he was impatient to see them, but was promised by the Drifter that he would make it home before Christmas. Tom smiled, for he knew their adventures would soon come to an end.

He lifted his binoculars for a closer look, when he spied the Drifter entering the small resting area. He watched his every move wondering why he was just now coming in to rest. *What was he doing? Does he know that I'm watching them? Did he see me?* These thoughts began to enter his mind until he feared that this man would once again spoil his plans. Tom noticed the Drifter stop, kneel down in the snow, and call his wolf. With curiosity, he watched the wolf as he approached this man and sat down in front of him. A few seconds later, after the Drifter whispered something that Tom could not hear, the wolf dashed back in the direction they had traveled. Thinking that he could be discovered before he was ready to carry out his plans, he slowly backed away from the tree and headed further east, away from the small group.

(The Drifter)

The Drifter walked among the passengers, checking on each of them, making sure they were okay and ready to continue. When he reached George, he stopped, and they shared eye contact for a brief moment; he nodded and slowly walked away. Jennifer and Amy were sitting close to Horse, so he attempted to have a conversation with Amy, but she gave no response. Jennifer could feel his heart breaking and offered him a place to sit, next to her. The Drifter took the offer and sat down. At first there was no conversation between them, until Jennifer broke the ice and asked how he was feeling. Moments later, they were in deep conversation until he was forced to leave and attend to the passengers. It was time to start the journey once more, as he gathered the small group of survivors together. He grabbed the reins of Horse and began walking slowly east, leading the group.

The small caravan passed the south fork of the small icy lake and slightly north of the wolf den. The air movement had shifted toward the south, carrying their scent across the valley. All were unaware that the wolves, south of them, had detected the scents and the wolf pack was on the prowl. The Drifter could not remember exactly where he had stumbled onto the den, so he had no idea how the events were beginning to change. Hours passed before the day finally came to a close. They had found an area large enough to sleep for the evening, and the routine began once more. The men grabbed the shovels and dug into the snow, creating four ice huts to sleep in. The Drifter and the captain gathered wood for a fire that was placed in the middle of the campsite. The women unpacked the food and utensils and began preparing dinner. The ice huts were built, the campfire was blazing, and dinner was served. After dinner, the group gathered close to the campfire and told stories of Christmases past. Some of them were giving their plans for the Christmas to come. The Drifter smiled as he heard the stories that brought his own memories of past Christmases with Amy and Janelle. As theses memories began to dwindle and fade away, they were replaced with his feelings for Amy. He could see her sitting next to Jennifer, with Dog on the ground beside her. He could not remember once where she paid him any attention, since that night of the confession. He was not sure how he was going to break his intense feelings of rejection, but somehow he had to. His time was running out and he had a promise to keep before it ended. One by one, the small group left the campfire to retire for the night. Soon, the only remaining passengers were Rachael, Jennifer, Amy, the captain, George, and Alice. The Drifter decided to approach Jennifer so they could continue their discussion from earlier. His admiration for her was growing, with a sense of hope that she could help repair the broken bond between Amy and him. She was his only hope of keeping his promise to Amy's mother. He slowly stood and walked around the campfire to sit next to Jennifer. As he was approaching her, she gave him a very warm, inviting smile, making him feel more comfortable with his decision. The two of them talked about Christmas and what their plans were. Their conversation dragged on until the others had cleared the campfire and retired for the night. Amy had laid her head in Jennifer's lap and had fallen fast asleep. This gave the Drifter the opportunity to speak to Jennifer about Amy's future. He quietly asked her about her plans with Amy, as he reminded her of his promise to her mother. Their conversation began to lean in the direction of adoption, and she was the only one who could take on the task. Jennifer immediately took to her own defense.

"I would love to, but I'm not sure the courts would accept me as a parent, and my job will make it hard for me to adopt. I travel too much and the cost of adoption … let's face it, I couldn't afford to hire an attorney. It will cost a fortune."

The Drifter agreed there would be that measure of risk, and a long, difficult road to travel. He thought for a while before he responded. "I assure you that I will help you any way I can. I've planned to go with you to Seattle and hire an attorney to take care of it. The promise I made to Jessica is mine to keep. I just need your help."

There was a moment of silence before Jennifer finally agreed to adopt Amy. The Drifter leaned back and smiled. Convincing Jennifer seemed like it would have been an impossible task, but now it was over and the feeling was wonderful. Before he would allow her to retire for the night, he made her promise, no matter what might happen, she would adopt Amy. After Jennifer slowly agreed, he carried Amy into the ice hut and laid her next to Rachael. When he returned, he gently picked her up and carried her to the ice hut, placing her next to Amy. Feeling relieved, he found a spot on the other side of the ice hut, where he and Dog could sleep. He was tired from the night before, and within seconds of lying down, he was fast asleep. Jennifer lay awake, thinking of the Drifter's proposal of coming to Seattle and helping her with Amy. Before she realized it, she was smiling at the very thought. There was a spark of life in Jennifer's eyes as she thought more about their conversation. She knew they started out moving in the wrong direction, and over time it seemed to propagate itself and get worse. She remembered the night the Drifter cared for her injuries, for that night her feelings began to change. She smiled once more as she put her arm around Amy and snuggled close to her. As she closed her eyes and fell asleep, dreams of the Drifter passed before her eyes.

Tears formed in Rachael's eyes when she saw the look Jennifer had given the Drifter as he walked away. She knew they had talked after she left, and could tell from the sparkle in Jennifer's eyes that she was falling in love with the Drifter. She loved Jennifer like a sister, and would never dream of getting in her way. Jennifer had her misfortunes with men, and this man would be a good catch for her. Rachael turned her face away from

Jennifer so she could cry alone. Her heart was breaking, now knowing she would have to give up the Drifter for Jennifer and Amy's happiness. She slowly closed her eyes as she cried herself to sleep.

 The night was quiet with a slight southerly wind. In the early-morning hours, the quietness of the night was broken by Dog's barking. The Drifter sat up and heard the sounds of wolves howling at the night sky. The sounds were close and followed by movement around the campsite. Fear struck deep as he launched his body toward the doorway. He frantically searched the ice hut for his rifle, only remembering that he left it by the campfire when he carried Jennifer to bed. He reached down to his bed of blankets to remove his handgun from its holster and headed for the entrance. Quickly and carefully, he scoured the campsite for wolves before dashing to the fire to retrieve his rifle. When he reached the campfire, all he could see was the soft glow of red coals. As he searched for his rifle, he heard Dog's barking and growling in the far distance. He called out his name, trying to get his attention and have him return to the campfire, but he did not respond. Briefly giving up on Dog, he quickly placed some logs on the red coals to get the fire blazing once more. After he was finished feeding the fire, he went back in search of his rifle. He searched long and hard but could not find it. It was not where he had laid it the night before. His fear turned to panic when he was faced with having only one weapon, plus his knife. The lives of the passengers were his responsibility, entrusted to him, and he was defenseless against the wolves. He quickly searched the entire area once more, but still came up empty. He shook his head, for he was unable to understand why it had disappeared. Giving up on the search, he grabbed a couple of bags of jerky from the supplies and left the campsite to find Dog. He had only traveled a few hundred feet into the dark forest before he found himself surrounded by wolves. He whistled for Dog again, as he stood very still watching the flashing of sharp, white teeth. The wolves slowly closed the gap between them as they growled, snarled, and snapped at their victim-to-be. Realizing Dog was not coming to his rescue, he slowly, without any sudden moves, removed several pieces of jerky from the bag and tossed them in front of the approaching wolves. They hesitated in their movement, as they begin to sniff at the jerky. Suddenly, one of the wolves grabbed a piece and devoured it in seconds. The others followed suit with the first wolf. Somewhat satisfied the Drifter tossed another handful of jerky toward the wolves as he slowly backed away. The wolves paid him no attention while they devoured the jerky. When the Drifter was far enough out of sight, he quickly turned and headed away from the wolves. Deeper into the woods he went in search of Dog. He continued to stop briefly and listen each time he whistled. His efforts to find Dog began to feel futile. When he stopped again to listen for Dog, he heard loud voices and screams back at the campsite. Being forced to give up his search, he returned to camp to fight off any attacking wolves. When he arrived, the campsite was swarming with wolves. Most of the passengers were standing close to the blazing campfire, huddled together, trying to fight off the wolves with some burning limbs. The Drifter raised his pistol and pointed it directly at the wolf closest to the campfire. He carefully squeezed the trigger. The bullet cut through the cold night air, hitting its intended target, echoing its strength, bringing fear to all. The wolf hit the ground and twitched briefly. Another shot was heard when a second wolf hit the snow and never moved again. A third and fourth shot, and two more hit the snow. Moments later, feeling sure of himself, the Drifter began to unload his gun. As he was reloading, he heard a fateful scream. He glanced toward the scream when he saw Amy backed against the west ice hut with an approaching wolf. Reaching down, unbuckling his knife, and without further thought to his safety, he ran toward the wolf. With the knife poised, he leaped into the air and collided against the body of the wolf. The fight for survival was on, as they both rolled in the snow. The Drifter was trying desperately to keep his grip around the wolf's neck, as he regained control of his right arm.

The wolf had clawed his chest and bitten him several times about the shoulder. The two wrestled as they each tried to gain control of the other. Time flew by as the two fought for their own survival. Rachael had run to Amy's side, and was now leading her back toward the fire. The captain had grabbed a branch from the fire and was running toward the Drifter, yelling and waving the burning branch frantically in the air. In a blinding flash of light, the Drifter had gained his control, and a loud "yelp" was heard as he plunged his knife deep into the wolf's chest. By the time the captain was standing beside the Drifter, the wolf was lying in the snow as his precious life-giving blood was coloring the snow with a deep red tint. The captain helped the Drifter to his feet, and without any warning, he was knocked backward a few inches when Amy lunged into his body. She wrapped her arms around his waist as she cried. The Drifter stood there with tears of his own, as he returned the affection he thought he had lost forever. Rachael approached them, shedding her own tears for a different reason, as she carefully checked his shoulder. The blood was forcing itself out of the gaping wound. With tenderness, she removed the clothing around his shoulder while he held on to the precious life that was wrapped in his arms. She could tell his heart was warmed by the love from Amy, which brought more tears to her eyes. The captain stood by the Drifter's side, searching the area for any signs of wolves that might venture into camp unannounced. Alice had brought some bandages with her, and the two women cared for the injuries of the man who had given so much for them. After they had bandaged his shoulder, he took a moment to kneel down next to Amy. He gave her a loving kiss on the forehead, as he broke away from her tightly clenched arms. He told her that he loved her, but needed to leave so he could find Dog. Amy stepped back away from him and ran back to the arms of Jennifer. The Drifter smiled for a brief moment before he stood back up and thanked the two women for helping him. He gave the captain a pat on the shoulder before he walked into the woods in search of Dog.

He walked the perimeter around camp, making sure it was clear of wolves before he stepped into a small clearing where his horse had been tied. The horse was gone with hoof- and wolf prints heading north. He dropped his shoulders with a slight disgusted sigh, for now he had to find his horse and Dog. He searched for what seemed hours with no results; neither could be found. As he called Dog's name, he would stand still and listen. He could hear the wolves howling in the distant south, but there was no response from his wolf. After countless tries, he decided to return to camp. He needed to check on them and assure them the wolf threat was over for the night.

When he reached camp, he saw them securely huddled by the fire with the captain steadily feeding it. The flames from the fire seemed to reach high into the heavens, lighting the night sky with its brilliance. As he approached, he forced a smile to his face to break the painful look of sadness for not finding his companion. He assured them that all was well for the rest of the night, and for them to try to get some rest. He sat on a log next to the campfire and laid his head inside his hands, while he thought about Dog.

Some of the passengers began returning to the ice huts to sleep, while others were uncertain about retiring again for the evening. As the Drifter drowned in his fears about Dog, he did not see Amy approaching. She shared her concern for Dog and asked about him. The Drifter lifted his head and cocked it to one side, to get a better look at her before he answered. "I'm not sure, Amy. He took off right after they showed up and he doesn't seem to respond when I call him. I'm sure he is okay and will come back soon. You go get some sleep, and by the time you wake up, he should be here…okay?"

Amy nodded, wiped the tears from her eyes, and gave the Drifter a long stare before she raised her arms in an attempt to get comforted. A tear found its way down the side of his cheek as he took her arms into his.

As the two embraced, and without any expectation of what was about to come, his senses went into shock when he heard Amy ask, "Are you and Dog coming home with us?"

The Drifter's eyebrow raised in surprise as his body twitched from excitement. His voice was somewhat shaky as he answered her question. "Yes, Amy. Dog and I will be coming with you. I promised your mother I would take care of you, and that is a promise I plan on keeping."

As he took his glance from Amy to Jennifer, he saw a smile break across her lovely face when she heard his words. The captain came over and put his arm around the Drifter and thanked him once again for all that he had done. The Drifter put his arm around the captain, and with a gentle pat on the back, responded, "You are more than welcome, and thank you for your support." He left the captain headed toward Jennifer so he could carry her back into the ice hut for some rest.

As he entered the hut, she softly whispered, "I love you and I truly believe I have always loved you." He looked down at Amy, who had a smile spread as wide as the Grand Canyon across her face. His heart was exploding with excitement as he lowered Jennifer onto the blanket. The three of them sat in silence, but all who had been awakened in the cozy little ice hut could sense their feelings.

He motioned for Amy to join Jennifer on the blanket, and waited for her lie down before he covered both of them with another blanket. He leaned over and kissed Amy once again on the forehead and wished her a good night. As he started to rise, he felt the soft, tender touch of Jennifer's hand. "I meant what I said." He smiled once more and placed a short but loving kiss against her lips, before he left the small hut to try to diffuse his emotions, which touched him so deeply.

The captain was sitting alone by the campfire, feeding it with logs. As the Drifter approached, he softly commented, "Afraid they will return?" The captain laughed softly without paying any attention to his approach. They both sat on the log close to the pile of wood that had been gathered, and fed the fire in silence. The Drifter was swarming in emotions about Amy and Jennifer, plus his concern about his friend and companion. He knew if Dog was okay, he would return soon. He again scoured the area around the campfire in search of his missing rifle. He gently shook his head, ashamed for misplacing it, even though he could not understand how he had lost it so easily. The Drifter attuned his ears to the night sounds, as he listened for anything that would give him hope of Dog's return. Hours passed as they maintained the fire in the silence of the night. When morning finally came, the other passengers joined them, one by one, for the warmth of the fire. Dog still had not returned by the time Amy was awake. The pain of having to tell her that Dog could possibly be dead began to greatly haunt his fears. It was not long after before the campsite was bustling with a crowd of people. There was excitement in the air, because today was the last day of the journey. The women were singing softly as they prepared breakfast.

Amy came from the south ice hut, running toward him. Rachael helped Jennifer through the cramped entrance and walked with her, supporting Jennifer's injured leg. Amy stopped in front of the Drifter, gave him a big hug, and looked around the campsite for Dog. As her search returned nothing, she sniffled and asked where Dog was. The Drifter, afraid he would lose her again, could only shrug his shoulders. With his heavy and painful heart, he softly said, "I'm not sure where Dog is, Amy. He did not come back last night."

Amy broke into tears, crying out, "He's dead, isn't he?" All he could do was bow his head and stare into the fire, for he too feared Dog might very well be dead.

When he attempted to reach out to comfort Amy, he heard, "What the hell is Amy crying about?" When he looked in the direction of the voice, he saw Jennifer standing on the opposite side of the fire. Before he had a chance to answer, Amy had run into her arms, crying soft murmurs. "Dog's dead."

Jennifer looked into his eyes as if waiting on an explanation, but all he could do was throw his hands outward, not wanting to argue the point. "Why haven't you gone looking for him? You could follow his tracks, couldn't you?" she asked.

The Drifter did not dispute her words, so he sat there as Jennifer berated him for hurting Amy's feelings. He tried to explain that it was impossible because of all the wolf tracks, and it would be easy to walk the woods for days trying to follow each of them. He went on to explain that when the gun went off, the wolves scattered in all directions and there was no way to determine which tracks belonged to Dog. As she listened to his explanation, she realized he was in as much pain or more than Amy. She lowered her voice as she softly apologized for her rudeness.

(The Last Day)

After breakfast, they did not bother breaking down the campsite. The ice huts remained intact, and the only supplies that were gathered were those required for their last day. Without Horse to carry them, they would be forced to carry the supplies themselves, but they were no longer needed. Being the last day, the Drifter instructed them to take the medical supplies, a handful of jerky, and to fill all the canteens with water. As they were breaking camp, the Drifter heard a wolf barking from the north, and it sounded very close. He was very excited as he ran toward the sound, into the woods to find his friend. Not long after his entrance into the woods, he passed by a large spruce tree. As he rounded the edge of the tree, he saw Dog limping toward him.

He ran toward Dog, shouting, "Where have you been, boy?"

When he reached Dog, he threw his arms around his neck. Dog whimpered for a brief moment, before the Drifter backed away from his hug and discovered a wound on his front shoulder. In his excitement to see his friend and companion, he did not notice Dog's limping. With love and passion, he carefully examined the wound. It was a large laceration beginning on his lower right shoulder and continuing across his back. Without a flashlight, the Drifter could not tell the full extent of the damage, so he decided to carry Dog back to the campsite. Amy was the first to greet him upon his arrival. She began petting Dog, even while the Drifter carried him. Never once did she question why Dog was being carried, for she was too excited, knowing Dog was alive.

As soon as the Drifter was close enough to the last remains of the campfire, he asked for a flashlight. Without any hesitation, the captain was there beside him, presenting him with a flashlight. As the Drifter slowly examined the wound, his expression turned from worry to anger. He asked the captain to bring him some bandages from the medical kit, while he rinsed the wound with fresh water from his canteen. When the captain returned with the bandages, he asked the Drifter about the angry look on his face. He ignored the question, as he finished cleaning and bandaging the wound. After he had taken care of Dog's wound, he lifted his head toward Rachael and asked her to gather everybody and prepare to leave. Rachael nodded.

When Rachael was out of earshot, the Drifter stared hard at the captain. "This cut is deep; it won't kill Dog, but it's the cut that bothers me." The captain shook his head, not understanding his statement. The Drifter motioned for him to get closer as he showed the captain the cut and how smooth the edges were.

Captain Joe was still confused by what the Drifter was showing him, so he said, "I don't know what you mean by this. It looks like it's a bite or possible cut caused by a tooth."

The Drifter shook his head, as he explained his concerns about the cut. "This cut isn't jagged, which would indicate teeth or claws ripping through the skin. This cut was too smooth, with sharp definitions of being sliced by a sharp object, like a knife." The captain backed away from the Drifter as fear lit up his face. The Drifter glanced around the campsite for anybody who might be close enough to hear, found no one, and started explaining to the captain what he knew. "I think we are being followed. I've felt it all day yesterday, but couldn't find anybody or shake the feeling. I dropped back away from the caravan to try to catch whoever it might be off guard, but still wasn't able to find them. I sent Dog out yesterday while we rested, to search, but he came up empty too. I believe Tom is alive and has been on our trail since we left my house. This would explain the cut on Dog's shoulder and my missing rifle." The captain's eyes opened wide, showing signs of worry as the Drifter spoke. "What does he want?" the captain asked.

The Drifter solemnly looked at the captain for a few minutes before he answered, "Me."

Captain Joe shook his head obtusely, saying very loudly, "Well he can't have you!"

Rachael overheard the captain and immediately joined them, asking questions. The Drifter waved her off and gave the captain a sign for him to remain silent.

The Drifter, not allowing Rachael's curiosity to grow, motioned to the captain and Rachael that it was time to leave. She had the look of a scorned woman, wanting to know what was going on, but realized she was not going to get any answers, so she agreed it was time to leave. As she was leaving, the Drifter grabbed the captain's arm. "I'm taking the rear and will slowly fall back further. Tom wants me more than any of you, so I need to head him off. If my luck holds true, I will join you in town."

The captain remained silent for a moment before he spoke. "What about your promise to Jennifer and Amy?"

The Drifter bowed his head as he said, "I made a promise to Anthony to have him home by Christmas. If I don't fall back and stop Tom, many of you might not make it home. If I don't show up in town before you leave, then I'm probably dead."

The captain hesitated for a moment before nodding and giving the Drifter a friendly pat on the shoulder. As he walked off to join Rachael, the Drifter spoke once more. "If I'm killed … please tell George to find my brother and have him carry out my promise to Amy's mother. Also Dog is to stay with Amy; he will protect her."

Captain Joe turned slowly, slightly confused by the Drifter's words. As he glanced into his eyes, they both remained silent. He felt the Drifter had placed a great burden on his shoulders, one that would be difficult to carry out. The Drifter finally motioned for him to join the others, but Captain Joe was reluctant to leave.

The Drifter glanced down at Dog, and whispered a few words into his ear. Dog barked once and limped to the front of the caravan, followed by the captain.

As Dog was leaving, the Drifter mumbled in a low voice, "Good-bye, my old friend." He turned and took up the rear of the caravan, which was now in progress. He steadily searched the area for Tom as he slowly dropped back further away from the caravan. After the first hour of the trip, the Drifter had dropped far enough behind that his disappearance was not noticed. Looking around the woods and through the trees, he still could not see Tom's presence. He decided to stop to allow the caravan to get completely out of sight before he continued his search. When the small group could no longer be seen, he turned northeast and slowly walked toward the south edge of the lake. He continued this direction for quite some time, before turning east and circling back toward the caravan.

He had almost completed a circle when he stumbled on a set of footprints in the snow. As he carefully examined the tracks, he could tell they belonged to a tall individual, from the depth and size. He followed the tracks, staying close to the trees to keep his movements somewhat concealed. With his pistol drawn, he anticipated running into Tom at any point, so he moved carefully forward, checking in all directions.

(Cyprus Springs)

The small group of survivors arrived in Cyprus Springs only a few hours after their early-morning departure. The lights were on in the small tavern, so the captain waved for everyone to follow. As he stepped onto the wooden sidewalk and entered the small tavern, he took the locals completely by surprise. The door opened, as a scruffy, large man entered the tavern followed by what looked like a ragged group of nomads who had been in the desert for months. The locals were not accustomed to strangers this time of year, so it was a strange sight for them to see. Their bewilderment turned to excitement, as each of the survivors entered the tavern, one by one. Dog limped into the bar behind the two men carrying Jennifer, followed by Rachael and Amy. As soon as Dog cleared the doorway, one of the locals name Jake recognized the wolf and yelled out, "Dog, where's that Drifter fellow?"

Jennifer was unaware of the Drifter's disappearance, and immediately she began worrying as she searched among the crowd and could not find him. The harder she searched, the more panicked she became when her results returned negative. Not finding him, she blurted out in a panic-stricken voice. "Where is he?" Amy was stricken with fear from Jennifer's reactions. She also began looking for the Drifter. When she too was unable to find him, she went running to Jennifer for comfort. Dog's whine was heard, for he too did not pick up the Drifter's scent. The captain felt guilty for not telling anybody about the Drifter's plan, and he could not withhold the information any further. He sat down next to Jennifer at a small table and began explaining to both Amy and Jennifer what the Drifter was forced to do.

"Tom ... that hunter fellow. The Drifter suspected he was following us and was afraid he would kill someone, so he went out to hunt him down. He told me that when he was finished, he would meet us here at the tavern."

The bartender, Peter O'Riley, an old Irishman, inquired about their presence and started asking questions. "What you people doing so far from civilization? You look like you've been through hell."

The captain stood up and walked to the bar to speak to Peter. "We need some help. Do you have a radio or telephone?"

Peter looked at him inquisitively as if his question was unexpected. "Phone lines are down, been down since that last storm. We could try to reach someone in Fairbanks on the radio; that's the closest city around here."

The captain thanked him and told Peter the reason they were there. "I'm Captain Joe of Flight 493 out of Seattle. Our plane crashed in the mountains before the storm hit, and our friend, that Drifter fellow, saved our lives. We have wounded who need medical help, and well the rest of us want to get home before Christmas."

Peter became very excited when he heard the captain. "I thought I saw a plane crash. It was northwest of here. Everybody thought I was crazy, remember Jake … I told you?" The captain waved Peter off as he asked to be shown the way to the radio.

Jake jumped up and headed for the door, saying, "I'll radio Byron; he'll know what to do." The captain was concerned about Jake's comment, not sure he was aware of the importance of their situation. He shook his head slightly before returning to Jennifer's table to impatiently wait for some good news. Peter saw the captain's confusion, so he explained that Byron was the local law in the area.

"He lives northeast and is the only law in the Denali Borough. It's about thirty miles from here, and it will take him a few hours, with the snow as deep as it is, but he will come. Now, I need to go get Mary. I'll be back shortly." Peter left the tavern to retrieve Mary from across the street at the Bread and Breakfast Hotel.

Shortly after his departure, he returned with Mary, who was elderly with a motherly touch. Seeing the state of the passengers of Flight 493, she immediately headed toward the small kitchen of the tavern to prepare a warm meal. The aroma of bacon filled the small tavern, along with the sweet smell of coffee. Dog lay by Amy's feet, with his eyes on the front door as he patiently waited for his master's return.

The door of the tavern opened once more, revealing a short, heavyset individual. Peter introduced the new arrival as Angus, the town doctor. Angus, carrying his black bag, began check each of them. When he got to George and examined his shoulder, all he could say was, "Hummmph." When he examined Jennifer's leg, he was amazed by how well it seemed to be stitched, but was overwhelmed by the smell of the ointment. He asked her about the ointment that covered the wound, and she just commented that it was a mixture of herbs the Drifter used. He nodded and continued his examinations of the other passengers.

(The Drifter)

He followed the footprints until he came upon a small opening. The prints crossed the opening and exited on the other side, beyond the trees. Caution was in order, so he searched the entire area very carefully, before he slowly walked around the opening, keeping to the trees. As he was getting close to the area where the prints exited the clearing, he found another set of prints walking up to the clearing from a different direction. *It had to be Tom walking through the opening and circling back trying to confuse me,* the Drifter thought.

He stopped again, taking more precautions as he scoured the area, looking for any movement among the trees. There was still nothing unusual he could see, except for the prints that ended where he stood. By the time he realized what was happening, a loud voice unleashed its discouraging words: "Drop your pistol and don't move, Mr. Drifter." The voice came from behind and above him. Without any sudden moves, the Drifter slowly dropped his pistol from his hand, letting it roll forward. A soft thumping sound was heard when the pistol hit the snow right below his feet. A few seconds passed in silence, before a scraping sound of bark being pulled from the trunk of a tree could be heard. Then there was a loud sound like something heavy hitting the snow, causing it to sink from a heavy weight. The Drifter could hear footsteps in the snow just before he heard, "Slowly turn toward me, Mr. Drifter. Any sudden moves and I'll blow a hole through you big enough to drive a car through."

He slowly turned his head toward the voice, as his body followed. Within a few seconds, he was facing Tom, his adversary, standing only a few feet in front of him. Slowly, their eyes lined up, each showing their aversion for the other. The Drifter had a sour look of despair with disappointment for being stupid enough to be captured once again. Tom had a look of defiance, for once again he outsmarted this man of the wilderness. The Drifter, with a slight uplifted smile, in a deep sarcastic voice asked, "Where do we go from here … Tom?"

Tom smiled a wicked smile. "For you, this is the end of the journey … for the others; well, let's say they're at the beginning of their crossroads." The Drifter stood firm, without showing any fear as he confronted Tom's meaning of, "the beginning of their crossroads."

Tom broke out into sinister laughter, showing his true evil nature. The Drifter became agitated by the laughter and boldly yelled what could be his last fatal act of defiance: "I should've killed you when I had the chance!" This only provoked Tom's sinister mood more, causing his laughter to grow even louder. The Drifter took a quick glance down toward his feet and saw where the pistol had landed. Tom's laughing was distracting him, causing a lack of attention to the Drifter's actions. Seizing the opportunity, he slowly buried his right foot underneath the pistol. Before he could take action, Tom had stopped his laughter as abruptly as it had started. The Drifter froze his movement of retrieving his pistol, suspecting that Tom had seen his feeble attempt. The two of them stood there for several minutes in close eye contact without either of them speaking. Tom was the first to break the silence when he began explaining his evil intentions. His words were cold and heartless. His eyes glistened as he spoke, as if he was taking pleasure in those words.

"Mr. Drifter. I want you to be the first to know my plans and feel how much pleasure I'm going to have carrying them out. So do not interrupt me or … I guess you'll never get to hear all my ideas. Now listen carefully." The Drifter sighed as he was forced to listen to a man he should have killed.

(Tom's Plans)

"First, of course, you have to die. You stopped me once and I can't afford to let you stop me again. Secondly, I am going to hunt down all of those passengers, one by one, and kill them. It will be the most pleasurable venture I have ever encountered. It may take a few years to find them all, but it will be an adventure of a lifetime. Third, last but most important, that little girl, I believe her name is Amy, you know who I'm talking about, the one you are so fond of. She and that crippled stewardess bitch will be the last ones I kill. I will save the little bitch until she matured some, then I will bring her, along with the stewardess, and do to them what I did to little bitch's mother."

The Drifter was fuming by this time. His rage had grown outside of its normal channels, and the more Tom spoke, the more it ravaged inside of him. As Tom continued to divulge his fantasies, he managed to completely bury his foot under the pistol. With a quick lifting of the leg, his gun rose straight into the air and lined up with his face. He reached out and grabbed the pistol with his right hand. Before he could completely get control of the gun, he felt a painful sting, followed by a loud blast. As he began to fall backward, he was able to squeeze off a round. Within a few seconds, he was lying in the snow, while his life-giving blood spewed from his chest, discoloring the snow. Tom staggered backward from the force of the bullet, grabbed his face, and dropped to his knees, screaming foul words of defiance.

The Drifter lay there with his eyes focused on Tom. He was hoping his one shot hit a fatal spot, keeping Tom from carrying out his dastardly deeds. While his strength slowly drained, he noticed the figure of a man standing behind Tom in the woods not far away. The plot thickened even more when the dark figure began his walk toward them. His vision was failing and the figure was blurred, so he could not make out who it might be. He steadily watched the shadow's every footstep. Unable to maintain consciousness, the Drifter slowly closed his eyes, as the warmth of his body continued to drain into the snow. The dark, shadowy figure stopped short of Tom, as it knelt down into the snow. With his arm around Tom's shoulder, the stranger helped Tom to his feet and the two of them left, leaving the Drifter to die.

(Back in Cyprus Springs)

The tavern was quiet, as the small group of survivors waited patiently for news of their rescue. Some of them were sitting on the floor along the walls, due to the inadequate chairs and tables, while others were comfortably seated at the tables. Dog was lying at Amy's feet, as she sat with Rachael and Jennifer. Without any warning, Dog stood up and began barking, as if someone was coming. The night air had been very still and quiet, so nobody understood the barking. He dashed toward the door of the tavern and began scratching against it with his paw, as if he wanted out. Rachael thought the Drifter was coming, so she dashed to the window to stare into the darkness in search of him.

Amy also ran to the window and stood by Rachael's side, as she too stared into the night. Dog was still scratching at the door, wanting out, and yet there were no signs of anybody approaching. Amy left the window to comfort Dog, when the sound of an engine was heard. Rachael saw a large man parking a snowmobile in front of the tavern. She watched as he stepped off the snowmobile and walked toward the front door. The door of the tavern swung open exposing Lawman Byron. As he stepped through the doorway, he was almost knocked off his feet when Dog forced his way outside. Dog rushed toward the west and soon disappeared into the night.

The End

Printed in the United States
62273LVS00004B/176